NIGHT TRAIN TO PARIS

BOOKS BY FLISS CHESTER

A Dangerous Goodbye

THE FRENCH ESCAPES ROMANCE SERIES
Love in the Snow
Summer at the Vineyard
Meet Me on the Riviera

NIGHT TRAIN TO PARIS

FLISS CHESTER

bookouture

Published by Bookouture in 2020

An imprint of Storyfire Ltd.
Carmelite House
50 Victoria Embankment
London EC4Y 0DZ

www.bookouture.com

ISBN: 978-1-83888-646-2
eBook ISBN: 978-1-83888-645-5

'Creativity takes courage.' – Henri Matisse

CHAPTER ONE

Almost in Paris, October 1945

Dear Mrs B, Kitty and Dilly,

I'm writing this on the train, so please excuse my appalling handwriting. Our carriage rattles so much, I'm wielding this pen with all the elegance of a sledgehammer! But – good news – I'm almost in Paris, although it has taken rather a long time to get here, due to the timetables being up the spout still and, of course, more importantly, trains of returning troops and prisoners of war taking priority on the lines. We've had so many delays, what should have taken us a few hours has stretched out throughout the whole night now. When some bright spark tells me there's no such thing as a night train from Dijon to Paris, I shall beg to differ, though, sadly, this one has none of the comforts of the couchette, more's the pity.

Still, I mustn't grumble, and I have just seen the most glorious sunrise over the fields and I hope a week or so in Paris might help me put the adventures of the last few weeks behind me. Although I miss Arthur and will love him for as long as I live, I hope to find a small part of me again here, in the City of Lights. (Remember that crossword clue I sent you a while ago, Kitty? Well, that's the answer – Paris! Let's hope it's the answer to my problems, too.)

I'm travelling with Arthur's friend, James Lancaster. I feel like he's a bit 'all at sea' now he's in this limbo that is demobilisation, so I can see why Arthur wanted me to look out for him. I hope he can stay with my friend Rose with me in Paris, but we'll see. And perhaps, if we travel to England together after this, you'll get to meet him, too.

I can picture you all, either sitting round the kitchen table, the kettle whistling on the stove, or, Kitty, you cross-legged in front of the open fire while Mrs B and Dilly are on the armchairs, but all listening to the wireless together.

I do miss you and hope my spare suitcase of summer clothes isn't too much in the way. I'll be back for it soon.

Anyway, I hope you're all well and the rationing isn't still biting too hard (bad pun, sorry!).

Here's another clue for you, Kitty: This Pullman took tea before his shower (5)... Here's a hint... I'm sitting on it right now!

Thinking of you all,
Fen xxx

Fen stepped off the train at Paris's Gare de Lyon station and walked forward a few steps to allow others off the train behind her. She took a deep breath and swiftly regretted it, as the mingled aromas of engine grease and coal smoke struck her lungs. She coughed into her hand and moved further onto the platform, away from the engine and its belches of steam and smoke.

The fresh air she had taken for granted in the countryside of Burgundy was sorely missing from this hub of movement and chatter, but the polluted air brought with it some compensation – this was Paris; dynamic, exciting Paris.

Fen tentatively breathed in again, this time accustomed to the tang of metal in the air, and a flood of memories washed over her.

She may not yet be home, but Paris and its particular aromas was almost as good as.

The letter she'd written to her former landlady – the indomitable Mrs B – and good friends was clasped in her hand. It was marked for West Sussex in southern England, which had been her base when she had worked for the Woman's Land Army in the war. Lots of young women from all walks of life had become land girls, as they'd been called, and meeting young Kitty, who was local to that part of England, and clever, kind Dilys, who had been posted there from Wales, had been light relief to the hard graft of field work. They'd been through so much together and, now, just holding their names in her hand, helped her feel close to them again.

Fen stifled a yawn and wiped the sleep from her eyes. It was early morning and the light from the sun, which was stubbornly showing itself time and again from behind equally as persistent clouds, was diffused through vast panes of glass, hundreds of feet above her.

Externally, the Gare de Lyon was one of Paris's most expressive stations, with its monumental arches, mansard roof windows and traditional continental clock tower, but here on the platform there was less ornamentation, and function trumped form, with only wooden benches and newspaper kiosks as decoration.

Fen looked at the other disembarking passengers around her, shielding themselves from the belches of steam and scurrying along with suitcases or unruly children grasped by their wrists. They seemed more solemn than Fen remembered the citizens of Paris to be. Had the gaiety she remembered from her childhood packed up and left as the first wave of enemy soldiers had arrived?

Fenella Churche, known to most as Fen, had had a rather unusual upbringing for a middle-class Englishwoman, in that she had grown up here in Paris, due to her father accepting a job at the world-renowned École des Beaux-Arts back in 1924. The family – that being her parents and older brother, plus the small menagerie of two cats, a dog, a tortoise and a gerbil – had left the leafy suburb of Oxford where they had lived and made their home in the artistic Left Bank area of Paris. And there she had grown up, in the somewhat louche world of artists and writers, until her father had moved them all back to Oxford to take up a new professorship in 1935.

She found herself back here now, in the city she had lived in until she was eighteen years old and had always loved, as it pulled itself back together, following the occupation and subsequent routing of the German army from its streets. This wasn't her first stop in post-war France. For the last few weeks she had been living and working in a small vineyard in Burgundy, on the trail of her fiancé, Arthur Melville-Hare, who had left her various coded letters that had helped her solve the mystery of his own disappearance.

It was never far from Fen's mind, however, that those clues were all she had left now of her clever, brave fiancé. He had been killed in the war, and although it broke her heart whenever she thought of him, at least she had found her answer. He was at peace now, the horrors of the war could no longer haunt him, as they did so many other men and women, and for Fen it had been not knowing if he was alive or dead, captured or wounded, that had been the very worst. In some way, slowly, now she could start to find her own peace, too.

Fen placed her sturdy brown suitcase down on the platform and waited for her travel companion to join her. Captain James Lancaster had been a huge help to Fen in solving the crimes they'd stumbled across in Burgundy and, what's more, he had been a good friend to Arthur. Fen felt comforted by his presence, and all the way since changing trains at Dijon, he had been telling her what he was allowed to about his and Arthur's certain style of war work. As members of the highly secretive Special Operations Executive, they had been parachuted in to aid the local Resistance cells, sabotaging the advancing and occupying German army in any way they could. Heartbreakingly, this brave work had cost Arthur his life.

'Here we are,' James pulled his own kitbag off the train and came to stand next to Fen. He stretched his long limbs out, reaching his arms up and ruffling his straw-like blond hair with one of his hands on its way down.

The journey had been a long one compared to pre-war speeds; as Fen had reported back to her friends, military trains took priority over civilian trips, and there were also still craters in some of the lines, due to either the retreating Germans or guerrilla-style subterfuge of the Resistance during the occupation. It was a stark reminder that although the war had officially been declared over in May, France was still very much feeling the after-effects of it all.

'Hats, gloves and coats?' Fen said, parroting the sort of thing her mother used to say whenever they'd travelled.

'Check, check and check,' James replied, holding up his long khaki-coloured dispatch rider's coat while checking its pockets for his leather gloves.

'You'll be pleased of that now the weather's on the change,' Fen remarked, wondering if her own thin cotton trench coat would suffice, and if she had sufficient funds in her pocketbook to afford a new, slightly warmer one. At least she had her thick wool jumpers: one was standard War Office issue from when she had been farming in the fields to help the war effort, and one had been hand-knitted by Mrs B and it had kept her warm on many a cold and muddy morning in West Sussex. *À la mode* they may not be, but the one from Mrs B now carried with it the distinction of not just being warm but having recently saved Fen from the worst effects of a bayonet.

She shuddered at the memory of that night up in the attic rooms of the château in Burgundy and pulled her trench coat around her, tightening the belt a notch. Using the glass windows of one of the kiosks as a mirror, Fen checked that her hair was still as neatly curled and styled as it could be after a night on the train – her chestnut locks were not known for their obedience to hairpins – and pursed her lips to apply some lipstick in lieu of a decent wash and brush-up.

Popping the tube of Revlon back into her bag, she turned to James again and said, 'I just hope I pass muster among the fashionable ladies of Paris!'

Her comment made James look down at his own outfit. He'd spent most of the war working undercover in the vineyard where Fen had met him, and his clothes hadn't been any smarter than they'd needed to be for that. She now noticed him frown slightly at his own woollen trousers and ill-fitting waistcoat, worn over a button-up shirt. He'd spent a few hundred francs at the local tailor in Morey-Fontaine, the small town they'd been staying in, but the result wasn't exactly high fashion either. Fen had to remind herself that 'a few hundred francs' wasn't worth that much these days, barely a pound, more like twelve shillings or so.

He's filthy rich... hadn't those been Arthur's words to describe his friend in the letter he left for her in Morey-Fontaine? Fen smiled as she thought about it – no man could look less like some wealthy heir than the one standing in front of her now.

'They'll just have to take us as they find us.' James shrugged and picked up his kitbag, then, without asking, picked up Fen's small suitcase too.

'Thank you, but I can carry that myself.' Fen stretched her arm out.

'If you insist,' James said, and Fen nodded.

'I do. If you can't carry it, don't pack it, eh?'

'Quite right,' James agreed and deliberately dropped her case on the ground and strode off towards the station concourse.

'How rude!' Fen called out after him, but then she laughed; only a week or so ago, she really *did* think his personality ran no deeper than the gruff countenance he put on – another warm protective coat as it were – and would have genuinely thought him devoid of manners or civility. Now, however, his gruffness had become rather a running joke and she knew he'd take her in jest.

She was proved right when he turned around and winked at her. 'Come on then, slowcoach, let's find this lodging of yours.'

CHAPTER TWO

Before they'd left Morey-Fontaine, Fen had written to an old family friend of hers, Rose Coillard, to ask if she and James could stay with her in her apartment near the École des Beaux-Arts. Fen had bunked down with her for one night last month as she'd changed trains in Paris on her way to Burgundy and they'd barely scratched the surface of what they wanted to catch up on. Madame Coillard – as she had first been introduced to Fen all those years ago – had been a colleague of Fen's father, Professor John Churche, but more than that, she had been – and still was – her parents' very good friend.

Fen would most likely lose count if she tried to remember all the times her family and Rose had dined together, or spent afternoons in the Louvre, the Tuileries Gardens or paddling on the sandy shore of the Seine at Île de la Jatte to the north of the city. Rose had tried, on those occasions, to teach the two unruly English children the wonders of the Impressionists, showing them with her own easel and brushes how those turn-of-the-century artists had marvelled at the dappled light and swiftness of moving time. More often than not, she'd come second in the race for their attention, narrowly pipped by the ice cream cart, but as Fen had matured from a young girl to an insightful and diligent teenager, she had grown closer to the mildly eccentric art teacher and even attended a few of her classes at the école, despite being by far the youngest in the studio. So, it was no surprise that Rose's apartment was the first place that Fen thought of when she realised they would be passing through Paris again.

Sadly, the postal system being not quite as efficient as it once was meant that Fen hadn't received a reply from Rose before they'd left Burgundy after bearing witness at the murderer's trial. With Arthur gone and his disappearance solved there had been no point in staying on at the vineyard, and James had offered to chaperone her to Paris. So here they were, walking together towards Madame C's apartment on the Rue des Beaux-Arts, with Fen hoping their early-morning arrival wouldn't be too much of a surprise.

The apartment was on one of the upper floors of a six-storey building. The road itself was an elegant, if not particularly long, one. At one end stood the famous college of fine art itself, its imposing stone gateposts topped with oversized busts of artists Nicolas Poussin and Pierre Puget. Fen had been through those gates a hundred times or more in her youth, going to see her father in his study and listening in to lectures on every aspect of art, from Byzantine icons to modern topics, such as the Fauves and Cubism.

The ground floors of most of the street's buildings were given over to shops and, due to the artistic nature of the neighbourhood, art galleries too. The war had taken its toll and some were now boarded up and others empty, while the lucky few still traded and displayed one or two decent-looking paintings in ornate gold frames in their windows.

There was a dressmaker on the street, too, with two lively-looking mannequins in the window wearing what must have been the latest in post-war fashions – cinch-waisted skirts and delicate swoop-necked blouses. Gold lettering above the door announced the services of a *Dufrais et Filles* – Dufrais and Daughters – and Fen wondered if the dressmaker and his or her daughters were there now, needles in hand, discussing trends for the autumn and winter season and planning spring fashions for 1946. She had a little money with her, and Fen knew the temptation to spend it all on something fabulous, rather than the more practical option of an overcoat, may well bring her back to that delightful-looking tailor as soon as she had a spare hour or so.

Each building on the street had a slightly different character, some with more ornate Juliet balconies, others with shutters at their windows or fancy classical-style podiums to their doors. They were all in what you'd call the French Imperial style, similar to many buildings built in the time of the great reformer Haussman, and, although suffering from a few years of neglect, elegant to the last.

Fen walked down the street a few steps ahead of James, clutching the handle of her suitcase in one hand, and the other she let trail along the rough, rusticated stone walls of the buildings. It was her way of connecting with her surroundings, 'seeing' something with her fingertips, almost as if she was reading the buildings as Braille. Stone would give way to glass, which would in turn change to wood… and even though she could see the street had shopfronts and doorways, she could feel it this way, too. Arthur hadn't laughed at her when he'd caught her doing this one afternoon down Midhurst's High Street (although Mrs Simpson from the bakers had given her a very strange look), as he said it all tied in with her love of cryptic crossword clues. 'Seeing' something in a different way, that was how puzzles were solved.

She pulled her hand back as they approached two large grey-painted doors, each eight or nine feet tall and easily three feet across. Together they made up one massive doorway. To either side of the building, there were private art galleries, the one to the left was already open for business, but sadly the one to the right was boarded up and closed. The name painted in beautiful gold curling script above the window was *Jacob Berenson*… a Jewish name, if Fen wasn't mistaken. Was that why this gallery, and not the one next door, was empty? Fen said a silent prayer for the absent owner, hoping that he hadn't been driven too far from his premises by the Nazis, or for too long.

James set his kitbag down and looked to Fen for confirmation before pressing his shoulder to one of the large grey doors, while turning the sturdy-looking cast-iron ring.

She nodded and the massive door shuddered open, scratching its well-worn arc across the encaustic tiles, and revealed the communal hallway behind. The daylight helped show the intricate patterns of the floor tiles, and as Fen's eyes adjusted to the darkness of the vestibule, she noted the set of tidy mailboxes, all named and numbered for the apartments and their occupants. A door the other side of the hallway led to a courtyard, which she remembered from her youth and attempts Rose had made to get her to 'draw from nature' by studying a bit of bark of one of the old lime trees. Now, though, Fen pointed James towards the cantilevered stone staircase, with its ornate cast-iron handrail that swirled and seemed to grow organically from the tiled floor.

'Ready for the climb?'

She picked up her suitcase and led the way, James following on behind as she swiftly made it up the first few storeys. By the fourth floor, she had started to slow down, and she was gratified to hear James's breathing deepen and quicken too as they climbed.

'A few more to go, I'm afraid,' Fen pointed up to where a ceiling lantern illuminated the landings of the uppermost floors.

By the time they reached apartment five, they were both a little out of breath. Fen paused before pressing the white button next to the door, wondering how old Madame C managed this climb every day. A moment later though they both heard the flat buzz of the electric doorbell sound in the apartment, followed by a rapid barking that was, in its turn, followed by a shushing and a voice calling out in a melodious tone, 'It's open!'

Fen pushed the door open and had barely got her foot over the threshold when the scampering sound of claws over wood parquet floor greeted them. She looked at James. 'Ah, yes, I forgot. I hope you're at home with dogs?'

'Dogs I'm fine with,' James muttered as the miniature poodle-like thing jumped up and clawed his knees, 'rats less so.'

'Bonjour, Tipper,' Fen leaned down and picked up the squirming little ball of fluffy energy. 'You're not a rat, are you, little one? Don't listen to the frightful man.' She was rewarded by a swift few licks to her nose, which made her laugh and James recoil in disgust. 'Tipper here is some sort of poodle crossed with… well, with whatever fancied his mother in the back alley. Maybe a Cavalier King Charles? He's a sweetie, though, you'll get used to him.'

'I'll probably end up sitting on him…' James was interrupted by the sight and sound of Rose, who appeared in the hallway to greet her guests.

'Fenella!' She approached, and Fen caught the familiar aroma in the air that she so associated with the older woman, that of floral ylang-ylang perfume teamed with turpentine and oil paint, and just a hint of some aromatic tobacco. 'Welcome, welcome.'

'Rose, it's so lovely to see you again. I'm so sorry we're so terribly delayed.' Fen met her hostess with a kiss on each cheek and then turned to introduce James. 'This is my friend Captain Lancaster.'

'James, please.' He stuck out his hand and was slightly nonplussed when Rose cocked her head on one side and proffered her hand as if to allow James to kiss it.

Fen noted how quickly James adapted to Rose's left-field greeting, bringing her hand close to his lips, but not too close, before gently letting her go. *He has been brought up the right way*, Fen thought to herself, as Rose arched her neck and brushed some unseen speck of dust off the front of her housecoat. She also couldn't help but observe how masculine and large James appeared in comparison to the supremely feminine apartment. The hallway was narrow and his frame seemed to take up most of its width. Just next to him was a spindly console table, painted white with delicate gold ring handles on its drawers, its puny legs like matchsticks compared to his bulk. The walls were painted a soft shade of pink and a delicately patterned Persian carpet covered a short length of the geometric parquet flooring.

'Do come through to the studio, my dears,' Rose beckoned them as she wafted off down the corridor, her voluminous velvet housecoat in the most jewel-like shade of amethyst purple, flowing out behind her.

Fen looked back at James and gestured for him to leave his kitbag with her suitcase where the hall widened.

'Quite the welcome,' James whispered to her, his eyes twinkling.

Fen raised a brow. 'Oh, James, you just wait.' She winked at him as they followed Rose into the light-filled room at the front of the apartment.

CHAPTER THREE

In most apartments of this size and style, the room they entered would have been a spacious salon or parlour. Here, however, the light streaming in from three floor-to-ceiling windows meant it was the perfect place for an art studio. Canvases were stacked up against the wall behind two large easels that faced one of the windows, while in between them sat a small table that was home to a couple of jars of dirty greyish-green-looking liquid, a precariously balanced palette and plenty of well-used paintbrushes. Some of the brushes were soaking in the jars, others were teetering on the edge of the table and looked as if they were about to join some of their fellows, which were lost in the ruched-up folds of a dust sheet, which was doing its best to protect the beautiful wood floor beneath it.

The smell of oil paint, turpentine and tobacco smoke was stronger in here and it instantly transported Fen back to a time when she would spend lazy hours reading Rose's art books and playing with jigsaws on the floor while Rose painted something or other at her easels. Nothing, it seemed, had changed from all those years ago, except that even more framed paintings now crowded the walls, hung between the panelling in a haphazard way, vying for attention and space, much like those at the summer exhibition at the Royal Academy.

Rose waved them past the tools of her trade to the other side of the room where a chaise longue and two comfortable-looking armchairs were placed around a low table.

'No need to apologise for the delay, Fenella dear. I was quite *at one* with the muse last night in any case. And it's simply marvellous to see you again. And meet your… friend.' She looked James up and down and indicated the oldest and saggiest armchair for him to sit on. 'Let me bring some refreshments through, make yourselves comfortable, dears.'

'I don't think she likes me,' James whispered to Fen.

'You're doing marvellously,' Fen reassured him, keen to alleviate his obvious concern that he might have put a foot wrong. 'She's just wonderfully eccentric. My brother and I used to play Madame Coillard Bingo, you know, after that game they play in America? If she said or did something silly or funny then we'd shout "bingo" to each other and roll around laughing. She must have thought we were feral animals.'

James chortled to himself and settled into the armchair and gazed around the room.

Fen looked around too, taking in the apartment's architecture and decor for the second time in as many months. The floor was parquet wood, smooth and bleached by the sunlight that filled the room from the three great windows. The walls were painted a pale eau de Nil with that beautiful light sea-green colour barely visible behind all the paintings.

'She is really quite the artist,' Fen explained to James. 'She was artist in residence at some rather smart château down in the Loire in the early twenties, then she started at the École des Beaux-Arts at about the same time as we moved here. That's where we met her. She knows everyone… Don't get her started on Picasso though. She still thinks he's a double agent apparently.'

James chuckled to himself again and shook his head. 'She does seem like quite a character.'

'She is. Pa always suspected she might be *Le Faussaire*, the art forger who was flooding the market with cheap, but seriously good, fakes in the thirties. I never bought that theory, but I did hear that some students called her lessons the École des Faux d'Art… She has a real eye for it though. Here, look at this,' Fen moved towards the windows and pointed to a small framed canvas that was hung between two of them. 'It's by an Impressionist. Deluca or Deland, or something. She's told me a hundred times, but I'm such a dunderhead at remembering artist's names.'

'One of the lesser-known ones, eh? Doesn't trip off the tongue like Monet or Manet.'

'I suppose so, that's my excuse anyway.'

Fen laughed and stepped back from the small painting, which, to the untrained eye, looked nothing more than a swirling mess of pastel-coloured paint strokes, devoid of composition or structure. To the more discerning viewer, however, it was a pretty little painting of a cherry tree in full blossom, verdant greenery around it.

'Gosh the light is stunning in here, isn't it?' Fen had wandered over to the middle of the three floor-to-ceiling windows and was caught in a trance by the view over the rooftops opposite. 'I think I can make out the dome of Saint Sulpice, and just behind it is the Luxembourg Gardens of course. Oh, I've missed Paris.'

'You had a happy time here?' James asked.

'Yes, rather. Slightly bohemian perhaps. And I was never really "one of the girls" at school. They called me Lily L'Étranger… Lily the Foreigner. But I learned the language and love the city. Did lose the gerbil in the catacombs once though, which upset Ma a bit. Ah, here she is…' Fen moved back towards the small table and perched on the edge of the elegant chaise longue as Rose flounced into the room carrying a brightly varnished papier mâché tray, on which was a small ornate silver teapot and three delicate teacups.

Tipper jumped up next to Fen on the daybed and snuffled his little nose into her lap.

'Afraid I don't go in for breakfast much myself. But I grow my own mint. Desperately good for the digestion and of course free, which is undeniably a bonus.' Rose sat herself down in the other armchair and began to pour the steaming liquid into the teacups. She passed them around and Fen inhaled the sweet, fresh aroma of the mint tea. 'It looks a bit insipid, but come the cocktail hour it goes marvellously well with a tot of rum and some molasses, if you can ever come by that sort of thing these days.'

'Oh Rose,' Fen reached over and gently touched her friend's arm. 'It is so lovely to see you.'

'And you, my dear,' Rose replied. 'Now, you must fill me in on what you got up to in Burgundy. You mentioned a murder?'

Fen sighed, and looked across at James. He gave a slight nod of his head, and she settled down to telling Rose all about what had happened since she'd last seen her.

'Tell me, dear, how long do you think you'll be staying?' Rose asked, once the conversation had moved on from Fen's most recent adventures. Condolences over Arthur's death had been offered and gratefully accepted and Fen had explained how she'd met Captain Lancaster.

'Well, I don't want to impose, but I'd like to visit a few of my old haunts,' she sighed. 'Hopefully, the city won't all be changed and boarded up like some of those galleries on the street below.'

'Same, same, but different, as they say in the Far East.' Rose twisted her long rope of pearls, which hung down from her neck, around her fingertips. 'It might not be quite what you remember, but then you were but a child, Fenella dear, an ingènue, a débutante!'

Fen laughed. 'And innocent as a babe in arms is what you're saying? Tell me, is it business as usual at the Deux Magots?'

'Oh Fenella, what do you know of that old dive?' Rose winked at her. 'But, yes, you'll still see Sartre propping up the bar if you're unlucky.' She placed her teacup down and from a pocket of her voluminous velvet housecoat drew out a long, black cigarette holder. She leaned forward, her pearls clanking onto the silver teapot, and pulled a cigarette from an open packet on the table. 'Don't mind, do you?' she asked, not waiting for an answer as she flicked open an American-style lighter and took a deep drag.

'Rose…' Fen paused.

The older woman raised her eyebrows and beckoned Fen to carry on.

'I was wondering, only because I never heard back from you, did you read all of my letter?'

Rose nodded as she exhaled a tight plume of smoke.

'Well, I was wondering would you be able to put James up for a few nights, too?' Fen looked over to where James shifted uneasily in the sagging armchair.

'Ah. No.' Rose then took another deep drag, eyeing up the man in her apartment all the time. She exhaled. 'I hate to be the proverbial bearer of… but I haven't told you another snippet of news.' She leaned back in the chair, giving Fen and James a masterclass in the dramatic pause. At last she spoke again. 'I have a lodger now.'

Fen tried to hide her disappointment and listened to Rose as she described her new paying guest. It wasn't that she was desperately upset to be separated from James, but she did feel embarrassed that the poor chap now didn't have a place to stay. Plus, she had been getting used to his company and liked the fact that he was a flesh-and-blood living link to Arthur. A comfort blanket in human form.

Before James could excuse himself and start looking for his own lodgings, a noise to the back of the room alerted them to the fact that someone else was in the apartment.

Fen turned to see one of the doors that led off from the studio open and a strikingly beautiful woman entered the room.

Tipper jumped off the chaise longue and snuffled around her feet.

'Aha! Here she is herself, Simone! Come in, my dear, and meet Fenella and her young man.'

'Oh he's not…'

'I'm not…'

Fen and James's protestations faded into the air as Simone came over to greet them.

James, who was already halfway to standing, almost fell over himself in getting fully upright. 'How'd you do?' He stretched his arm out and the svelte, terribly chic young woman giggled, not understanding the typically English greeting. James said hello again, this time in French and Simone shook his hand.

Fen looked at her. *Her waist can't be any larger than my thigh*, she thought. *And that skirt, it's beautiful!*

Simone turned to face Fen and introduced herself. 'Simone Mercier, hello.'

Fen introduced herself in her own near-perfect French.

'Oh this is marvellous, such clever English folk!' Simone laughed again and went to stand next to Rose, who placed a maternal hand on her shoulder.

'Off to work, dear girl?' Rose asked her.

'Yes, and I must hurry, I am late again… *tch*, my bag?' Simone cast her eye around the room and then sashayed towards James and bent over next to him, retrieving a small leather handbag from next to his chair. '*Oop la*, here it is!' She giggled and waved an air kiss to each of them as she left the room.

Rose looked at James and not unkindly said, 'So you see, Captain Lancaster, it's just the most desperate of timing that you've both descended when darling Simone is already in residence. She's a poppet, isn't she?'

'No, I mean yes, absolutely. Quite understand.' James fluffed his words a bit and Fen shook her head in disbelief. She'd heard of pretty girls turning men's heads, but this one seemed to have twisted James's noggin right off.

With the excitement of Simone's entrance, and almost as swift exit, over, the three of them sat back down and finished off their mint tea.

'I hope you don't mind me remarking, Fenella dear,' Rose said, narrowing her eyes in concentration as she looked at Fen's face. 'But you look like death, darling one.'

Fen touched her cheek and could feel the heaviness of the skin under her eyes. All of a sudden, the lack of sleep on the uncomfortable train caught up with her and she stifled another yawn, then replied, 'I must admit, I do feel rather tired.'

James pushed himself out of the armchair. 'I'll take my leave then.' He bowed a goodbye to Rose, and Fen couldn't help but smile as she noticed Rose slightly incline her head in reply.

'Fen will see you out, won't you, dear. And don't let Tipper escape! Tipper!' Rose called to the little dog as Fen and James left the room.

'Will you be all right – finding somewhere to stay, I mean?' Fen asked, feeling slightly responsible for his predicament.

'Don't worry, I can fend for myself. I'll probably hit the hay all the way through till sun-up anyway.' He paused in the hallway and picked up his kitbag, giving her a reassuring smile. 'I must say, though, I'm a bit jealous of the company you'll be keeping tonight.'

'Honestly,' Fen rolled her eyes and pushed him out the door. 'But, James, do call round later or tomorrow morning. And drop me a line to let me know which hotel you find.'

'Will do.' He threw her a quick salute and disappeared down the stairs.

Fen waved and then slipped back into the apartment. She had become fond of him, especially now he was a lot less gruff than he used to be, but she had to agree with him, if anyone could fend for themselves in this world, it was ex-SOE operative Captain Lancaster.

CHAPTER FOUR

Fen picked up her suitcase from the hallway and carried it back into the studio room. Light was streaming in through the three large windows and Fen blinked a few times, her eyes smarting with tiredness.

Rose stood waiting for her, holding open one of the doors that led off from the room.

'The smaller of the two again, I'm afraid,' Rose explained. 'Dear Simone has taken the suite…' she laughed to herself '… as I like to call it. I mean, it has a basin, that's all.'

'I thought that was your room, Rose?'

'Ah, well, Tipper and I do just fine in the box room at the front of the apartment, you know the one between the studio and the kitchen. Closer for midnight snacks and you know…' The older woman rubbed her thumb and forefinger together to indicate that Simone might well be paying a little bit more for the privilege of the larger room.

Fen nodded. 'Understood, and thank you so much for letting me stay. Of course I'll pay—'

'*De rien*, dear girl, I wouldn't hear of it.' Rose raised her hand to shush Fen. 'And Simone being here is more of a favour to my friend Henri. He took pity on the girl during the war and asked if I could help her out. Poor thing had nowhere to stay after her last, well, *dalliance* broke down, if you understand my meaning. Now, pop yourself in there and grab forty winks or so. I'll be quiet as a mouse out here, though I can't vouch for Tipper.' The dog woofed on cue and Fen laughed.

'Don't worry, Rose,' she stifled another yawn. 'I think I could sleep through the fall of Rome at the moment.' She pressed her hand against her mouth again as another yawn came out.

'Of course, dear girl.' She turned to leave, then said, 'Oh, and before I forget, a letter arrived for you yesterday, from England it looks like. I've left it on your bed. Unpack and settle in, dear. I'll see you for a little drinkie later, and there's some bread and pâté and yesterday's soup I can heat up for you if you wake up in time for lunch. You know where the bathroom is, make yourself at home.'

Fen smiled at her hostess and set her case down on the floor of the bedroom as Rose left and closed the door behind her. Fen looked at the bed – a double no less, with a pretty upholstered bedhead – and then noted the other, familiar, pieces of furniture. Opposite the bed there was a chest of drawers and a makeshift hanging rail for any longer garments. Just like in the studio, the walls were covered in a patchwork of paintings, some framed and some just canvases stretched across their wooden frames. A few looked familiar, as if they were copies of more famous works that Fen might have seen in art books or exhibition catalogues.

Perhaps Rose was a famous forger after all, thought Fen as she crossed the room to the window that overlooked the courtyard of the apartments.

As Rose's flat was on the fifth floor, Fen could look down and see the crown of the tree below her and countless other windows, some still shuttered or with curtains closed and some allowing a direct view into the lives of the people waking up to the day in the flats around her. The window in this room was of a more normal size to the ones at the front of the building and Fen pulled the heavy curtain across it to block out the morning light. She turned towards the invitingly made-up bed and reached down to pick up the letter that was lying on the floral counterpane. She glanced at the handwriting and knew at once that it was from Kitty, her dear friend to whom she had only just sent a letter from the station.

Fen shook her head slightly at the inconvenience of having letters cross in the post but opened it up, and despite having to practically force her eyes to stay open, she devoured the news from West Sussex.

Mrs B's kitchen table, Midhurst,
Boring old West Sussex,
October 1945

Darling Fen!

PARIS! I mean, that's where you are by now, and it's the answer to that clue you put in your letter from Burgundy. Do send more, and more letters too in general please, they're a heck of a lot more interesting than reading whose sheep have got stuck in whose ditch as reported in the Midhurst Herald, that's for sure.

By Jove, what a time you've been having!! Mrs B says we should never have let you go gallivanting across the continent only to find bad news. And Fen, we are all really, really sorry about Arthur. He was such a nice and clever man. I hope you hurry home soon, dear friend, so we can give you one of these big mugs of tea and an even bigger hug. Gosh, now you've got me crying.

Not much else to report here. Dilly has decided to move to London and learn secretarial skills. I'm sure she'll be ace at it, she's so good at everything. Mrs B says she'll be wasted in town as she'd make such a good farmer's wife, but Dil is adamant. I think I'll stay on for a while longer. Mrs B's knees

> *crack every time she bends over to hang the washing from the basket and she's slowing down on her knitting too. Still, cows to be milked and fields to be tilled. Yawn. But having Dilly in London will be a riot. We must go and visit her once you're home and she's got settled in lodgings.*

Kitty's news trailed off and Fen read the couple of clippings from the local newspaper that Kitty had deemed worthy of the postage. She couldn't work out if she was meant to be impressed or shocked at the size of Mr Rivers's prize-winning marrow, photographed complete with bow and rosette, or if the piece about Reverend Smallpiece losing his spectacles at the church fête was meant to be comical or not. The mental image of the kindly old vicar from their local church on hands and knees under the cake table in the tea tent did make her smile though.

Midhurst, West Sussex… Fen sighed as she pushed aside one of the heavy curtains and looked out over the skyline of Paris from her window. *I couldn't be in a more different place.* As keen as she was to see Kitty, Dil and even old Mrs B, she was glad to be back in her favourite city, even if right now all she wanted to do was sleep.

She clicked the catches of her suitcase open and fished out her nightdress. It felt odd undressing and putting her nightie on at the wrong time of day, but she hated the thought of getting in between those beautifully clean sheets in her travelling clothes.

Folding the letter and slipping it back into its envelope, Fen slid in under the counterpane and crisp white sheets and, within moments, her eyes had closed and she had fallen asleep, the letter from her best friend still clasped in her hand.

CHAPTER FIVE

'Well, that just sounds incredible,' Fen was listening to Simone talk about her work in the fashion atelier. She had slept all morning and most of the afternoon, and had finally roused herself as she'd heard Simone return home from work. Rose had been good enough to heat up the soup and fetch out the pâté from the refrigerator and the three of them had eaten together.

Now the two younger women were washing up the dishes in the kitchen and Fen was running out of superlatives in reply to Simone's stories. Hearing about the swathes of fabric in the cutting room had been 'super', the idea of modelling clothes for the wealthy aristocrats who came to purchase them was 'simply splendid' and Fen had even blurted out a 'by Jove' when Simone had told her about the possibilities of travelling abroad for photo shoots.

'I swear, it is the most fun a girl can have, no?' Simone asked rhetorically, describing a fashion shoot in which she had modelled recently.

'A beautiful girl like you maybe,' Fen blushed a bit. Her old land girl friends back at the farmhouse in Sussex would have *died* to be able to talk to a real-life model and hear about her day from the cutting room to the catwalk. Fen made a mental note to write to Kitty and Dilys and tell them all about this glamorous creature.

'Fenella...' Simone laid a slightly soap-sudded hand on Fen's arm. 'It is all a mask, see...' She pouted her lips and raised her eyebrows and mimicked putting on lipstick, rouge and mascara.

Fen laughed at her, but didn't disagree. Simone may be stunning, but Fen wondered if she was actually one of those quite plain girls underneath, who just knew exactly how to accentuate their best features. She took another sopping plate from Simone and started to dry it.

'I can show you some tips. You have very dark eyelashes, which I would *kill* for…' Simone winked at her and Fen smiled, '… and such good skin, if maybe a little weather-worn.'

Fen put down the plate she had dried and raised her hand to touch her cheek. She felt like she was on a slide under one of Madame Curie's microscopes and wasn't sure she entirely liked the scrutiny she was getting from Simone, who now pursed her lips and narrowed her eyes to fully gauge Fen's pores and wrinkles.

'A few too many days in the fields, perhaps,' Fen agreed and turned her face back to the drying rack, hoping Simone would stop analysing her. At twenty-eight she wasn't exactly old, and she did rather pride herself on her appearance, albeit not in an overly vain way. She did wonder, though, if her nightly ritual of just putting on Pond's cold cream and hoping for the best would pass muster here in Paris among the ultra-chic urbanites.

Luckily, Simone turned back to the washing-up bowl and changed the subject. 'Oh it was terrible though, you know, last week. We were posing on the steps of Montmartre modelling a new look, much fuller skirts, like this one,' she swayed her hips at the kitchen sink to indicate the folds in the skirt, 'and women – not men, mind you – *women* started shouting at us! Can you believe it? Every name under the sun!' Her soft brown eyes looked imploringly at Fen, and Fen found herself just nodding along while she dried up one of the soup bowls. 'It is a world gone mad. And you know why? Because apparently we flaunt the fabric. And it's not *de rigueur*, you know, it's not done. But it's progress, it's victory, that's what we're celebrating. Victory over oppression, victory over poverty.'

'And victory over the Germans?'

Simone shrugged. 'Yes of course, and that too. After all, fashionable people suffered like everyone else. Models and designers were going missing all the time. Like Catherine, my friend, she is only just back from Ravensbrück, you know, and the things she tells me, *ooh la la*.'

'Ravensbrück…' Fen knew of the concentration camp since its name had been splashed on the front of the newspapers back home when it was liberated by the Soviets in April.

'A camp.' Simone looked imploringly at Fen. 'A *death* camp.'

'Oh my word.' Since news of the death camps had filtered through to the allied press, Fen had wondered what it must have been like to live in fear of being plucked out of your home, or from the street, and condemned to that terrible fate. She wasn't so naïve as to not realise that the grainy pictures she'd seen in the newspapers must have shown only a glimpse of what those ghastly places had been like. And to now hear of someone who had survived… Fen couldn't imagine what it would be like to have survived such terror. 'Is she quite well now? She must be traumatised after being held there.'

Simone fell silent for a moment, then said, 'She is well. But she said God never showed his face inside the camp. She was on one of the last prisoner convoys out of Paris to that hateful place, but that only meant that the camp had had time to become a complete cesspool.'

'It's so hard to imagine.' Fen shook her head, unable to visualise the horrors of a death camp.

'We should count our blessings that imagination is all we need. Catherine still wakes in the night, she tells me, and screams out loud; she is not freed from the camp, not fully, not while she is still there in her dreams.' Simone jabbed a slender finger against her temple.

Fen shivered.

Simone turned back to the sink and carried on. 'But she survived, heaven save us, and she's back at the fashion house now, though she's not so quick to laugh or make a joke as she used to be. Her brother Christian is our chief designer. He tried all he could during the last months of the war to help his sister – we had the wives of Nazi officers shopping in our atelier, you see – and he asked all of them for help, but he couldn't secure her release any earlier. It's all very close to home, you know?'

Fen nodded, aware of how close to home losing someone really was. She almost couldn't bring herself to ask another question, but it was out of her mouth before she had time to stop herself. 'Why was she taken?'

Simone stopped washing for a moment and turned to Fen. '*Resistance*,' she whispered. 'As if they ever needed a reason. She was caught carrying a pistol by the Gestapo. She resisted their torture, so they sent her to what would certainly have been her death, if the Allies hadn't marched in just in time.'

'Poor, poor thing.' Fen shook her head, her heart full of pity for Simone's friend.

'She could have betrayed us all, but she didn't.' Simone looked thoughtful.

'Us all?' Fen looked up at Simone, who slowly turned to face her. 'Were you…?'

'Oh yes…' Simone said and Fen thought for the first time how much older her make-up and fine clothes made her look. She must only be in her early twenties, but she suddenly looked world-worn, the weight of experience heavy on her powdered brow. After a pause, she added, 'I was in the Resistance, too.'

CHAPTER SIX

'Ladies, ladies!' Rose called from the other room. 'Come through, come through, you must be done by now and I'm simply yearning for some conversation!'

'Coming!' Fen and Simone called in unison, which made Simone laugh, breaking the tension that had built up as they had spoken. Her words still resonated with Fen, however, and she couldn't help but think of Arthur and the part he played in the Resistance. *Would he still be alive now if he'd been sent to a camp, rather than the firing squad? Alive maybe,* she thought, *but a different man, perhaps.*

Simone flicked the water off her hands and Fen, still deep in thought, passed her the already damp tea towel. A few moments later Simone touched Fen on the shoulder. 'Coming?'

Fen nodded and together they walked back into the studio to attend on Rose, who was draped over the chaise longue, cigarette holder in one hand, the other stringing out her long rope of pearls and winding it between her fingers.

She had dressed up for the evening by adding a splendid orange silk turban to her outfit, and the light from the side lamps made it glow like a setting sun atop her head. Unlike the ancient château in Burgundy, where Fen had stayed most recently, this chic apartment had electric lights and the room was bathed in a warm glow as the incandescent bulbs did their best to illuminate through the dark, red velvet, gold-tasselled lampshades. Shadows now crept across the high ceiling and accentuated the pattern in the carved mouldings and ornate ceiling rose, from which hung a beautiful crystal chandelier.

Fen sank into the sagging armchair that James had sat in a few hours earlier and Simone took the one opposite her. The gold of the many picture frames caught Fen's eye and she tried to take them all in. They were hard to categorise and varied from landscapes in the style of Turner and Constable, to Dutch-style still lifes and more modern abstract pieces. Fen's eye was drawn to several self-portraits, all of which held her gaze as keenly as if she was looking at the woman herself.

'Now tell me, ladies…' The real Rose took a deep drag of her cigarette and then flicked the ash in the vague direction of the ashtray on the coffee table. 'What is your plan for tomorrow?'

'Back to the cutting room for me.' Simone smoothed out her full skirt over her angular knees. Fen looked down at her own pair (winners of a Knobbly Knees Competition in 1943, no less) and patted her tweed skirt down too. 'We have a new design being cut and I'm the model they're showcasing it on.'

'Wonderful, dear, wonderful. And you, Fenella?'

'Well, I'll see if James, Captain Lancaster, drops me a line, then I… well, I rather hoped to visit some of the galleries, the Rodin museum perhaps, and it might sound silly, but I've a hankering for just walking along the Seine and finding a café or two…'

'Charming. Most of the cafés are open still and the Louvre is reopened now… and it *even* has some artwork in it.' Rose took another deep drag from the elegant long black cigarette holder and laughed, waving at her own walls. 'Not quite as much as I have, mind! I could come with you, though, I need to see Henri anyway.'

'Who's Henri?' Fen quizzed her, while wracking her brains. She couldn't remember an Henri from their shared past, but Rose had already mentioned him once today.

'Henri Renaud,' Rose replied and sat a little more upright. 'I can't remember what I told you when you stopped by last month, Fenella dear, but Henri and I worked together during the war.'

That made more sense. Fen knew that sometimes one's wartime acquaintances were on a 'need-to-know' basis. Her talks with Arthur, and latterly James, had taught her that. Still, she was curious as to their relationship. 'You worked together? At the école?'

'No, not there. Henri has his own art gallery, you see, quite close to the Louvre, which is where he is also a consultant, if you will, a sort of roving fine art curator.' She waved her cigarette in the air as she tried to find the words. 'Put it this way, he is very well connected and the Louvre was very lucky to have him on board when it came to finding places to squirrel away their works before the Germans came.'

'Was the Louvre raided by the Nazis?' Fen asked and looked at Simone too for confirmation.

She stayed silent but raised her eyebrows.

'Not raided so much, but leaned on rather heavily to send its masterpieces to the Fatherland for "safekeeping". Ha! Safekeeping my *derrière*!' Rose flicked ash across to the ashtray on the table and tutted to herself as she just missed. 'Anyway, after all of that excitement, he was asked by the Germans to help with what they called the *sequestration,* or what we normal people would call the looting and pillaging.' She paused for a moment, her brow furrowed. 'The Germans wanted to steal as much art as they could from our galleries, both public and private, and from our homes.'

'Not *our* homes as much,' Simone added softly, following Rose's eyeline up to the little Impressionist painting on the wall, the one between two of the grand windows that Fen had pointed out to James earlier.

'Simone is right.' Rose leaned forward and stubbed out the cigarette, replacing it in her hand with a glass of crème de menthe. 'Those of us of a Christian persuasion got off lightly. But the Jews, oh dear Lord, what those poor people went through.' Rose knocked back the green liqueur and winced slightly as she swallowed it down. 'Those Nazi *bastards* would arrest the families on *no charge* save that of being Jewish, then commandeer the apartments and strip those homes of their valuables! Strings of pearls, diamonds, paintings, sculptures, furs! Everything was put in boxes and sent back to Germany for the pleasure of who knows who…' Rose set down the thick glass tumbler rather heavily on the table and Fen noticed a shake to her hand as she poured herself another slug of the mint liqueur. 'You want some?' Rose asked and Simone, without being prompted, got up and went towards the kitchen. She returned a moment later with two more glass tumblers.

'Just a little bit then,' Fen murmured and accepted a shot of the crème de menthe. She was taking in what Rose had just told her, and it shocked her. She had known, of course, that the Nazis had routed out the Jews, and their treatment of that faith had been one of the reasons the Allies had joined the war, but now hearing more about death camps and sequestrations… it was becoming much clearer to her quite what terrible atrocities had been committed here in France.

'So, what did you and Henri do together then, Rose?' Fen was more curious than ever, a trait of her personality that at times landed her in the soup, but more often than not meant she got to the bottom of what she wanted to know. She posed her question and then leaned back again in her chair, tucking her stockinged feet up under her and, unlike Rose, nursed the eye-watering liquid, taking small sips as the older woman continued.

'Henri Renaud is a well-connected man. And it is always *who* you know, not *what* you know, that gets you anywhere in this life. Not that Henri isn't very clever, for a man, but he was definitely the right person in the right place, at the right time. He was married, you see, to a wonderful woman called Heidi, from Bavaria, but she died and the baby with her, oh, this must have been in '35 or '36. Anyway, Heidi had struck up a friendship with the wife of the

German ambassador here in Paris and even after her death, Henri maintained a friendship with Otto and Susanne Abetz.' Rose paused and picked something from her teeth, before changing tack slightly.

'Now, don't get me wrong, I'm as patriotic as the next eccentric artist, but I trod that fine line between collaborating and surviving.' Rose looked at her and Fen wondered if she was trying to gauge Fen's own reaction. She carried on a moment later. 'You see, I didn't refuse to paint the portraits of the German officers. Such vain men, the Germans, so interesting to paint.' Rose lit another cigarette and inhaled deeply.

'Wasn't that frowned upon?' Fen wouldn't have dared asked anyone else, but there had been something about Rose's telling of the story that invited it.

'Frowned upon?' Rose pulled a face. 'Everyone should have access to art, dear girl, we are all equal in the muse's eyes. And anyway,' she raised just the one archly plucked eyebrow as she looked at Fen, 'they paid handsomely and there's nothing more insufferable than a starving artist.' She winked. 'And it got me into their trust.'

Fen nodded and smiled. *Bingo*. It was obvious now that all Rose's talk of treading fine lines was just her cover story. But why she needed one was still a mystery to her. 'So, you and Henri were both trusted by the Germans… then what happened?'

CHAPTER SEVEN

'The Germans found themselves needing an art specialist to value and catalogue the art they were stealing from the Jewish homes and galleries. Abetz recommended Henri for the job, not realising that Henri was as passionately patriotic to France as I was.'

Rose paused as if taking the time to consider what she'd just said.

'Henri spoke to me of Abetz's offer to him one night and we came up with a plan. I was to be his assistant and follow him around noting down his evaluation and, more often than not, his *valuation* of the paintings that the Germans wanted. They saw everything in terms of francs and Reichsmarks; it was heartbreaking.'

Rose took a moment to collect her thoughts, then continued. 'I would then come home here and type up my shorthand notes, creating a list of the paintings. In the meantime, they were moved from the apartments to a warehouse.'

'Not just any warehouse,' Simone nudged Rose.

Fen wondered if she knew the story so well due to Rose telling it often enough or if it was common knowledge among the Resistance fighters in the area.

'Not just any warehouse, that's right. The German officers could be cruel beasts and shout at you until spittle came out of their mouths, but they were also a pushover once they trusted you and fundamentally lazy. If you could offer them an easy, *collaborative* plan, they would more than likely say yes. So, Henri suggested they used his own warehouse space, just to the north of the city, to house the paintings as they awaited transit to Germany or to the auction house.'

'Auction house?'

'Yes,' Rose stubbed her cigarette out and played with her long rope of pearls again. Fen wondered if it was the artist in her that always had to have her hands occupied in doing something but tried not to let it distract her from what Rose was saying. 'It seems war is an expensive business and the Nazis decided to *sell* the paintings they didn't deem worthy of the Reich. Modern pieces, valuable, to be sure, but what they deemed "degenerate" art. That's why they brought in Henri, an esteemed dealer of modern and contemporary art as well as an expert in the classics, to tell them what to keep and what to sell, and *how* to sell it. The trade here was booming throughout the war, with less scrupulous dealers asking no questions regarding the provenance of works.'

'That's so terrible.' Fen could imagine the crates of packed-up paintings being shipped away from their rightful owners, or worse, sold to pay for the cruelty that was being visited upon them. It pained her to think of what those families had so recently been through. 'But you didn't let them get away with it, did you, Rose?'

'What could I do?' Rose shrugged, but Fen noticed a twinkle in her eye.

'Rose?' Fen was on the edge of her seat.

'You're right.' The older woman sat forward now and let her long necklace dangle between her knees as she lit another cigarette and spoke animatedly about her plan. 'I was there, you see, in those apartments. And if I didn't know whose apartment it was, I would look for clues: unopened letters on a console table, a labelled postal box in the communal hallway, or maybe I just listened to what Henri and the officers said. And when I typed up the list of all the paintings and sculptures, I came up with a code. A cipher, if you will. Not a complex one, but enough to disguise the name of the family whose apartment we'd been in that day and who owned the art.'

Fen waited, impatient to hear more of the story as Rose took another sip of her drink. 'Then I hid that coded name *into* the list, disguised as a transit number or some such. The Germans, so in love with pointless bureaucracy, never even noticed it there.' She chuckled to herself as she inhaled from her cigarette, then coughed, but laughed again. 'I even managed to code in where I heard Müller – he was the man in charge, you see – say the art was destined for, like "this one for Hitler himself" or "my wife loves the countryside, she can have that one of the haystack", you know the sort of thing.'

Fen felt her jaw drop. 'So you knew exactly what was stolen, and from whom?'

'And sometimes where it was going.'

'You were a brave woman,' Simone said approvingly.

'Wasn't it terribly dangerous? What if you'd been caught?' Fen asked.

Rose shrugged. 'What could they say? I was an assistant. A mere woman, a clerk just parroting what the men said. To all onlookers, I was helping the Reich. Ha! The thought of it.' She took a deep inhale from her cigarette in its holder and flicked away the ash. 'And what would they find? You know what manifests and transport lists look like, they might as well all be in code, they look so like double Dutch anyway. Of course, if I'd been caught at the time actually writing down who the paintings belonged to, while we were there in the apartments, I probably would have been shot.'

'Or sent to Ravensbrück,' Simone shuddered.

'Yes, so I kept it all up in here,' Rose tapped her head, 'until I was alone with my typewriter and cipher and then I came up with these bogus columns of "transportation serial B", or whatever, and then handed the list over to Henri to mark up which were to be sold or sent to Berlin. That was when the real work happened. Henri had the list rubber-stamped by Müller, then gave it to his warehouse manager, who, under the Germans' own noses, chalked the codes onto the back of the paintings before they were crated up!'

'That's so clever, Rose. I still can't believe some were just sent to auction though. Were many sold?' Fen was still shocked that local dealers and auctioneers would do such a thing, though she had to admit the proverbial gun to the head was always a persuasive reason.

'Yes, too many. Some of the Jewish families had some beautiful paintings – Matisse, Mohl, Braque, even that Picasso's daubings. We called it *avant garde*, the German called it *degenerate*, but they knew enough to know that they were worth something. So, Henri took my list and marked up which paintings would delight the Führer and which ones could just help line the Reich's pockets, but knowing full well that I had already snuck my code in. And now the war is over, it's safe to decipher the names and start tracking down the art. Some of our dear friends are returning to Paris and I can now help them, thank the Lord.'

'You've decoded the list, Rose?' Simone seemed put out that she didn't know this already.

'No, dear child, I'll have it back from Henri tomorrow. He saved it from the fires that the Nazis lit as they retreated.'

Fen toasted her. 'I'm so impressed, Rose.'

Rose shrugged the praise away. 'We all did our bit. You tilled the fields in rain or shine to help feed your countrymen and women, Simone here took potshots at Germans and I… I just typed up a list.'

CHAPTER EIGHT

Fen slept well that night, despite her almost all-day nap earlier. Whether it was the crème de menthe, the exhaustion of last night's journey or the comfortable bed, she couldn't tell, but there was a bit of her that was sure it was because she felt, in some way, that she was home. Not home as in Oxford with her parents, or home with Mrs B in the old farmhouse near Midhurst where she'd spent the war, but home in the sense that everything around her was familiar. She had spent hours in this apartment as a girl, either painting alongside Madame Coillard (as she had always called her back then) or playing with her brother as her parents left them to amuse themselves running marbles along the smooth parquet floor while they talked and laughed with their eccentric friend.

She'd also reread her letter from Kitty and she could almost hear her voice through the words as she sent condolences and local news. Fen missed her friend terribly. Simone seemed nice enough, but Fen would give anything for Kitty to be here now, sharing her room like they did at Mrs B's, giggling into the night about some fancy man or other, or just companionably going about their work. Still, it was good to know that Kitty, Dilly and Mrs B were safe and well. It all helped to ease the pain of knowing now that her beloved fiancé Arthur was dead.

By 8.30 a.m. the next morning, Fen was up and dressed and sitting in the studio, a hot cup of mint tea steeping in front of her. She'd been woken by Tipper scratching at her door an hour or so earlier and rather than let him wake the rest of the household up, she'd taken him for a quick run around the tree-lined courtyard in the centre of the building. The early-morning blast of chill air had been good for her and she felt far more alert than she had the night before.

Now, sitting in the sunlight streaming through the windows, a newspaper caught her eye... the name Sartre – hadn't Rose mentioned him last night? She picked the paper up from the floor where it had been doing a grand job of protecting the wooden blocks from splashes of white spirit and oil paint. She read the headline properly: 'France Seen From America, by our special correspondent Jean-Paul Sartre'. She read with interest about the journalist and philosopher tasting Coca-Cola for the first time and meeting President Roosevelt.

'Well, Tipper,' Fen said, as the little dog padded into the room and nuzzled her outstretched hand, 'if I do come across this Sartre chap in the bar of the Deux Magots, I shall ask him all about this Coca-Cola drink!'

She read a few more articles, enjoying the challenge of testing her French and stretching her vocabulary. There had been a rise in Mafia-style gangs, it seemed, according to one article at least, which blamed American films for giving Frenchmen ideas, while there had also been a scandal in the Bois de Boulogne, where a painting had been stashed in the racehorse stables. Paris was certainly more exciting than Midhurst, that was for sure.

Simone's bedroom door opened and the young woman crossed the studio to get to the bathroom, which was on the other side of the apartment. Seeing her now in her nightdress and without a scrap of make-up on, Fen realised that the assumption she'd made last night over the dishes about Simone being plain under her lipstick and powder wasn't entirely correct. Her skin glowed and her poise was as elegant as anyone's who had spent years at the barre. No, she wasn't unattractive without make-up, far from it, but her rouge and mascara had emphasised her features, which were actually more delicate and less striking in the clear morning light.

'Good morning, Fenella,' she spoke and raised a hand in greeting.

'Good morning, Simone,' Fen replied and went back to reading the newspaper.

Gradually, the apartment came to life. First, Simone dressed and breakfasted, if you could call just a small cup of coffee breakfast. Fen decided that Mrs B, her old landlady in West Sussex certainly wouldn't. She had always said that a breakfast wasn't a breakfast without at least one of the freshly laid brown eggs from the 'ladies' on the farm.

Fen was just thinking about those early-morning stints in the fields when Rose appeared from her bedroom, wafting into the studio with her hair in a bright-pink chenille turban and the rest of her draped in another voluminous velvet housecoat, this one turquoise in colour. A more different landlady to her last, you could not imagine.

Fen remembered the history of how Rose came to be in this apartment. Her parents had left it to her, their only daughter, after they had died, prematurely and devastatingly for the young woman, of the Spanish flu that had swept through Europe after the end of the Great War. Rose had become a financially independent young woman, and one not inclined to marry, it seemed. The artistic life suited her, and she only took the honorary title of *madame* on as she got older, as a way to distinguish herself to her pupils and clients.

A buzz of the doorbell, followed by the scrabbling of Tipper's claws on the wooden floor and his yapping, announced a visitor.

'That will be your young man, Fen dear.'

'Oh, he's not—'

'Simone!' Rose interrupted Fen and called out to her lodger. 'Be a dear and let the poor man in.'

'I suppose it might not be James,' Fen looked at the ormolu clock on the console table, it was still only 9 a.m. and remembering how he used to like drinking with the men at the vineyard, she wouldn't have put it past him to have found a bar rather than a hotel last night.

The sound of girlish giggles, and a deeper more earnest voice in the hallway, put paid to that idea, though, and, soon enough, the masculine bulk of James appeared in the studio, this time carrying the squirming Tipper in his arms.

'You see, he likes you,' Simone was still stroking the small dog as it strained against James's muscles. She kissed the pooch's head and Fen couldn't help but notice James's cheeks redden slightly at the attention, even if it was directed at the dog.

'Ahem,' James coughed as Simone ran her fingers along Tipper's back, brushing them against James's chest at the same time. 'Good morning all,' he continued as he placed the small dog down and gave it a little shake as its needle-like teeth hung onto his sleeve.

'Tipper!' Rose snapped and clicked her fingers and the dog obediently let go and shot off around the legs of the easels, upsetting a couple of paintbrushes from the side table between them. 'Oh, that stupid dog,' Rose sighed, as if this was a near-daily occurrence.

Fen stood up to greet James. Before she could cross the room to offer him a friendly handshake, Simone had reached up and given James a kiss on both cheeks. She then waved to the women.

'*Ooh la la*, I must go. I'm due at the atelier and I'm late. Simone, Simone...' she tutted to herself and riffled through her stylish little handbag. 'Key!' She held her quarry aloft. 'Not that I need it, you never lock the door, madame!' She waggled a finger at Rose, who raised her eyes ceiling-ward, letting the accusation glance off her.

'Have a good day,' James said to her as she left the room and then Fen watched as he followed her into the hallway. She couldn't catch their conversation, but she heard Simone giggling again. She shrugged her shoulders and sat back down with Rose.

'Beauty is such a transient power, don't you think?' Rose asked her, rather rhetorically. 'And yet such a strong one.'

'Oh to be young and beautiful, indeed.' Fen flapped the newspaper open again and ignored James when he walked back into the room. He came and sat down on the saggy old armchair and nodded a hello to the ladies.

'Captain Lancaster, good morning.' Rose reached forward and pulled a cigarette out of the packet. 'And to what do we own this pleasure?'

'Just checking in. *As asked.*' He put a certain emphasis on the final two words and Fen was shamed into lowering the newspaper and finally smiling at him properly.

'Thank you, James. Did you find a hotel yesterday?'

'Yes, all tickety-boo. Decent little place round the corner in fact. Close to that Deux Magots place you were speaking of, so, after a nap, which seemed to last most of the afternoon, I popped in there and shared a drink or two with some of the locals. Decent chaps.'

'Good. I was worried about you,' Fen smiled at him. 'I'm glad you didn't get lonely.'

'Not at all. And Simone has offered to show me some more hotspots tonight, so, all in all, my trip to Paris is really looking up.' He leaned forward in his chair and rubbed his hands together, obviously very pleased with himself. 'So what's the plan for today. Art galleries?'

'Definitely,' said Fen with enthusiasm, then raised an eyebrow at James and carried on, 'if you think you'll be interested? Rose has offered to take me to the Louvre. We can meet her friend Henri Renaud too and see if there's anything we can do.'

James looked puzzled, so with Rose's nodded permission, Fen filled James in on her certain style of war work.

'Blimey, Madame Coillard, bravo.'

The older woman allowed herself a smirk. Then she sat upright and stubbed out her cigarette. 'Come, let's not tarry here with war stories. What's done is done. I need to get that list from Henri and you two can get some culture.' She paused and looked at James purposefully. 'I feel at least one of you will be greatly improved by some time in our wonderful national collection.'

Fen stifled a chuckle. She was pretty sure James could take a joke, but she caught his eye just to check. Luckily, he looked more rabbit-in-headlamps than annoyed and Fen really wanted to snort out a laugh. Instead, she gabbled out something along the lines of going to get ready and slipped back into her bedroom to check her reflection and fetch her coat.

CHAPTER NINE

The short walk from the apartment to the famous Louvre art gallery took the three of them down the appropriately named Rue de Seine, a road that led towards the city's great, wide river. As they neared the embankment, they passed the magnificent Institut de France, a building as ornate and embellished as anything you might see at Versailles.

Fen wanted desperately to go and explore, or even just to linger and run her fingertips along the rough stone wall as it met the cast-iron railings, but Rose kept them on a short leash and soon they had circumnavigated the building and were finally crossing the river via the wooden slatted bridge known as the Pont des Arts. This simple bridge joined the quaysides between the great building of the Institut de France and that of the Palace of the Louvre.

Once over the water, the three of them entered the art gallery through a nondescript side door, an intriguing thing in itself given the magnificence of the building, and Rose led them through corridors and doorways that would never usually be visited by mere tourists.

'What a maze!' Fen exclaimed at they climbed another staircase, having been up and down two already.

'These would have been the suites and bedrooms when this was a palace in Louis XIV's day,' Rose explained. 'Before he waltzed off to Versailles, that is.'

'I never knew this was a proper palace,' James was trying his best to make conversation.

Rose shook her head in despair as she carried on at pace along the grand corridor. 'Well, why did you think it was built? The clue is in the name, young man, *Palais* du Louvre! This is our equivalent to your Buckingham Palace.'

'Except we let our royals keep their heads,' James muttered, but luckily it seemed it was only Fen who heard, and mouthed a 'how rude' at him, much to his amusement.

Finally they came to a stop outside a beautifully painted white-and-gold door. Rose turned the handle and called out as she entered, 'Henri! *C'est moi*!'

Fen and James held back until Rose called them in.

'Come, come! Meet Henri Renaud, my partner in crime.'

A bespectacled man, who had been sitting behind a large partner's desk, was rising out of his seat as Rose pushed Fen and James forward to meet him. He was smaller than average, perhaps only as tall as Fen, and dwarfed by Rose with her magnificent pink turban. He was well-dressed and Fen guessed him to be in his mid-fifties, about the same age as Rose and her own parents. In fact, he had that sort of paternal look about him, and it saddened Fen to think that he'd lost his wife and child.

'Partner in no such thing,' he said warily, regarding the people in his office over the top of his spectacles. He shuffled the papers on his desk, and if Fen and James hadn't been so stunned by the beauty of the palatial room, with its floor-to-ceiling windows, ornately gold-framed mirrors and shiny parquet flooring, they may have noticed him subtly turn those papers upside down so they couldn't be read.

'We are safe to talk openly, Henri.' Rose collected herself and sat down in front of the large partner's desk. For this visit, she had chosen to replace the turquoise velvet housecoat with a long patchwork overcoat, while the pink turban had been securely fixed in place with a feathered pin. She looked uniquely suited to the grand apartment that they now found themselves in, the rest of them so dull and under-dressed by comparison. She gestured for Henri to sit himself down again too and introduced Fen and James to him.

'Ah, Fen Churche, like the station in London, yes?'

'Yes, monsieur,' Fen was gracious enough to say no more about the joke she'd heard a thousand times or more in her lifetime.

'And Captain Lancaster. Enchanted to meet you both. Although I can't think why Rose here would suggest we were doing anything *criminal...*' He cocked his head to one side and looked at her, turning the accusation back to her. 'Even in jest.'

Rose held his gaze, Fen noticed, then laughed. 'Henri, you take everything too literally.' She spread her coat out around her and sat more comfortably in the chair.

'I suppose I'm still too wary, even though the danger of being found out has passed,' Henri said, noticing that Fen was looking at a small bronze statuette of a female reclining nude, which was on his desk. It was simply rendered, and not explicit in any way – angular, but elegant – she reminded Fen of Simone.

'She's beautiful,' Fen murmured as Henri reached over and picked up the small figurine and handed it to her to look at properly. The bronze was heavy in Fen's hands, its solidity at odds with the elegance of the sculpture. Fen could just about make out a signature on the flat underside of the piece but didn't recognise the artist's name.

'She's a degenerate,' Henri said, shaking his head. 'I mean that purely in the artistic sense. She is beautiful, you are right. It takes a good eye to see through labels and experience art for how it makes you feel. She's been on my desk for several years now and is very dear to me.'

Degenerate... Rose had used that word last night to describe the works of art sold by the Nazis to fund their war effort.

Fen carefully placed the small statuette back down on the desk and smiled at Henri. It must have taken quite some bravery on his part to champion this artist while he carried on his work with the Germans, and she said as much to him.

'Yes, I received a fair few *comments*, let's say, from Müller and his goons,' Henri sighed. 'But I was only brought on board because I could see the value in artworks they would have otherwise assigned to the rubbish pile of history.'

'Or worse, burned,' Rose said. Then she flicked her hand in Fen and James's direction and carried on, 'Now, run along and enjoy the exhibits. Henri and I have work to discuss and you both need some culture. There's a door to the main galleries at the end of this corridor. I'll come and find you soon. Enjoy the *Mona Lisa*, though do remember the poor lady has been on her travels recently so might not look as dewy and fresh as she might.'

Fen shook her head in amusement. 'We will, Rose, *adieu*.'

She and James took their leave of Henri too and left Rose and her partner – of whatever sort – to their business.

'Culture for me then,' James breathed out a sigh once they were standing in one of the main galleries.

'She's just teasing,' Fen raised her eyebrows at him and he smiled. 'Come on, let's find da Vinci's finest and check she really is all in one piece. Apparently she's been in hiding everywhere from Chambord to Montauban before coming home to her palace.'

The pair followed their noses to find the famous painting, but all the while, Fen noted how empty the gallery was. There certainly wasn't as much on the walls or plinths as there had been the last time she'd been here, albeit that was probably in 1934, long before the Nazis decided they wanted most of the exhibits for themselves. There were some other tourists, however, or perhaps they were Parisians using the gallery as a good spot for a tryst. The thought reminded her of Simone's offer to James and she asked him about it.

'So where's Simone taking you later?'

'She mentioned some jazz café, I think, perhaps a bar or two. You should come, too.'

'Oh, I... well, I'm not really up to it after, you know... I mean, I don't want to intrude.'

James gently touched Fen's elbow and said, 'Arthur would want you to start living again, you know.'

The mention of her darling fiancé, now dead thanks to a Gestapo firing squad, brought tears to Fen's eyes. She quickly rubbed them with the heels of her hands and smiled up at James, his kindness reminding her of how kind and patient Arthur had been too. Hadn't it been Arthur who had asked her to look out for James? Perhaps, in his infinite wisdom, he'd asked James to look after her, too.

'Thank you, James,' she managed, while fishing around in her pocket for a handkerchief. 'Perhaps I will.'

'Good. I think it's what Arthur would have wanted.'

'You like her, don't you?' Fen asked James, as much to change the subject and give her eyes time to dry before they moved on from the Rubens they had been admiring.

'She's a classical depiction of the feminine form, but if you're talking about Simone and not the painting, then yes, she's quite a looker.' James winked at her, making her laugh a little.

'She was in the Resistance too,' Fen told him, then added, 'Brave and beautiful. The whole package.'

This didn't elicit as much agreement from James as Fen had expected and instead he gave a half-smile and wandered on to the next painting. Maybe he wasn't looking for love after all and, like her, just wanted a friend to show him around Paris. That they could do it together was a comforting thought. If Arthur could never share her experiences of being here, then his best friend would have to do. And perhaps, if they went somewhere terribly *à la mode*, they might even get to try a Coca-Cola.

*

Fen and James had just about taken in all the culture they could wish to when something caught Fen's eye in one of the smaller galleries.

'James, look here.' She pointed at the small oil painting. It was a still life, its dark background a foil for the vase that was spilling over with colourful flowers, greenery, grasses and wheat fronds. Looking closer, there were bugs and insects hidden among the exotic blooms, butterflies and spiders, an alert lizard and a snail, leaving a delicate silver trail.

'Very nice, if you like that sort of thing,' James muttered, rather non-committally.

'It's not the merits of the painting I'm interested in,' Fen replied, leaning forward across the stanchion rope to get a better look, 'although those tulips are beautiful.'

'Imported from Turkey apparently.'

'Excuse me?'

'Tulips,' James stated. 'Everyone assumes they're native to Holland, but the Dutch imported them from Turkey.'

'That's interesting,' said Fen, standing back again from the painting. 'But not as interesting as the fact that there is an almost identical copy of this painting on my bedroom wall at Rose's apartment. Down to that little snail and everything.'

'Hmm,' James took more of an interest in the exquisitely rendered Dutch still life. 'Perhaps Madame Coillard was *Le Faussaire* after all?'

Fen shook her head and elbowed him in the ribs.

'Excuse me,' a woman's voice interrupted their play-fighting and Fen and James apologised and allowed her to look at the painting. 'Any idea who it's by?' she asked them.

Fen looked at her. She was probably in her late forties and dressed smartly, a fox fur slung over one shoulder and a natty hat set at an angle. *So Parisienne*. And too vain to wear her reading glasses, Fen thought to herself as she leaned in and read the small card that was attached to the wall next to the painting.

'Ambrosias Bosschaert – 1573 to 1621.'

'I see, thank you,' the smartly dressed lady said and peered closer at the painting. 'I can't believe it,' she muttered, 'down to the ladybird and everything.'

'Madame, do you have a copy of this painting?' Fen recognised her own thoughts in the woman's words.

The woman stopped leaning and straightened her back. The fox's legs swung to and fro as she walked off, having not answered Fen at all.

Before James could venture their usual response to such behaviour, the familiar scent of ylang-ylang and tobacco alerted them to Rose's presence.

'Come, come!' She waved at them from the other end of the vast, empty gallery space and her voice echoed through the air.

'She's not a shy, retiring flower, is she?' James whispered out of one side of his lips to Fen as they got closer. For this, he received another elbow to the ribs.

'Hurry, you two, we have work to do!' Rose ushered them out of the gallery and into the fresh air, striding out before them so swiftly it left Fen no time to pose her question over the identical paintings.

The day was a mild one for the time of year, and as they crossed the Pont des Arts back to the Left Bank of the Seine and towards Rose's apartment, Fen noticed the many couples strolling around together, enjoying the crisp autumn weather. The leaves of the large lime trees were just starting to turn, their fruit dangling like large fluffy cherries. Fen had a pang of grief; she would have so loved to have brought Arthur here and walked arm in arm along the river, just passing the time of day, like those couples were doing.

Rose hurried them both along. 'No dawdling, my dears,' she called back to them as she swept her way along the pavement like a ship in full sail.

'What's the hurry?' James stopped walking and rested his hands on his hips as the three of them were nearing the end of Rose's road. 'It's just there's a rather good-looking little café there and I might stop in for a bite to eat, if you don't mind.' He looked at his watch. 'You're more than welcome to join me. It is lunchtime after all.'

When he said that, Fen became aware of her own rumbling stomach and looked towards Rose to see what she would say.

Surprisingly, to both Fen and most likely James too, Rose did an about-turn and headed into the café. 'Fine,' she said. 'But lunch is on you, Captain. And I'm hungry.'

CHAPTER TEN

The café was an utter delight. Fen tucked into an *entrecôte* steak, glistening with a herbed butter, while Rose lived up to her promise – or threat – of being exceptionally hungry and dug into a *coq au vin* that looked so rich and hearty, unlike anything Fen had seen in the days of deprivation throughout the war. James had joined her in having the steak, but she could see he was also wolfishly eyeing up the steaming pot of stew in front of the older woman.

'You think I didn't know the best thing on the menu?' Rose looked at them both with a definite twinkle in her eye. 'I had to spend my ill-gotten gains from painting all those German officers on something.'

'I'll trust your recommendation next time,' James said, and Fen nodded, though she couldn't fault the juicy steak that was on the rarer side of medium. She remembered this style of cooking from her schooldays and her initial horror at seeing the bloodied juices seep out of a lightly cooked piece of red meat. She'd become not only accustomed to it, however, but realised now how much she'd missed it once they were back in England where the *haut*-est of cuisine had been boiled beef and cabbage in her college refectory. And then, with the outbreak of war and the years of rationing, this sort of luxury had been hard to come by at all, however it was cooked.

'This is delicious,' she murmured, in between mouthfuls, and wiped a piece of pan-fried potato around the garlicky juices on her plate. 'Ma and Pa would be so jealous. Real French cooking!'

'The best!' Rose raised her wine glass – she had insisted on a carafe of the *vin de table* too – and clinked it with the others. 'There was a silver lining to being occupied,' Rose continued, 'with the German army in town, they made sure that the restaurants had enough food. But it takes a local to know which cafés have true artists in the kitchen.'

'I thought it had all been rather hard-going?' Fen asked, before popping another piece of the succulent steak into her mouth.

'Oh, it was and it wasn't,' Rose sighed and then took another sip. 'Don't get me wrong, the war was terrible and it destroyed many, many lives and businesses. But Paris was a bubbling crucible of opportunity, for some at least. I sold more paintings during the occupation than ever before. We,' she gestured around the room and Fen took it to mean the whole of Paris, 'were still the centre of the world's art market and there were fortunes to be made. Still, thank the heavens, it's over now.'

The three of them toasted the end of the war, and being in each other's company, absent friends of course, and anything else they could think of until their glasses were empty and their plates cleared too. Not a scrap was left anywhere by any of them, a testament to how grateful they all were for the bounty that they'd just enjoyed.

'You said we had work to do?' Fen asked Rose as the waiter piled their empty plates up his arm and placed a small coffee and dessert menu in front of them.

'Yes,' Rose answered Fen but was looking more interested in the list of puddings in front of her. '*Garçon*!' she called across to the waiter who had returned to the bar. 'Three *tarte Tatin* please!' She waved the small menu at him and he came and picked it up, not bothered in the slightest by Rose's eccentric ways. 'You'll thank me, believe me,' she said to Fen and James as they sat back in their chairs, already feeling more full than they had in a while.

'We'll need a kip after this,' James rubbed his stomach and leaned back in his chair.

'No time for idling, chickadees,' Rose straightened out the place mat in front of her. 'We do indeed have work to do. Fenella, I have a wonderful surprise for you.'

Fen couldn't help herself and, before Rose could announce her surprise, took the opportunity to ask her about the Dutch floral still-life painting that had intrigued both her and the woman with the fox fur.

'Ah, you spotted that,' Rose said, a glint in her eye.

'Yes, and, bravo really, as it's incredibly good. I mean, I don't think there's chance we could ever compare them side by side, but from what I can remember from both, it's a near-identical match.'

'Indeed. Down to the little creepiest of crawlies...' Rose inched the fingers of one hand across the table as if they were an insect. Then she laughed. 'Of course, I had them side by side before the war and, if I say so myself, my copies are rather fine.'

'Copies... that makes sense. But how did you...?' Fen was flabbergasted. *It couldn't be that... No, Rose would never have swapped them over, would she?*

'That Bosschaert would have been right up Herr Göring's street, it had to be rescued along with the others.' Rose looked at Fen, and smiled coquettishly. 'And no, dear girl, I was never left alone with the original, if that's what you're asking.'

'Why do you do it?' James asked, rescuing Fen from her blushes.

'Why? Well, it's a discipline, isn't it? Anyone can daub some paint on a canvas and call it art. But looking at something, examining it from all angles so you can be absolutely sure that you can copy it, tiny piece by tiny piece, well, that is an achievement.'

'I think I understand,' Fen sucked in her cheek as she thought of what to say, then carried on. 'It's like the crossword puzzles that I love solving. Arthur taught me how to do the cryptic ones and he always said, "if you can't solve your five down, check your six across," or suchlike. What he meant was that sometimes you can't work something out just on its own, you have to really look around and find something else that fits in with it.'

'Exactly,' Rose waved her hands around and emphatically agreed. 'To copy something, you have to really look at it, really understand it. Decode it, if you will. Now, do you want to know what this surprise is, or not?'

'Oh yes! Sorry, please do tell.'

'Well, guess who is coming to see me, us, this afternoon?' Fen barely had time to think of a name before Rose continued. 'You'll never guess, stupid game that one really. Anyway, it's the Bernheims. Joseph and Magda.'

Fen rocked back in her chair, and the tears that had only recently subsided after her memories of Arthur threatened to reappear, but this time in joy. 'Magda! And Joseph. Oh my word, they're safe? They're here?'

Rose nodded. 'Recently back from New York, if you can believe such a miraculous thing.'

'Oh Rose, this is super news. James,' she turned to explain her evident joy to him, 'Magda and Joseph Bernheim were some of our dearest friends when we lived here. Ma and Pa knew Joseph's parents and went to their apartment for dinners and dances. Rose, what happened to them?'

'Magda and Joseph made it out in 1940 when it became obvious what was happening. Well, I don't need to spell it out for you, I'm sure.'

'And the Bernheims senior?'

'Not so lucky.' The three of them sat silently and Rose pulled a packet of cigarettes out of her bag by her chair and inserted one of the Gauloises into its long holder. 'You don't mind, do you? *Eh bien.*' She lit it and inhaled deeply before Fen or James had had a chance to reply. 'Do you remember their apartment in the eighth, Fenella?' She was referring to the number of the *arrondissement*, or neighbourhood, in which Joseph's parents' apartment had been. It was one of the smartest districts in Paris, encompassing the Champs-Élysées and Place de la Concorde.

'Yes, very well. They kindly invited us to the wedding party, it must have been just before we left Paris in 1935. I remember it so well, having never been to a Jewish wedding before.'

'That's right, yes. What a party that was, I think it went on for most of the night, didn't it?' Rose inhaled and blew her smoke out in near-perfect rings. 'And that apartment, oh it was a marvellous place, *magnifique*! The light! It would stream in through the windows... and the Bernheims were such astute collectors. Old masters, yes, but some more contemporary art, too. After their wedding, Magda, on old Mrs Bernheim's insistence, came to me for lessons, much like you used to, Fenella, dear.' Rose seemed lost in her reminiscences.

She took another deep drag on her cigarette and then stubbed it out in a small glass ashtray as the waiter brought over three small plates, each with a slice of deeply caramelised brown *tarte Tatin* on it. There was even, to Fen's absolute delight and astonishment, a small scoop of the softest whipped Chantilly cream on top.

'*Ooh la la*,' Fen couldn't help herself admiring the pudding.

'Dig in, I say,' James was the first to take a fork to the glossy apple tart.

'I'm sorry,' Fen blew on her forkful of warm pie before putting it to her lips, 'do carry on about the poor Bernheims, Rose.'

'Well, that was the thing. They weren't *poor* then. They were incredibly wealthy, with not just art but furniture from the time of the revolution, great ormolu clocks, and Madame Bernheim senior's jewels were exquisite. She had a sapphire from Ceylon that was a big as a gull's egg, I swear.'

'Dare I ask?' Fen knew she didn't really want to know what the fate had been of the Bernheims senior, the human tragedy of this war already being too much to really take on board, and knowing the family in question so well made hearing of their suffering so much worse.

'The Germans arrested them and deported them, only days after we'd got Joseph and Magda out. They were due out on the next boat.' Rose took a deep breath, her anger over their arrest still burning strong. She sucked in her lips and smacked them out again, then continued. 'Their apartment was stripped of all of its furniture, its Persian carpets, and of course their clothes, her furs, her jewels...'

'The sapphire?'

'Probably adorning some Nazi *hausfrau* in Munich.' Rose prodded her apple tart, her appetite seemingly vanished. 'And their art... oh, it was the most terrible of days when Henri and I were summoned to *their* apartment to catalogue the sequestration of their collection. I could barely bring myself to do it.'

'And now Joseph wants it back?' James asked, putting two and two together.

'Wouldn't you?' Rose glared at him. 'Of course he wants it back. He'd like the apartment back too, but the deeds have mysteriously disappeared deep into the depths of the Vichy filing cabinets, and though he has tried and tried, he can't claim it. Damn weak government. He can't find the furniture, the carpets, the furs, the jewels... but the art! There at least we can help!' She took another cigarette out of its packet and lit it up.

'And he's coming to your apartment this afternoon?' Fen gently probed.

'Yes,' Rose seemed deflated after her outburst. 'Yes, they both are. Here, *garçon*!' She beckoned the waiter over again. 'Give this young man the bill, we're leaving soon.'

'*Bien sûr*, madame,' the waiter demurred and slipped a paper stub onto the table next to James's resting arm.

To Fen's amusement, James mouthed the words 'how rude' back to her as he pulled his wallet from his pocket and thumbed out several notes. Rose hadn't noticed as she had busied herself packing her cigarettes back into her bag. She did at least deign to thank James for lunch and, moments later, the three of them were back out into the fresh autumn air.

Fen gave an involuntary yawn; she was unused to such a heavy meal in the middle of the day and James noticed.

'Good idea, Fen. Ladies, I shall take my leave and go and have a little nap back at the hotel. I better stay fresh for young Simone later.'

'Come then, Fenella, it seems it is just us women who have the appetite for work, as much as for other things.' Rose looked at James curtly and then chivvied Fen back down the road towards her apartment.

'Cheerio, James,' Fen waved to him. 'Thank you for lunch!'

Unlike James, her mind wasn't on their evening plans at all, and instead she was excited about seeing Magda and Joseph again, albeit in such tragic circumstances.

As they walked at pace back towards the apartment, Fen took in the sight of Rose, her coat flapping behind her in the wind, her turban wrapped tightly around her wayward hair, and she realised what a truly remarkable woman she was and what a very good job it would be to help the young Bernheims to regain even a fraction of their former property. A jolly good job indeed.

CHAPTER ELEVEN

The genuine joy that Fen felt as she hugged Magda Bernheim was like something she hadn't experienced since she had been carefree and mucking around with Kitty in the fields of West Sussex. Seeing the woman who had been such a role model to her when she was a teenager, with her eye for fashion and elegant wardrobe, and who had suffered so much in the time since they last met, was almost overwhelming.

Fen's family had moved away from Paris a few years before the rise of the Nazi party in Germany and the outbreak of the war. Back in the early 1930s, the Bernheims senior had been some of the wealthiest patrons in Paris, commissioning modern artists and collecting old masters, while curating their own collection and hosting artistic and literary salons in their beautiful apartment.

When Magda, a student at the École des Beaux-Arts, had been introduced to the Bernheims' son Joseph at the synagogue, it had been love at first sight, much to the joy of their parents, who had orchestrated the match, and within months they were engaged and soon after married. Fen had been lucky enough to have been invited to their wedding, which had been the most joyous and sophisticated party that she, as a slightly gauche seventeen-year-old, had ever been invited to.

In the Bernheims' apartment in the eighth arrondissement, she had first tasted champagne and, excepting the happy marriage between her own dear parents, had first witnessed true love between a newly-wed man and wife.

Pressing her cheek against Magda's now as they held onto each other brought back all of those memories, and Fen did her best to keep her tears in check.

'Oh Magda, how are you?' Fen looked at her old friend and saw that time, and the war's worries, had taken their toll on her. She had always been willowy but now she looked brittle in a way that suggested her life over the last few years had not been easy at all. Her hair was prematurely thinning, no doubt through stress and grief, but she wore it with élan and neatly swept back into a chignon at the nape of her neck. Her cardigan could have been that of a child's in size and still it amply covered her. It was cashmere, though, and her skirt looked to be of good quality too, if a little dated and worn.

'Much, much happier to see you, dear Fenella.' Magda hugged her again. 'You remember Joseph of course?' She ushered Fen over to where Joseph was talking to Rose, who was pouring her special mint tea out into dainty little teacups.

Joseph Bernheim looked every inch the American, in his natty pinstripe suit and Homburg hat, though he too looked thin and strained. He put down his teacup and stretched out his hand to shake Fen's.

'So super to see you both again,' Fen reiterated, stumped for anything more to say that could possibly bridge the gap that ten years, and one atrocity-filled war, had created.

Magda smiled at her and changed the subject. 'I see you still have the Delance, Rose?'

'Yes, *my* little Impressionist.' Rose kept pouring the mint tea from the same silver teapot she'd used yesterday, until all four cups were full.

'You had me copying it for weeks, do you remember?' Magda said softly. 'So much so, I think I managed a near-perfect replica when I was in New York.'

'Some people say that copying something isn't *real* art.' Rose winked at Fen and handed her a steaming teacup.

Before Fen could answer, Magda got in there first. 'Oh no, madame, I quite disagree. You only realise how intricately something's been put together when you try and replicate it yourself.'

'A bit like a crossword in a way,' Fen mused. 'Really looking at something does make you see it from different angles.'

'The Impressionists were the finest puzzlers of them all,' Rose, who was looking rather satisfied with herself, declared. 'What's this, a pink splodge, look again, it's a face.'

The women all laughed, but Joseph looked more serious.

'We had a Cezanne, you know?' he asserted, before taking a sip from his cup.

Magda came to sit down next to him on the chaise longue and gently laid a hand on one of his knees. Rose sat herself down in the less saggy of the two armchairs.

'I know, dear boy, I know.' She took a sip of her tea and swallowed. 'And I know exactly how much Henri valued it for and I think I finally know who has it now.'

'Who?' Joseph suddenly looked more animated.

'I just have a few more enquiries that I need to make, Joseph dear. And I swear to you, we will get the art back to you.'

'It's all gone, you see,' Joseph explained to Fen.

'Yes, I'm so sorry. Rose told me. I can't imagine… I mean, I'm just so very sorry for your loss.' Fen never felt she was very good at comforting people. Practical help she could do, but she was often lost for words when it came to trying to offer some sort of solace to those grieving. 'Your parents, I mean, I remember them very well. Has there been any news?'

Joseph looked across to Fen, who was rather hoping at this moment that the saggy old armchair would eat her up, but there wasn't any anger in his voice, just sadness. 'No. No good news at any rate.'

'It was all planned, Joseph…' Rose leaned over and touched his leg too. 'They should have been on that train to Le Havre…'

'I know, I know.' He rubbed his eyes and ran his hand through his oiled hair. Then he looked up at Rose and across to Fen. 'The Chameleon.'

'Do you think?' Rose asked him.

'I'm sure of it. Who else could have betrayed them at the last minute.'

Fen looked from Joseph to Rose and then back to Joseph as they spoke. Her curiosity was piqued. 'Who, or what, was the chameleon?'

'The Chameleon,' said Magda, speaking up for the first time since they sat down, 'was a double agent. We think. He must have worked within our networks, but for the Gestapo too. No one ever found out who he was. He just faded into the background, unseen until he struck, hence the name.'

'And he struck out at my parents,' Joseph continued. 'And Magda's. They were hours away from leaving the city when the officers raided the apartments we'd moved them to just days before. They were all arrested and sent to one of the camps. I still don't know which one, but I have a meeting with the Red Cross tomorrow. Hopefully they'll know more.'

'Let's hope indeed,' Rose reassured him. 'Now, however, dear boy, we have art to trace. You know my list, the one the Germans thought I was making for them? I wrote to you about it in New York?'

'Yes,' Joseph looked more hopeful.

'Well, I have it back from Henri Renaud today.'

'Oh, Henri Renaud,' Magda shook her head, the name obviously meaning something to her.

'He used to come to Mama and Papa's parties,' Joseph nudged her.

'Of course, of course. He loved that Degas your parents had.'

'And said the Gainsborough was the peak of British civility.' He laughed, but it caught in his throat. 'Still, Rose, please continue…'

'I need to find my cipher, I know I stashed it around here somewhere... Anyway, once I have decoded the "transport serial codes", we will have proof that those paintings belonged to you. And I remember that cabbage-breath Müller said something as the paintings were being pulled off the walls.'

Fen saw Magda blanch at the expression and grip the top of her blouse close to her neck.

'So that Degas, I can tell you without deciphering it, as I remember,' Rose said with some pride, 'was destined for the Führermuseum itself, but with that monstrosity never built, it was likely stored at Schlosskirche in Bavaria. I've recently spoken to the Art Looting Investigation Unit – they're the nice American chaps who discovered all the plunder in that church – and asked for an inventory and to see if my codes are still chalked on the back of the paintings. When I finish decoding the list, together with their stocktake, I'm sure we will find your painting, and maybe some of the others, *and* have the proof that it was stolen from you!'

Both Rose and Joseph seemed to fall back into their seats with relief. Even Magda loosened her grip on her collar slightly and seemed to relax.

'Thank you, Rose,' she said, almost in a whisper. 'I can't tell you what this means to us. To me and Joseph.'

'Well, it's not a done deal yet. But we have the proof. Once deciphered, my list will show the world *who* had their paintings stolen, and *where* their artworks are now.' She straightened her back in her chair. 'More tea, anyone?'

CHAPTER TWELVE

Fen closed the door behind the Bernheims, having promised Magda that they would find a time to visit some of their old haunts together, and went back into the studio. Rose was straightening the small, Impressionist painting and muttering something about it never hanging properly when there was rain on the forecast. Fen shook her head at her friend's little eccentricity and sat back down on the chaise longue.

'Was she a good student? Magda, I mean.'

'Oh so-so. Better than you, I dare say, though perhaps with less raw talent.' Rose sat down on the saggier of the armchairs and twiddled her beads around her fingers. 'You were always too practical to be a true artist, though you had flair. Magda was a good student though, she practised and sketched and drew all she could, but she never accomplished a great deal beyond what you might call *holiday art*.'

'Holiday art?'

'You know, the sort of souvenir watercolour you might bring home from a sojourn in Italy? But she was a good student of mine. She was never one for coming up with her own compositions and she enjoyed the tasks I set of copying the greats. I wouldn't be surprised if she does indeed have a rather robust version of my little Delance.' She waved her hand towards the painting on the wall. 'I do enjoy the challenge of taking something and copying it. Even if I do add my own artistic flair sometimes. What was it your father always said about me?'

Fen wasn't sure it would be polite to mention all the things her father had said about his flamboyant colleague at the école, so just widened her eyes in curiosity at her old teacher.

'He said, "Rose, I would as soon have your sunflowers on my wall than that Van Gogh chap's. He might have pushed the boundaries of fine art, but your copies allow time for the soul to catch up"!'

Fen laughed. Her father's specialisms were Florentine architecture and draughtsmanship, and he rarely talked about the more emotive side of art, but she loved that he had made Rose feel special, which was so typical of his generous spirit.

'And on that cheery note,' Rose winked at Fen, 'shall we have another, what you English might call, cuppa?'

'Oh yes, let's,' Fen replied and helped Rose clear up the tea tray.

A few moments later and the pot of mint tea was refreshed and Rose had brought out some garishly pink wafer biscuits from the back of a cupboard, saying, 'Contraband no doubt. But a very grateful ex-student of mine sent them from Holland. Now, dear girl, let's sit down and have a proper catch-up. Tell me all about your dear parents and that dashing brother of yours…'

A couple of hours later and the mint tea had morphed into champagne ('a payment in kind', Rose had explained, from a grateful portrait client) and the teacups replaced with crystal coupe glasses.

Simone had come home from her work at the atelier and Fen had enjoyed the half-hour they'd spent wafting in and out of each other's bedrooms, deciding what to wear for their evening jaunt. James's kind words in the gallery earlier had persuaded her that joining them could be rather fun after all and as she hadn't packed much in the way of fancy clothes, Rose had lent her a brightly coloured tea dress, which Fen now cinched in at the waist with the matching fabric belt. The gaudy red roses on the yellow background made Fen feel cheered, and she didn't care that it was probably a few years out of date, and possibly a few sizes too big. She pulled on the sleeves to make sure they puffed out like they should and she set her hair in the victory rolls she'd learned to do for the dances at The Spread Eagle in Midhurst.

'You should try this colour,' Simone said, nudging Fen out of the way in front of the bathroom mirror and pouting as she applied the deep red tint to her lips.

'It's rather fabulous,' agreed Fen, pursing her own lips and accepting the lipstick from Simone.

With her hair done, lipstick on and new dress just about fitting, she felt like a different person. A person still grieving, but one who would enjoy seeing a new side of Paris; a Paris liberated and full of hope, a Paris that she was old enough now to experience properly, but also a Paris that might hopefully remind her of the simpler days of her youth.

James buzzed the doorbell and caused Tipper to yap at him.

'Shush, you little brute,' Rose slurred slightly as she wobbled in front of one of her paintings, a paintbrush in one hand, a champagne coupe in the other. 'Come in!'

Moments later, James was in the studio, having picked up the squirming little ball of fluff that was Tipper and winced as his teeth dug playfully into his forearm.

'He's a feisty chap, isn't he?' James said to Rose, who had put her paintbrush and glass down and was pouring James some champagne.

'Like all men, he bares his teeth to get what he wants.'

James let Tipper jump out of his arms and accepted the proffered glass from Rose. 'Are we all so bad?' He raised his glass to his hostess, who in turn arched an eyebrow at him.

'Oh women are quite, quite worse.' She winked and grinned at him. 'Thank you for a splendid lunch today, Captain. I do hope the bill wasn't as painful as one of Tipper's little love bites.'

'Not at all, my pleasure.' He raised his glass again and then took a sip. 'Ah, this is the good stuff.'

'I didn't know you were a connoisseur?' The voice was Fen's, who had emerged from her bedroom, the first of the two young ladies to finish her toilette.

'I've had my share.' James smiled at her. 'You look very nice by the way. Like the dress.'

Before Fen could make a joke about him being a real Champagne Charlie, Simone opened her bedroom door and Fen wondered, if she had had a yardstick handy, if she could have measured to the eighth of an inch how far James's jaw dropped at the sight of the beautiful young woman.

'Good evening, Mademoiselle Mercier,' James blurted out slightly and Fen watched with increasing embarrassment on the poor man's behalf as he accidentally spilt a few drops of champagne on himself as he reached over and took Simone's hand to kiss it.

Rose winked at Fen and gave the pair a withering look, before pouring the dregs of the bottle into Simone's glass, which she'd brought with her from the bedroom. 'Now drink up you three and be off with you,' she said, barely concealing the almost maternal smile. 'And don't wake me up when you come in falling over yourselves later.'

CHAPTER THIRTEEN

The bar was noisy and boisterous, and mostly, Fen noticed, full of men. James led Simone and Fen through the fug of cigarette smoke and Fen wondered if it was the smoke or the language that turned the air a certain shade of blue. Simone seemed unfazed and walked tall, and Fen guessed that she was just pretending not to notice the eyes of the men follow her as she gently nudged them out of the way.

'Here,' James pointed at a booth-style table, where two men were already sitting.

Fen furrowed her brow as she felt something wet against her leg but accepted the slurred apology of the drunk man with a tilted glass who had filled the space she'd left in her wake as she'd followed her friends through the bar. She wasn't sure if the two men sitting at the table looked any more salubrious than the other chaps in this bar. *Not that it would take much to be so*, she thought to herself as she smiled at them and let James introduce them all.

'Fen, this is Gervais Arnault and his brother Antoine—'

'Or should that be the other way around?' the taller of the two men, who was wearing a grubby cloth cap, said in mock indignation before James could complete the introductions. 'I am the elder Arnault brother.'

'And the uglier,' countered the shorter, fatter brother, who did, to his credit, have the more handsome face, even if it was slightly smudged and dirtied with what looked like engine oil and grease. His blue denim dungarees were similarly dirtied, and his shirtsleeves were rolled up to his elbows to reveal arms covered in tattoos, those also obscured by streaks of grease.

The brothers play-fought while Fen and Simone slid into the banquette seating opposite them. James took drinks orders and left Simone to finish off the introductions.

'Fenella, you must ignore the children over there,' she winked at the men, who both threw their arms up in mock disgust at being so tarnished.

'We are both old enough to be your father, young Simone.'

'And bald enough,' she answered back, tartly, before laughing at poor Antoine, who now rubbed his pate and jammed his cloth cap back over his bald spot.

'It's OK for you,' he said back to her, 'you are young and beautiful and can make a living doing fancy things, whereas I am stuck in the warehouse all day—'

'Getting balder and balder!' laughed his brother Gervais.

Fen was slightly bemused by this buffoonish pair, yet her natural curiosity took over and she asked them about themselves.

'I have a fleet of lorries,' Gervais announced proudly, ramming his thumbs under the straps of his dungarees and pushing his chest out.

Simone laughed and shook her head. 'A fleet? Is that what we're calling it now?'

Antoine interrupted and introduced himself in similarly flattering terms. 'And I am the boss of a large team of workers.'

'You're both liars,' Simone wagged her finger at them. 'But I shall forgive you as I know you're only doing it to impress a pretty stranger.'

'Oh, I see,' Fen felt a bit flustered. 'Please don't exaggerate anything on my account.'

'Antoine works in a warehouse in the north of the city and Gervais is a lorry driver—'

'And mechanic!' the plump Gervais chipped in.

'And a mechanic,' Simone added to appease him. 'So I assume you two met Captain Lancaster last night?'

'We did,' Antoine replied, beating his brother to it. 'And we shared a good few drinks with him.'

'You mean you fleeced him for a few drinks?' Simone asked, a note of disapproval in her voice, but a smile playing across her lips.

Fen thought this all rather amusing; a young slip of a girl telling off two burly much older men. But the two men seemed to take it all in their stride and laughed at her joke. *Perhaps she proved herself during the war*, Fen thought, *made herself their equal?*

Just then, James came back to the table and set down a round of beers for him and the men and a glass of wine each for Fen and Simone.

'To our British friends and allies,' Antoine led the toast once James was seated, having found a chair to bring to the head of the table.

'To friends and allies!' They all chinked their glasses and finished the toast with a few '*saluts*' to each other too.

As James talked cars with the Arnault brothers, Fen asked Simone how she knew the two men.

'They are just local characters. I'm not surprised James bumped into them last night. They could probably sense the very moment when his wallet opened...' she raised her eyebrows and then laughed when Fen did. 'I think they mean no harm though.'

Fen nodded. 'Did you grow up around here then, on the Left Bank, I mean?' She asked her, wondering how their paths might have crossed.

'No, no. I was raised in the north of the city. But Antoine and Gervais are pretty friendly to all the new faces round here.'

'Especially a pretty one, no doubt,' Fen said and took a sip of her wine. It was only when she put her glass down did she realise that Simone was looking at her.

'As you yourself have just found out. *Tsch*, really, Fenella, you are very pretty too. I assume that's why Captain Lancaster is here with you, *non*?'

'Oh, no.' Fen could feel the blush rising in her cheeks. 'It's not like that between us at all. No, no. We're just chums. Sort of thrown together.'

Simone grinned, then seemed to check herself and brought her lips back into a much sexier pout. 'That's good. So you won't mind if I, well, if we…'

'Oh no, absolutely. Crack on.' Fen hid herself in her glass of wine again and wondered why everyone seemed to think she and James Lancaster were a couple. Nothing could be further from the truth. All that muscle and slightly unshaven look did nothing for her. But that combination was obviously like nectar to Simone, who turned away from Fen almost as soon as she'd received 'permission' and commandeered James's attention away from talking about cam belts and air-cooled engines.

Fen knew when she was dismissed and instead struck up a conversation with the brothers. 'So, what did you both do in the war?' It wasn't the most original of conversation starters, but a fairly ubiquitous one, she'd realised over the last few months.

'Ah, this and that,' Antoine said, smiling slightly as he did so.

'I kept France moving,' Gervais puffed out his chest again, 'single-handedly fixing the French army's vehicles.'

'As long as those vehicles were never any further than 200 yards from your garage, brother!' laughed Antoine.

'Hey! So what if I have flat feet and cannot fight,' Gervais looked like he might have taken offence as his brother's slur, but then laughed. 'But I could drive and I drove all sorts of things to freedom.' He tapped his finger against his nose and winked at Fen.

'How interesting,' she replied, 'do tell?'

'Well, it's not a well-known fact that the Louvre needed its paintings moving around—'

'Oh yes,' Fen interrupted, 'to Montauban and Chambord...' She was cut off by Antoine's laughter.

'You see, brother,' he said, jabbing Gervais in the shoulder, 'everyone knows about that. You would have made a useless Resistance agent, your secrets are so well known!' He chuckled again and took a long slurp from his beer.

'It's not my fault Monsieur Renaud told me it was a secret.' Gervais shrugged his shoulders, but Fen could see he looked a little crestfallen.

'You're friends with Henri Renaud?' she asked, directly to Gervais, to try and build up his ego a little again.

'Yes, of course. I know you wouldn't think it, as we are, how would you say... from different sides of the track,' he laughed. 'But we are good friends.'

Fen's ego fluffing had worked. Gervais all of a sudden looked very pleased with himself.

'And did you work with him throughout the war?' she asked, innocently enough.

'Yes, I did. I drove the lorries that took art everywhere, to the galleries, from the galleries, to the auctioneer, to the warehouse, from the Jews' apartments...'

Fen suddenly got a shiver down her spine and remembered that not all of Henri Renaud's war work had been on behalf of the French Resistance.

Antoine must have picked up on her sudden change of countenance and interceded on his brother's behalf. 'We were not all lucky enough to have the ability to stand up to the oppressors,' he said thoughtfully. 'Sometimes you just had to get by. It was an honour for us to work with a man like Monsieur Renaud, though, the war at least gave us that. Gervais would drive the lorries and

I worked – I still do – in his warehouse. There were times we had to kowtow to the Nazis, but in the end, I think we did the best we could, to do the best we could.'

'Amen to that,' James added and they all clinked glasses again.

Simone, who had been leaning in very close to James, turned her attention back towards Fen and changed the subject. 'Fenella, why don't you come and visit me tomorrow, at the atelier. It would be fun, no?'

'Oh, rather! Thank you. What a treat.'

From that moment onwards, the talk that evening kept to the lighter side of life, albeit each person's stories were tinged with the scent of the war. It had been such a large part of everyone around that table's lives, whether they'd fought, spied, dug the fields or kept the engines ticking over, that it was hard to ignore it. One person's laughter, however, became infectious and by the time the barkeep called for last orders, they were all flushed with the warmth that good humour and good drinks bring to the table.

CHAPTER FOURTEEN

Fen awoke the next morning to the sound of the front door of the apartment closing. She sat up in bed and swung her legs out, stretching out the last of her sleepiness as she did so. Once the curtains were open and her old land girl jumper slipped on over her nightdress, she ventured out of her room and into the light of the studio. Rose was already at her easel, the curtains long drawn back and the morning light streaming in through the tall panes of glass.

'Good morning, slug-a-bed! Can I put the wireless on now? I do so like some jazz while I work.'

'Good morning, Rose, and yes, I'm so sorry, of course – fire her up!' Fen headed towards the bathroom but paused and asked, 'Did I just hear the front door go?'

Rose sighed and dragged her eyes away from her canvas and met Fen's own enquiring look. 'Young Simone has just returned. I thought you both might have come home together, but…'

Fen rubbed her eyes again and tried to remember what had happened after the fourth or fifth glass of wine. She remembered all three of them trying to get the big grey door open downstairs, but perhaps it was just her on her own who practically pulled herself up the banister to the fifth-floor apartment.

'I'm sure James looked after her,' Fen said, by way of an explanation.

'It's not his *hospitality* I question, dear girl.' The look in Rose's eyes implied she knew all too well what two young people might get up to alone in a hotel room and Fen nodded, before leaving Rose to carry on with her painting as she headed into the bathroom.

*

'Ah good morning, young lady,' Rose eyed up her lodger as she rather sheepishly left her room and closed the door behind her. Fen looked up from the daily paper and Simone winked at her. 'I'm not sure I should condone this sort of behaviour…' Rose continued as Simone walked into the centre of the room and helped herself to a cup of coffee from the pot.

'Urg,' she swallowed it in disgust. 'It's the chicory stuff again.'

'It was all I could find,' Fen shrugged her shoulders.

'It's all we have,' Rose spoke over her. 'And I'm sure it's nothing so good as one can get at the breakfast tables of the Hotel de Lille.'

Simone was modest enough to finally blush a pretty shade of pink and lowered her eyes to the coffee pot.

Fen knew that Rose was cross with her, whether for her loose morals or just that she had been worried about her, she wasn't sure, but she knew she should say something to ease the tension. 'Simone, is a visit to your atelier still on the cards today? I rather fancy a walk out and about.'

'Of course. I will warn my friends Christian and Pierre that they will be meeting one of the famous English land girls!'

'Rightio!' Fen clocked what Simone had said and smiled, cheered at the thought. 'Though I didn't know we were such celebrities.'

Simone just laughed and took another sip of her coffee. She wrinkled her nose in disgust at the ersatz brew. Fen took a sip too, but couldn't say she disliked it. Real coffee was such a luxury these days and Fen had grown rather fond of the woodiness of the chicory drink.

'Mind if I bring a chum?' Fen remembered her promise to Magda and thought it might be friendly of her to ask if she'd like to come along as well. Simone merely shrugged and Fen wondered if perhaps an audience to show off her glamorous workplace to was always welcome. 'Wonderful. See you later then.'

With the rendezvous arranged, Simone bid her goodbyes and donned her coat before leaving the apartment.

'If she were my daughter…' Rose began, before leaning over to pick up her cigarette holder and light one up. Her long beads clanked against the jars of white spirit next to her easel. She had wrapped her hair up in a navy-blue turban today and paired it with a striking bejewelled peacock-feather hatpin. She inhaled deeply and then laughed to herself. 'Who am I kidding, if she were my daughter, she'd be twice as bad and thrice as ugly.'

'Oh Rose.' Fen laughed at her. 'Still, I'm rather intrigued by seeing this fashion house. I'll put in a call to Magda's building and, then, is there anything I can do for you in the meantime?'

Fen had slightly regretted asking Rose that a few hours later. Her hands were now red raw and reeked of white spirit. Cleaning oil paint off brushes in the freezing cold of the kitchen sink was not fun at all, but Fen couldn't begrudge her friend the favour – she was staying with her free of charge after all.

'Reminds me,' Fen said to Tipper as he sat on her feet like a fluffy hot-water bottle while she stood at the sink, 'I must see if there's anything particularly tasty at the shops this afternoon. I think we could all do with a bit of a treat.'

The little dog had agreed with her, or so she thought by the yapping, followed by a particularly energetic bout of tail chasing. She looked at the ball of fluff as he skittered around the kitchen, bumping into her ankles, and couldn't help but smile at him. Perhaps it would be nice to get a dog once she was settled back in England? The rather pleasant daydream of choosing a breed occupied her until she'd finished washing out the brushes, and once she was free of oil paint splats herself, she put her mind to what she should wear for this adventure into the heart of haute couture.

Visiting a fashion house hadn't been on Fen's agenda when she'd packed her old brown case in West Sussex last month and headed off in search of Arthur. At that point, she'd figured her luggage would be more usefully filled with rugged work overalls and sensible jumpers; which indeed had been just the ticket as she'd taken up the role of a vineyard worker to aid her search.

Now, though, she felt like her Sunday best of a smart tweed skirt and nice cream-coloured blouse just wasn't going to cut it, while the Victorian cameo brooch of her grandmother's that she'd so almost lost to a thief in Burgundy, as precious as it was to her, wasn't exactly *à la mode* either. Plus, Rose's dress she had worn the night before hadn't had a chance to air out and still smelt of tobacco smoke and stale beer, more's the pity. Luckily, Rose was as generous as ever, and although Fen had only her sensible shoes and trench coat, she was glad to have borrowed another one of her friend's less-exuberant tea dresses, this one in a rather fetching blue with little white daisies on it.

As Fen put it on and pulled the belt tight around the waist to give the dress a bit of definition, she started to feel a little of her old self come back. Fen had never been a vain woman, but she did follow her mother's mantra of 'it's nice to look nice' and had been known to check her headscarf and victory-rolled hairdo in the passing wing mirror of a farm vehicle when she'd been working in the fields. Perhaps this trip to the heart of the Parisian fashion world would be the boost she needed after losing her darling Arthur had knocked her for six.

A few hours later and Fen and Magda walked along arm in arm towards the atelier.

'This is such a joy,' Magda exclaimed, 'not just being here with you, although that is wonderful, don't get me wrong,' she squeezed Fen's arm, 'but I mean just being in Paris again! Home.'

'It must have been terrible, having to escape from your own city, I mean.'

'I cried all the way to New York,' Magda said and released her arm from Fen's. 'Poor Joseph had to almost carry me onto Ellis Island.'

'You knew then that your parents hadn't made it?'

'Yes. They should have been on the same voyage as us, but... still, Rose did all she could to help then, just as she is now. At least the war was good for one thing.'

'What's that?' Fen turned to her friend in bewilderment.

'Rose. She was getting in some hot water just before we left.'

'Rose?'

'Bless her, you know how she loves copying paintings?'

'Gosh yes, the paintings in my bedroom in her apartment could fill a wing of the Louvre and barely anyone would notice the difference!' Fen suddenly remembered the woman in the fox fur saying something similar and was about to tell Magda all about it when she stopped herself. Gossiping about her most generous hostess had its limits.

'Exactly.' Magda carried on talking anyway. 'Well, you know the old rumours about her being a forger? They were surfacing again and Rose was about to be hauled in front of some sort of committee. Apparently a few too many of her "homages" were on the open market and the auction houses were feeling the heat. Some of the news even made it to the *New York Times*. There really were some cross people out there who'd thought they'd bagged a Rembrandt or Degas for silly money and hadn't realised they'd been duped.'

'But not by Rose, surely? She always says they're copies. She even adds her own flourishes at the end to prove it.'

'I think that's the point. She's never anything but upfront about it. But once they're sold on once or twice, and what with the art all being stolen and shifted around,' Magda shivered and threaded her arm through Fen's again, 'well, I think she might have been investigated. It certainly made some of the art world and a few patrons very cross indeed.'

'Poor Rose. All she ever wants to do is paint and create art. It's not her fault if someone else sells it on as the real thing.' Fen felt aggrieved for her eccentric friend.

'I'm just glad to see her still with us now. I couldn't have borne it if she had been killed too.'

'Killed?' *Surely Magda was referring to Rose's war work now?* Fen checked. 'You mean if she'd been caught by the Germans with her codes and ciphers and things?'

'Oh yes, there was that too. What I meant, though, was that she had received quite a few threats, if you know what I mean. People don't like being made fools of, and don't you find it's always easy to blame us women for everything. Just before we left, she was in a real pickle, almost about to go underground, then Henri Renaud vouched for her and… well, there you go. I'm just so glad she's safe now.'

Fen thought about Magda's words. Rose hadn't mentioned any of this. Perhaps she was embarrassed, falsely accused or not, mud often stuck. Maybe, as Magda had said, the war in its crazed crucible of fire and heat had at least saved one person – Rose. Like a phoenix from the flames, she was reborn as just another artist. Had the war done anything to silence her detractors though? Or was that just another pot waiting to boil over?

CHAPTER FIFTEEN

Fen and Magda chatted away about less serious subjects until they arrived at the address printed on the very smart little calling card that Simone had passed to Fen that morning. The atelier didn't have a showy shop window and was in fact only recognisable from the discreet brass plaque next to the door. Fen was about to rap on the door when it opened and Simone appeared behind it.

'Hello, Fenella, and...' Simone stopped and stared at Magda for a brief moment before introducing herself to her. Pleasantries were made and Simone ushered the two women into the building. 'Did you have any trouble finding your way?' Simone asked as Fen and Magda hung their coats up on the stand in the vestibule.

The entrance hall of the building was sparse in its own way, black-and-white tiles chequerboarded the floor and the only furniture was the stand, on which they'd just hung their coats, an upholstered bench seat and a mahogany receptionist's desk, which was currently unoccupied.

'No, not at all. We found it quite easily in fact.' Fen's sense of direction was something of which she was quite proud, plus she'd been to this neighbourhood before, as a girl, accompanying her mother on jaunts to her dressmaker. She had remembered the way, even if so many of the once-familiar shops and dressmaker's ateliers had been closed now and some even boarded up.

Magda spoke up too, echoing Fen's thoughts. 'This was always such an exciting part of Paris to come to, in the old days, I mean.'

'As it is now,' Simone said rather coquettishly, placing a hand on her hip.

'Yes, of course,' Magda agreed, 'and I'm sure it will be just as delightful as it ever was, even if perhaps my purse strings need to be pulled a little tighter these days.'

Fen reached out and squeezed Magda's hand, before realising that Simone was still waiting for them at the partially opened door, which led to the rest of the atelier.

The atelier itself was a hive of buzzing sewing machines and scratching pens on drawing boards. Simone showed them into what she called the cutting room. Here, on one side, there were draughtsmen sitting at large white drawing boards, while seamstresses dressed mannequins and stood over large, wide tables measuring and cutting fabric. There were great windows, like those in Rose's apartment, letting in the early-afternoon light, and drawings and sketches filled the walls. The whole place felt industrious and purposeful, and Fen could now understand Simone's outrage at the way fashion models like herself were attacked and sworn at in the street. Here in the atelier of Lucien Lelong, for that had been the name on the brass plaque by the front door, progress was being made one stitch at a time.

'Come, let me introduce to you to my friends. They will simply adore that crazy dress you're wearing, Fenella. Is it one of Rose's? She's a scream that woman. Christian, Pierre!' Simone led a rather self-conscious Fen and obviously rather awkward Magda through the cutting room to where two middle-aged men were sitting at their drawing boards. 'Miss Churche, Madame Bernheim, may I introduce you to my mentors here at Lelong, Monsieurs Christian Dior and Pierre Balmain.'

'Bonjour, mademoiselle, madame,' the rather handsome Christian leaned over and kissed Fen's hand, then that of Magda, while Pierre laughed and saluted them both from behind his drawing board.

'These two men are geniuses,' Simone gushed. 'Their designs are so full of life…'

'... And luxury,' Pierre laughed. 'Luckily for Mademoiselle Mercier here we like to dress her up like our younger sister and parade her around.'

Simone tutted and huffed in that particularly Gallic way, but Fen could tell she was in her element, being the darling of these two trailblazing designers.

'Next let me show you the pattern designs,' Simone pulled Fen along with her as the two designers waved them all off. Once out of earshot, she pulled Fen and Magda into a huddle and said in a conspiratorial whisper, 'Don't you dare tell anyone, but Christian is leaving soon, he says.'

'Oh dear. That will be a loss for Monsieur Lelong.' Magda sounded genuinely worried for the proprietor. 'My mother used to come here in the twenties...' her voice trailed off and Fen looked at her with concern. 'I'm all right, I'm all right,' Magda confirmed as she fished around in her handbag for a handkerchief.

Simone waited for Magda to finish blowing her nose and then carried on with her juicy piece of gossip. 'It will be a disaster for this atelier, yes. Christian's designs are out of this world, you know? They are in the new style, so fresh.'

'Promise we won't say a word,' Fen assured her.

'Good. I'm hoping that he might take me with him. If I'm still living in Paris by then, of course.'

'Are you planning on leaving Paris?' Magda asked but didn't wait for an answer as she put her handkerchief back in her handbag and carried on. 'I don't think I could ever leave, not again. Never again.'

Fen slipped her arm into Magda's and gave it a squeeze as Simone merely shrugged and led them into another room, this one full of rolls of fabric, all standing on their ends, like a vibrantly coloured version of the Giant's Causeway.

Fen wanted to ask Simone what she meant about leaving Paris but was swept up by the sight of so much fabric. She remembered repurposing a pair of Mrs B's old curtains to make a skirt during the war, and how Kitty had laughed at her as a rogue curtain hook had fallen out during a tea dance. Put it this way, the fabric in this room would have dressed the whole of West Sussex for the entirety of the war, with spare left over for the VE Day bunting.

'Gosh aren't these patterns wild!' Fen ran her finger along a wide roll of brightly coloured silk, feeling the texture as much as seeing the pattern. 'My friend Kitty would be in seventh heaven here!'

'These are the fabrics for Christian's new look, he's very particular about them.'

'I can see why, one yard of this is probably worth more than my entire wardrobe!'

'Can you imagine,' Magda joined in, 'I used to come here and think nothing of ordering dress after dress. And now… well, same as you, Fen, dear, just being in this room is about as close to bespoke tailoring as I'll get any time soon.'

Simone smiled and carefully tucked a stray few strands of her hair behind her ear. 'I know what it's like to be poor, too. Though I've never resorted to borrowing old lady's clothes.' She touched the fabric on the slightly unfashionable squared-off shoulder of Rose's tea dress and laughed. 'So thirties!'

'Oh, well, I mean…' Fen trailed off as Simone carried on talking, her manner suddenly less carefree.

'Still, I would have only dreamed of a dress like yours back then. I was a young girl when Paris was in crisis, you know? The depression?'

Fen knew it well. It was The Crisis of Paris that had weighed on her mind heavily when she was deciding what to do for the war effort. She had witnessed the poorest in Paris starve back in 1934 when the shops ran empty and even bread was hard to come by. Her family had moved back to England the year after, but it had always haunted her, how it was the worst off in this world who suffered the most during times of depression, and how economic depression so often followed war…

'We were starving. My father was out of work and my mother had died in the winter of '33 from pneumonia. You might have been buying dresses here at Lelong, Madame Bernheim, but I was dressed in rags.' Simone looked intensely at Magda.

'I'm so sorry.' Magda dropped her eyes and seemed to carefully examine the floor.

'*Tch*, it is what it is. We have all been through hell and back these past few years. Back then, we were alley rats, vermin on the streets of Paris. My sister and I were old enough to help our father ply the streets but too young to realise what was happening. You could say that we were dying, but we didn't know it.'

'What happened?' Fen couldn't help but find it hard to tally the story Simone was telling her to the cosmopolitan young woman standing before her.

'I realised I was beautiful.' Simone paused as if waiting for Fen and Magda to agree with her, and sure enough they did both nod. 'And I traded it as my best asset.'

'Oh, I see…' Fen was slightly shocked, while Magda took to examining the floor again.

'No, not like that.' Simone stood taller, more proud. 'I was barely seventeen when the war started. A woman, yes, but not worldly, you know? But I modelled for artists and became a waitress and then I worked for the Resistance in the war as a lure for the Germans.'

'A lure?'

'Yes, you pretend you want, you know, *jiggy-jiggy* with them and then lure them into an alley where others were waiting.' She ran her finger across her throat and Fen instinctively raised her hand to protect her own neck.

'Cripes!'

'No more than they deserved,' Magda crossed her arms, looking more defiant than Fen had seen her.

Simone laughed and pulled a scrap of fabric out from an end of one of the rolls and draped it over Magda's shoulder. 'Suits you,' she said and then coolly carried on with her story. 'Of course, there was always that temptation to let them go, or accept their offers of money and ration books… like The Chameleon obviously did.'

'That brute.' Magda practically spat the words out, then hurriedly fetched her handkerchief out of her bag and blew her nose again.

'Were there many double agents, do you think?' Fen was curious, and while not wanting to upset Magda by dwelling on the subject, she wanted to know more.

'Yes. More than you'd think.' Simone looked thoughtful, and Fen watched as she took in the obvious sadness in Magda's eyes. 'Anyway, now my life is full of silks and brocades, not mouldy bread and rat droppings. Oh, this fabric is so beautiful, don't you think?' Simone seemed easily distracted, even from her own story.

The other two women murmured their agreement over the prettiness of the fabric and Fen, her natural curiosity still burning, willed Simone to continue. She wasn't in luck, however, as Simone walked them out of the fabric room and back through the cutting room to the salon where smart *Parisiennes* would come to watch girls such as Simone model the latest fashions.

'Here, I have a gift for you both.' Simone slipped down behind the raised walkway and pulled out two neatly tied packages. She handed one each to Fen and Magda. 'Pop them in your handbags, quick. Don't let anyone see on the way out,' she winked at Fen. 'They keep these scarves here for important clients. A little sweetener to encourage *les madames* to buy the clothes.'

Fen couldn't help but have a quick peek and peeled open one end of the brown paper and gasped. Magda had done the same but couldn't even manage to make a sound. Fen quickly closed the paper up and offered the parcel back to Simone.

'Oh Simone, I can't possibly take this.'

Simone pushed the parcel back into her hands. 'Honestly, it's not a big deal to us. I have two or three of these scarves in the new patterns. Take them, take them.'

'This is too much,' Magda had found her voice. 'I… I don't know what to say.'

Fen could see that Magda very much wanted to keep the pretty silk scarf that was wrapped up in the brown paper, but was torn, like her, by the morality of accepting such an expensive and luxurious gift from a near stranger.

But Simone all but forced them on to the women. 'Catherine says I have an eye for design,' she explained. 'I cut the fabric for these scarves myself. To me, fashion is a disguise, you know, like a mask. You can wear something beautiful now and for a moment you can forget your past.' Simone ran a finger down the sleeve of her own blouse, which Fen noticed was pure silk and utterly divine. Simone looked up again, awakened from her own reverie. 'Please, have them. I am glad to be able to bring a little joy, especially to you, Madame Bernheim.'

'Thank you, Simone,' Fen touched her arm, careful not to snag the silk, while Magda gathered Simone into an impromptu hug.

Simone smiled at them both. 'I will do anything, you see, *anything* to not go back to the poverty of my childhood. But I know I am the lucky one now, being here among this luxury. You've both suffered too, and sharing a bit of this good fortune, well, it's the least I can do.'

'Thank you, again.' Fen said, feeling the softness of the silk inside the packet. 'And, well, yes, you've landed on your feet here, I think. Pierre and Christian obviously think very highly of you and—'

'And maybe I can marry well now the war is behind us and I look so smart, yes?' Simone winked at Fen, who smiled back at her, finally realising what she meant about not being in Paris much longer.

Oh you'll marry well, all right, she thought, knowing exactly who she had her sights on. *I think I may know just the chap…*

CHAPTER SIXTEEN

'She's right, I suppose,' Magda said to Fen as they stood at the northern end of the Pont des Arts. Magda and Joseph had found a reasonably priced apartment to rent in the Marais district, which was on the northern, or Right Bank, of the Seine, while Rose's apartment was over the river in Saint Germain.

'What do you mean?' Fen asked her, unlinking her arm from that of her old friend.

'Just that fashion is a type of disguise. I mean, even before the war when we dressed up for occasions, well, what did we mean by it?'

Fen thought for a moment. 'It was different then though, wasn't it? We just followed conventions. I would never have worn trousers or work overalls before the war, but now I feel rather useless in a skirt. And somewhat exposed in a way!'

The women both laughed as Fen juggled her handbag and the bag of *patisserie* they had stopped to pick up, so she could keep her dress from floating up thanks to a stiff autumnal breeze.

'Here, you take these.' She passed the brown paper bag of bread and strawberry tarts to Magda. 'I know for a fact that Rose has more than enough bread in the apartment. I think the *boulanger* at the end of the road has a soft spot for her. Maybe she painted him a nice picture of a croissant or something?'

'Are you sure?' Magda asked, ignoring Fen's little joke. She sounded as serious as if Fen had offered her the use of a diamond tiara.

'Of course. And send my best to Joseph, tell him the tarts are particularly good.'

The two women embraced and Fen was able to walk across the bridge with one hand free now to keep her billowing skirt at bay. She was pleased that Magda had accepted the bread and tarts, as she knew they were struggling to make ends meet from what Magda had said as they queued up in the patisserie for the treats.

Fen thought about it as she walked over the bridge. She had wanted to visit one of her favourite patisseries, which she knew lay only a few streets from the atelier.

Her mother had taken her to Patisserie Cambon on the occasions that Fen had had to wait patiently for her to be fitted for whatever dress she had ordered, and worse, sometimes Fen herself had had to stand on the funny little box in her underwear as the long tickling tape measure had dangled down from shoulder to ankle. Even now its red awning and window, filled with sugary pastries and tempting glazed tarts, had made her eyes much bigger than her stomach. She had asked Magda if she didn't mind the diversion from their way home and both ladies had feasted their eyes on what the talented pastry chef had put in the window.

There had been cream-filled *religieuses*, their choux pastry tops daubed with chocolate and nuts, delicate pale green *macarons* and elegant slices of chocolate *gâteaux*, but it was the bright-pink strawberry tarts, their glaze almost dazzling in the sunlight, that had caught Fen's eye. They were at least affordable; food shortages and rocketing inflation making the other treats most expensive. Magda had pointed out as much and Fen had remembered that her friend had lost everything and cakes that would have once been part of life were now an almost impossible luxury. She hadn't really wanted a loaf of bread or those strawberry tarts for herself, and was pleased to be able to send Magda home with them.

Fen carried on across the bridge, her thoughts mostly occupied by how she would wear the jazzy new scarf that Simone had given her, when she noticed a very familiar person on the quayside, no more than thirty feet or so away from her, talking to a man. She was about to call out to Rose when something made her stop. There was something about Rose's countenance, the way she was talking to the man, that made Fen pause and take note. *Were they arguing?*

Fen sidestepped a mother who was dragging a querulous child along by his hand and leaned against the rail of the bridge, hiding herself behind a lamp post, hoping Rose wouldn't look over and see her.

They were definitely arguing. The man was waving his hands around, while Rose stood her ground and occasionally pointed a finger at him, jabbing it towards his chest as she seemed to make a point. Fen was unsure as to whether she should go and help Rose, but she looked very much to be in control of the situation.

The breeze that was still trying its best to embarrass Fen was blowing Rose's velvet coat large behind her, helping make her look authoritative, while today's choice in coloured turban elevated her height by another few inches. The man she was arguing with, however, seemed small in stature and smartly dressed. Fen could make out what looked like a blazer and light-coloured slacks. Maybe not the right clothes for the season, but smart in their own way nonetheless. Something about his slicked-back hair and slightly receding hairline reminded her of the portrait of Napoleon she had seen in the Louvre only the day before, and Fen suddenly worried that this Frenchman might be just as aggressive.

Fen was about to grit her teeth and enter the fray when the conversation between the two combatants ended, each turning on their heel and heading off in separate directions from the end of the bridge. Fen trotted across the rest of the wooden slats, but by the time she'd got to where they had both been standing, there was no sign of either of them. The temptation to follow Rose's Napoleonic adversary was strong, but Fen knew finding him down the many and varied routes he could have taken from the river would be a fool's errand – plus, what would she say to him if she found him?

Instead, she carried on her way back to Rose's apartment, wondering as she did how she might bring up the subject of this mystery man with her old friend, and if there was a story to be heard behind it all.

'Nothing of the sort,' Rose snorted as Fen questioned her on him later that afternoon. She had walked the few streets back to the Rue des Beaux-Arts and climbed the stairs up to the apartment, all the while posing theories in her head as to who the man might be. A rogue supplier who wanted his bill paid? A spurned lover of Simone's wanting Rose to pass on a message? Possibly even one of those duped buyers wanting his money back?

Fen had rather tumbled all of these theories out over a cup of tea and now Rose was laughing it off.

'He was just my art dealer, Fenella, dear. Michel Lazard.'

'Oh.' Fen thought back to what Magda had been saying earlier about Rose's dubious links to the less salubrious art dealers. 'What did he want from you? You seemed quite peeved with him, if you don't mind me saying.'

Rose looked at her and Fen got the impression that perhaps Rose did mind, just a little, what she was saying. 'Michel is a rough diamond. You know my art falls between genres, not elevated enough to be taken seriously by Henri, yet too good for those roadside tinkers. Michel fills that space, if you know what I mean.'

'I see.' It still didn't explain to Fen why he and Rose had been arguing and she said as much.

'Oh, he's a weaselly fellow all right, wanted more commission. As if everything in this life comes down to grubby francs. If only Valreas hadn't stopped dealing with him.' Rose huffed out a sigh. 'Didn't use to all be about money, of course, not when Michel still had hold of his moral compass. Used to hide all sorts of paintings for us, from the Germans, you see? Quite the daring chap. Probably sold his morals for a few francs now. Wouldn't trust him with his own grandmother, but he does get things sold.'

'What changed for Michel?' Fen asked, intrigued.

Rose sucked in her teeth. 'Enough now, let's talk of more erudite things. Did you perchance see the Roman galleries when you and Captain Lancaster perused the Louvre yesterday?'

Fen let Rose talk as she listened, though admittedly with only half an ear. Her mind was gnawing over something and it was only as Rose was describing the great sarcophagus from the mausoleum of Anicii that Fen realised what it was. Michel Lazard… what a name. And only one small vowel away from Lizard… Had perhaps that moral compass of his been sold not after the war, but during, enabling him to become The Chameleon?

CHAPTER SEVENTEEN

Apartment 5,
15 Rue des Beaux-Arts,
Paris, October 1945

Dear Mrs B, Kitty and Dilly,

A few days have passed now since I arrived in Paris and, boy, do I have some stories to tell you. Kitty, you would never believe it, but I have been to a bona fide fashion house and met some real designers. I'd watch out for names such as Christian Dior and Pierre Balmain – both lovely chaps, who I met at their drawing boards at the atelier my new friend Simone works in. Such beautiful fabrics too – if I can, I'll see if I can get hold of some of Simone's hand-me-downs for you all. I'm afraid I'm keeping the rather jazzy silk scarf Simone gave me for myself!

Paris is alive, though perhaps not totally 'well'. At every turn, it seems you meet some brave person who was in the Resistance, but equally there are stories too sad to tell of loss and hardship. Still, I plan to see and do all that I can and I'm really trying very hard not to miss my dear Arthur too much.

Simone and James took me out last night and tonight we're off again to see the marvellous Josephine Baker in revue. She's recently back from North Africa and I daresay as fabulous as ever! I'll write again soon and tell you all about it.

Kitty – did you get the answer to the clue? It was a play on words you see, a Pullman is part of a train, while 't' or 'tea' fits in just before a shower, i.e. a rain shower! TRAIN. How about this one, it's called a letter clue – so look to the starts of the words (initially, see?) to help solve it. Here goes: I watched it dry initially, perhaps an idler notes time? (5). Let me know how you get on.

Much love, etc.,
Fen xx

Fen hurriedly sealed up the envelope and caught up with James and Simone as they trotted (in James's case; more of a glide in Simone's) down the cantilevered staircase of the apartment building. They were indeed off to see the marvellous Josephine Baker, the American singer and dancer who had made her home in Paris many years ago. Fen felt a little as if she were just 'hanging on' as she had done when she was seventeen and snuck along to see Miss Baker at the Théâtre Marigny with her brother in those heady days just before they left Paris to return to Oxford.

Josephine Baker had been something of a favourite among Fen's school friends, who all collected pictures of her extraordinary menagerie in their scrapbooks. And that night at the theatre back in 1934 had been an eye-opener, to say the least, not only because Miss Baker was really quite daring in her dancing, but also because Fen had never seen her nineteen-year-old brother blush such a deep shade of crimson when she was on stage. The memory made her smile and James asked her why she was grinning to herself quite so much as she closed one of the big grey doors behind them all.

'I think sneaking out to see Josephine Baker when I was seventeen was quite possibly the naughtiest thing I ever did.' Fen shook her head, 'It was a blast though. That dancing!'

'If you think that's *naughty*,' Simone emphasised the last word, 'you should see what I had to do as a seventeen-year-old!'

'Speaking of naughty,' James said rather quickly, and Fen wondered if Simone had told him what she'd had to do as part of the Resistance, and if he disapproved. 'I had a shirt stolen in the hotel.'

'Really? Have you asked the laundry?' Fen asked.

'Well, that's the darnedest thing, I don't remember leaving it out for the maid. I'm sure it'll turn up. Aha,' he raised a hand and called out to the man walking towards them. 'Ahoy there, Gervais!'

'I didn't know he was coming too.' Fen pulled her coat tight around her, the chill autumn air of the evening cutting right through to the blue, flowery tea dress she was still wearing, with Rose's blessing, from the outing to Atelier Lelong today.

'We thought it might be nice for you to have some company, Fenella,' Simone trilled as she slipped her arm into James's. The slight shrug to her shoulders gave Fen just the message Simone intended and Fen opened and closed her mouth like a goldfish a few times as she tried to think of what to say to put Simone off trying to matchmake her. Arthur was barely cold in his grave – the thought of replacing him with someone else was as far from her mind as it was possible to be.

Still, Fen thought, *manners maketh man, or in this case woman,* and she waved a cheery greeting to the chubby Frenchman.

Miss Baker *was* astounding. Though not in her first flush of youth, she was as dynamic and as dazzling as ever before, if perhaps slightly less flamboyant. She held the audience in the palm of her hand, her beautiful voice filling the theatre as she sang songs by Cole Porter and Vincent Scotto. Her dress was covered in gems and sparkled under the stage lights.

Fen was transfixed and loved every second of the virtuoso performance. She would have enjoyed it even more if Gervais had stopped trying to talk to her throughout it all.

'So you've known Madame Rose Coillard for many years, you say?' was one such question.

'Yes, since I was a girl,' Fen had turned her face back towards the stage as soon as she'd spoken, hoping that she hadn't missed a beat of the show. But still Gervais persisted.

'She is a proper *bourgeoisie*, you know. Society connections. But even I, Gervais Arnault, have met her a few times.'

Fen had smiled at Gervais, acknowledging his slight brag, and then turned her attention back to the stage, bobbing her head around to try and see past the annoyingly tall man sitting in front of her.

'A good lady though, you think?' Gervais had continued.

'Oh the best, absolutely. Why?'

'No reason, no reason.' Gervais had raised his hands off his lap in mock defence. Fen had given him another quick smile and then faced back towards the stage, hoping that would be the last of his chit-chat.

Gervais did indeed stay relatively quiet for the rest of the show, but afterwards as the four of them retired to the bar of Deux Magots, he asked Fen again what she thought of Rose and if she knew Henri Renaud at all. Henri had been a particular hook of Gervais's to hang his conversation from and Fen had barely sat down at the small round table in the Deux Magots bar that James had found for them all when Gervais enquired all about him.

'You'd not think that a lowly mechanic like myself would know such grand people, eh?'

'I thought you said you had a fleet of vehicles?' Fen had cheekily reminded him.

'Well, fleet, you know it is a wide definition…'

'I'm only teasing,' Fen had unconsciously reached over and touched the mechanic's arm as she said that, as a way to reassure him, but withdrew it quickly as she saw his cheeks redden. He had carried on talking, though, regardless.

'Yes, yes, well you see, just like in the old days when everyone needed a farrier or stable boy, well now, you see, everyone needs a mechanic, or driver.'

'I do see, yes.'

'So, you see, I get to meet all sorts of important people. Like Petain himself.'

Fen raised her eyebrows at the mention of the Vichy army general and stifled a laugh as James caught her eye. His attention was quickly drawn back by Simone, however, who rose from the table and led James across to the bar, no doubt to find somewhere more private for the two of them to talk.

Gervais continued, unfazed by their leaving and puffing his chest out more as he spoke. 'And celebrities, you see, I have driven Judy Garland and Clark Gable.'

'Really?' Fen wasn't convinced he was telling the truth.

'Yes, yes. You don't believe me, I'm hurt!'

'It's not that I don't believe you, it's just—'

'And your friend Henri Renaud, he wouldn't have been able to save all the artwork without his trusted driver, that's me.'

'I'm sure he's very grateful.' Fen was unsure where this conversation was going, but she could see that Gervais was keen to keep telling her about his society connections.

'He *is* grateful, France is grateful. He is a good man though, you think?'

Fen thought about it for a moment. 'I don't have any cause to think otherwise. He seems as straight as anyone I've met. And a patriot—'

'We are all patriots!' It was on this little outburst that Fen, not unhappily, realised that Gervais was growing tired of their conversation and only a few moments later she had bid him *adieu* as he'd made an excuse to join some other friends over the other side of the bar.

Fen looked back at her own drink and saw that it was empty. A second wouldn't hurt and she cast her eyes around to see if James or Simone fancied getting another. At first, she couldn't see them, and wondered if they'd gone back to the bar already, but she scanned the louche types propping it up and resting their backsides on the fixed-in-place stools – James and Simone, it seemed, weren't among them. She was just starting to feel like a little bit of a lone poppy in a muddy field when she caught sight of them, having a smooch behind the telephone kiosk at the end of the bar.

'Looks like James is getting his own round in,' Fen murmured to herself, as she collected the empty glasses from her table.

Slightly unsteady on her feet, she realised she'd probably had quite enough to drink for one evening, so leaving James and Simone to it, and with a cheery wave over to where Gervais was now standing with a group of men, including his taller, thinner, and balder brother Antoine, she picked up her coat and bag and headed for the door.

Paris nightlife was definitely an experience, she thought to herself as she walked out of the bar. But, she had to admit, maybe it had been a little more thrilling when she'd been seventeen…

CHAPTER EIGHTEEN

Fen wondered when the marching band would stop doing a tattoo on her head and carefully rolled herself over in bed to face the window. She peered through bleary eyes to see the curtains still closed, but a bright chink of light was shining through where they didn't quite meet in the middle. She closed her eyes again and sank her face into the pillow. *What had she drunk last night?*

She remembered James and Simone catching up with her outside the bar and James walked them both home, saying a rather lingering goodnight to Simone. Then she remembered that Simone had suggested just one glass of Calvados from the decanters on Rose's sideboard.

'It's for our own good,' Simone had said as she'd sloshed the golden liquid into two of the chunky tumblers. 'It will help us sleep.'

'If you say so,' Fen had gone along with the plan, buoyed up by Simone's gaiety and pleased, on Rose's behalf, that Simone hadn't stayed the night with James again. Still, he had been the focus of most of Simone's conversation as she'd tucked her long legs up underneath her on one of the saggy old armchairs.

'I like him very much. I think he's a very generous man.'

Fen had thought to back to the lunch he'd bought her and Rose just the other day and had to agree.

Simone had continued to wax lyrical. 'He's a gentleman, I think, and rich. The way he speaks French, it's not like you, you obviously learned here in Paris, but his accent is southern. I think he learned to speak French on the Riviera, yes?' She laughed and sipped her apple brandy.

Fen had been about to speak when Simone had carried on.

'And his manners are very formal, and his conversation really very highbrow.'

'I don't think his manners were terribly formal tonight,' Fen had said as she thought about the clinch she'd seen them both in behind the telephone kiosk.

Simone had just laughed. 'He is a passionate man, but that's good, eh?' Simone had leaned forward and gripped her hand together in a fist. 'A fighter, a lover. He's my type of man.'

'He's kind too…' Fen had thought about it. He was really. And kindness was something she thought was far more important than fighting or passion, or indeed money. Arthur had had kindness in bucketloads.

'Yes he is, as you say in England, "perfect husband material". Let's drink to me being the next Lady Lancaster!'

'Lady Lancaster?' Fen had almost choked on the small sip she'd taken when Simone had said that.

'Yes, he's a viscount. Didn't you know? He's inherited a fortune, I think.'

He is filthy rich… Arthur's playful words had come back to Fen as she had pondered this new information. If this was the case, though, then James might need to be a little bit careful about how he conducted himself around impressionable young women like Simone. Still, Simone herself seemed truly excited by the prospect of joining the English aristocracy and Fen remembered her reaching for the decanter time and again, as she had filled both their glasses and spoken of her dreams of being a fine lady among the British upper classes.

Fen rolled over and mustered the mental strength to push herself up and out of bed and, head thumping, find herself a dressing gown and head to the bathroom. Arthur's words still careered around inside her head, along with another favour he'd asked of her. *Look after James*. Well, he was doing quite well at looking after himself… but Fen made a note to try to talk to him later, just to check in on his intentions, as she reached for her toothbrush.

Once a steaming, sweet mint tea was in her hand and she was sitting in the saggy armchair, chosen as it was the one with its back to the light streaming in through the windows, Fen felt better. The clock on the mantel ticked constantly and reminded her that the day was not now young; and if this reaction to a bit of alcohol was anything to go by, neither was she. She was just about to rouse herself again into action when the front door of the apartment clicked open and, moments later, Rose strode into the bright studio.

'Good morning, slug-a-bed!' she bellowed, and Fen was fairly sure the raised voice was specifically designed to set that marching band off again. And if the voice wasn't bad enough, it was accompanied by the rhythm section of Tipper's staccato barking.

Rose moved towards the console table where the spirits decanters were kept in a tantalus. She picked up the one with a small silver tag hanging around its neck that spelt out CALVADOS and held it up to the morning light to better see exactly how much, or how little, was left.

'Good thing I'm not planning on a morale booster myself later!'

'Gosh, sorry.' Fen felt terribly guilty. 'I'll replace it later as soon as I…' She pressed her hand against her forehead and sank even further into the chair.

'Ah, you know what I say, live life.' Rose put the decanter back and came and sat down opposite Fen, basking in the light of the windows. Tipper scampered in too and scrambled up onto her lap. 'We have all been through so much. I'm not surprised you let your hair down last night, *ma chérie*. It's only natural.'

Fen thought about it. She'd heard of people self-medicating with alcohol, and she always assumed it was just those poor unfortunate souls addicted to the spirit who did it. But perhaps Rose was right, perhaps there was pent-up emotion in her and she had needed the brandy to dull the pain? She nodded at Rose and sipped her tea.

'As for me, I find my expression in art,' the older woman continued. 'And my work has become dark, very dark indeed.'

'I can imagine.' Fen looked over at the easels, one of which was covered with a sheet, shielding the painting from the viewer, or perhaps it was the other way around. She looked at back at Rose. 'So, where have you been this morning?'

'Ah, just to see Henri.' Rose let Tipper nibble at her fingertips as she sat back in the chair. Fen thought she looked sad. No, not sad. Disappointed perhaps.

'At the Louvre?'

'Yes,' Rose then became more animated. 'And blow me, I was ambushed!'

'Ambushed?' This all sounded rather dramatic, Fen thought, and shuffled herself a little more upright in the saggy armchair.

'Madame Adrienne Tambour no less! Accused me of selling her a forgery!'

Le Faussaire… Fen wondered to herself, but kept quiet.

Rose continued. 'She thinks the little Dutch one, like the one in your bedroom, Fenella, was missold to her on purpose.'

'Did she buy it through Lazard?'

'Yes, more's the pity, and he probably fleeced her. Still, she can afford it, the fox-murdering old wotsit.' Rose extracted her hand from Tipper's mouth and used it to pull her long rope of pearls out from under him, then she started twisting them round her fingertips. 'That naughty man though. He gets me into all sorts of trouble and he never passes this untold wealth onto me!'

'Why do you use him then, Rose? I agree your art is far superior to the quayside kiosks, but maybe Lazard isn't the dealer for you? Surely others exist.'

'I suppose I could have a word with that Arnault chap.' Rose sank back into her chair. 'Though his brother is… Well, Henri can deal with that.'

Fen remembered Gervais's comments from the night before about how much he thought of Rose. Apparently she didn't feel as warmly.

'Will Madame Tambour want her money back?'

'How did you…? Oh never mind.' Rose gesticulated as far as the rope of pearls would let her. 'Michel can deal with that. He sold her the daubing. Anyway, in better and much more exciting news, I have Magda and Joseph coming again later today. I think I've tracked down their Cezanne to a farmhouse in the Rhineland.'

'Good gosh! How did you manage that?'

'I have my ways, dear girl. Some less legal than others. But it usually comes down to the military wives and their big mouths. They can't believe their luck that not only is *Herr Bosch* home from the fighting, but he brings a little souvenir back with him too. And not just the clap!' She laughed at her own joke, but then became more serious again. 'These rumours start and eventually they find their way to me. I shall prepare to leave for Germany soon, after I've… well, I need to finish deciphering the list and I need to speak to Henri again.'

Fen pushed herself up from her chair. 'I feel this is my cue to head back to London then.'

'No, no, dear girl. Stay as long as you like. You might be able to teach that young Simone a thing or two about morals and manners if you stay under the same roof as her.'

Fen laughed a little. 'I'm not sure I'm much of a good example after last night.'

'You're still *you* though, and all the better for it.' Rose paused. 'Will you stay and see the Bernheims again? They're coming after lunch.'

'I'd love to, but the forecast is for rain this morning, then brightening up this afternoon. And I'm desperate to go and see if Shakespeare and Company is still there.'

'Oh yes, that dusty old bookstore. I'm sure Magda will quite understand. Be back by six though, *chérie*! Cocktails!'

Fen smiled for the first time that morning. She wasn't sure she'd be up for whatever concoction Rose would come up with later, but if she was going to be able to manage one sip, she better go and clear her head in the autumn sunshine and take in some fresh air on the banks of the Seine.

CHAPTER NINETEEN

The Seine worked its magic on Fen's head and served to remind her too of how much she loved this city, especially in the autumn. The light from the low-lying sun shone through the orange and yellowing leaves of the horse chestnut and lime trees, creating a golden glow over the pavements on which she walked. She'd left Rose to prepare for her meeting just before lunch and had wandered the streets of Paris from the Île de la Cité down to the Rue de l'Odéon.

Fen had pressed her nose up against the dusty window of the sadly closed Shakespeare and Company bookstore, but took a moment to remember how her father would take her and her brother there on Saturday afternoons to browse the shelves and catch conversations between the owner, Sylvia Beach, and her many distinguished literary guests.

Arthur had often talked of the shop too – it had been one of their many plans to come back and visit it together when the war was over – and Fen tried her best to hold back a tear or two as she saw the empty bookshelves and out-of-date posters stuck to the window. *I wonder where they've gone?* She thought of the books and of the stories she'd heard of rallies in Berlin where books were burned on huge bonfires. She hoped the tomes from Shakespeare and Company's shelves hadn't suffered a similar fate, or perhaps worse, been sold to line the pockets of the Führer.

To cheer herself up, she ducked into a café, just as a few unforecast raindrops started to fall. Fen had the letter she'd written the night before with her and thought about unsealing it and adding in a postscript about her night out. Kitty would love to hear about Josephine Baker, and would groan if she heard that Fen was being matchmade with an overly friendly mechanic.

'... But I don't much fancy writing about it,' she said to herself as she paid her bill and slipped the letter back into the pocket of her trench coat. Of course, she'd only been matchmade with Gervais so that Simone and James could act more like a couple.

Simone's words were still echoing around her head and Fen had to admit that for some reason or another she was feeling slightly uneasy about the pairing. It wasn't that she didn't like Simone, but she did wonder if Simone saw James as more of a meal ticket than a real, true and honest man to love and to hold. Perhaps having her own dear Arthur so cruelly taken from her made her more sensitive to it, but she detected more than a little ambition in the young woman's attitude. Equally, she was very young and Fen only hoped James knew what he was doing, leading her on so much.

She checked her watch against the great tolling bell of Notre Dame and saw that to her relief if was now 5 p.m. Rue de l'Odéon wasn't far from Rose's apartment and Fen was glad to be getting back; cocktails aside, she just rather fancied putting her feet up.

As she neared the end of the Rue des Beaux-Arts, Fen heard a familiar 'what ho' from behind her.

'Oh, hello, James.' Her thoughts of a few minutes ago were still fresh in her mind. 'Not with Simone?'

'No, she's at work, I assume.' He looked guarded, or at least Fen thought that might be the reason for the sudden crossing of his arms in front of him. 'You're not jealous, are you?'

His question struck Fen right in the chest. It was absurd. *Jealous?* 'Ha, no. I mean, absolutely no. You're a very nice man—'

'It's just you left in rather hurry last night, and dammit, Fen, I don't want you to think badly of me, as, of course, I was happy to walk you both home, but a man's entitled to have a bit of fun and—'

'Bit of fun? Should I tell Simone that's all she is then?' she snapped at James, which was as much of a surprise to her as it was to him, and due in part to the fact that her thoughts regarding it all were still rather fresh in her mind. She stopped, only yards now from the large double grey doors of the building, and took a stand. 'Or will you tell her yourself, like a gentleman, that she's nothing more than…' Fen looked around her and in the dying light of the autumnal afternoon caught sight of the tailor, *Dufrais et Filles*. The mannequins in the window were dressed in the sort of outfits Simone revelled in. Fen pointed towards them. '… Well, nothing more than window dressing?'

'Oh, that's just ridiculous.' James followed Fen as she entered the building and started climbing the many steps up to the fifth floor. 'She's not a child, she's an adult.'

'She must be a good ten years younger than you, James, if not more.'

'So?'

'So… you should know better than to take advantage of her. Unless you plan on marrying her?' They both paused for breath as they climbed.

'God no, it's not like that. She's just showing me the sights.'

'Oh, so that's what they're called.' Fen thought of the telephone kiosk clinch last night.

'Well, who are you to say who I can and cannot see?' James crossed his arms.

They stood face to face now, slightly panting, outside the door to Rose's apartment.

'Arthur told me to look out for you, but if you don't want me to, then that's fine. Really.' Fen fumbled in her purse, trying to find the key, but her hand was trembling, she wasn't used to confrontation and hated that she and James were having these cross words. Maybe it really was none of her business who James had fun with?

'Dammit, I can't find my key.' Fen felt flustered. 'And you breathing down my neck won't help, James.'

'Breathing down your neck? You're the one giving me the third degree on propriety.'

Fen snorted and was about to say something about the *noblesse oblige* of his lordly status when she remembered that Rose seldom locked the door. She grasped the doorknob and, as expected, it clicked open. Fen exhaled with relief and let them both into the dark hallway, hoping the change of scene might also change the direction in which the conversation was heading.

'She's not that interested in me anyway…' James said, pulling Fen very much back into the discussion.

'Not *you* perhaps,' Fen took a deep breath, 'but she seems to think there may be a pot of gold hiding under your sunny disposition.'

'What?'

'Oh, James. You know what I mean. Mixed metaphors aside, I'm worried that if you rush into something with her… well, she might just be seeing you as some sort of golden-egg lay—'

James was following Fen through to the studio when she stopped suddenly. He almost toppled over her and grasped her shoulders to steady himself. Fen didn't move though. She just stood there, her hand now clasped to her mouth as she took in the scene in front of her. One of the easels was on the floor, its canvas lying awkwardly on top of it. And next to it, with a paintbrush jabbed fully into her neck, piercing her throat, was the lifeless body of Rose Coillard.

CHAPTER TWENTY

Blood pooled around the body, spreading over the dust sheets and mingling with the oil paint on the canvas and palette, which must have been in Rose's hand when the killer struck.

'Dear God!' Fen looked on in shock and reached out for James to hold onto.

'Oh Fen,' he was there, his arm immediately around her shoulder, their ever-so recent argument all but forgotten.

'She's dead.' Fen could barely believe it. This vibrant woman who had only a few hours ago been talking of cocktails… here she was now, her long beaded necklace draping limply over her velvet dress, her eyes glassily staring up at the crystal chandelier.

'Here, boy.' James let go of Fen's arm and looked over to where her little dog was quivering behind the saggy armchair.

'Oh Tipper,' Fen knelt down and beckoned him over, but James beat her to it and walked over to the small dog and scooped him up. 'The poor thing, he must have seen it all happen.'

'If only you could talk, huh, pup?' James rubbed his head between his ears and held him tightly.

'I suppose we should call the police.' Fen was still kneeling by Rose's body. 'I'm so sorry, Rose,' she said to the recumbent figure and carefully closed her eyelids.

'I'll do it.' James carried Tipper with him as he walked into the hallway, where Rose had a telephone. 'Come on, Fen, you need a cup of tea and a shot of something stronger.'

*

A few hours later and the apartment was quiet. *Deathly quiet*, Fen thought to herself and shivered. She had decided to stay on once the police had taken the body away and sent in a cleaner, having photographed the scene, and she and James had given their statements to the businesslike inspector.

A preliminary inspection by the police surgeon suggested Rose was killed earlier that afternoon, although Fen was given a sharp look by the police inspector when he caught her earwigging on their conversation.

During this time, Simone had come home and, upon seeing the bloody mess and sheet-covered body, had fallen into a faint, rather conveniently close to James's open arms. She was now asleep, the police surgeon having had a handy dose of sedatives in his medicine bag. James had offered to stay with Fen, but she'd sent him back to his hotel, not because she didn't want the company, but because she thought he might need an hour or two to himself. He'd promised to return with a bite of supper for them all later.

She got up from the old armchair and moved towards the windows. The sun had disappeared over the rooftops and it was long past the time when Paris's famous street lamps were lit. It was a relief in a way to see a city ablaze with light again, after the blackouts of the Blitz, but tonight Fen didn't want to relish in the life beyond the windows. She pulled the heavy red curtains to, switched on the side lamps and turned to face the scene of the crime again.

'I will find out who did this to you, Rose,' Fen swore, addressing the place on the floor where her friend had fallen. 'And if Arthur were here, he'd help me work it out. What would he say? "If you can't solve your seven across, check your two down" or some such thing. So, what do I need to solve? Who murdered you. Well, I have no idea. So what's my two down that might help me...?' Fen pondered the question as there was a knock at the door and Tipper started yapping from the hallway. 'I'm coming, I'm coming.'

Fen followed the little dog to the front door and opened it cautiously, grateful to find it was only James with a baguette and a bag of groceries.

'How are you holding up?' he asked.

Fen shrugged and led him through the hallway into the galley kitchen. 'I just can't stop thinking about poor Rose and looking at the… well, the spot where we found her.'

'Are you sure you two should be here tonight?'

'Simone's out like a light and I don't think I could leave her to wake up alone. Plus I'm not sure a hotel would take me and Tipper at this late hour. No. I'll be fine. Thanks for the tucker.'

'My pleasure. I would offer to look after Simone for you, but…' James paused, obviously expecting some sort of reprimand. 'Are you all right, Fen? I thought that might get me a telling off. You didn't even tell me I was rude earlier either, I was waiting for that one.'

Fen tried a weak smile, but it didn't really come out as much more than a thin grimace. 'Sorry, James, I know you're just trying to cheer me up.'

James looked at her and she could see the sincerity in his eyes. 'What would help? Really?'

'Finding out who killed dear Rose.'

James put the groceries down on the side. 'Well, that's going to be a little harder than just telling you a few jokes, but let's see what we can do.'

'You'll help me?' Fen felt a wave of relief come over her.

'Of course. But where do we start? I know you, what's your five down then?'

Fen smiled. 'Tried that. Didn't get very far, I'm afraid. From what they told us earlier, the police seem to think it could just be a burglary gone awry – some of her paintings are gone, including the little Impressionist one, and although I don't know how much jewellery Rose had, there is none left now *at all* in her room.'

'Shame they didn't steal Tipper.'

'James... now, that *is* rude.' Fen gave him a look and he smiled back at her. 'But I don't know, I just don't buy it. Yes, things were stolen, but why Rose? Why this apartment? When there are art galleries and shops on the street just below us, full of artworks of equal, or probably far greater, value to Rose's collection. Those buildings could so easily be broken into and the art taken without having to risk coming across someone. And there are plenty of other well-to-do apartments twixt here and there, too. Rose told me the other night that the lady downstairs is a Russian countess, for heaven's sake! So, no, I don't think it was a burglary.' She paused. 'So I suppose to work on my two down or whatever, we have to start talking to those who knew Rose the best.'

'Well, Sleeping Beauty is dead to the world.'

Fen frowned at his choice of words and shook her head.

'Sorry.' James dug his hand into the shopping bag and pulled out a tin of coarse pâté, then started riffling through the drawers, trying to find a tin opener.

'Asleep or not, Simone has only lodged here for a matter of weeks, so I'm not sure she would have much more to share on Rose than I know already.' Fen furrowed her brow in thought. 'There's Henri Renaud...'

'And?' James pulled the cork on a bottle of *vin de table*.

'She brushed it off, but I saw her arguing with her rather dubious art dealer, Michel Lazard. That was only yesterday. What if he—'

'Killed her?' James posed the question they were both thinking. 'Why would he do that?'

'I think he'd been miss-selling her paintings and getting her into the soup with some customers.'

'Miss-selling how?'

'Let's just say there's a fine line between *homages* and forgeries.'

'Blimey,' James pondered. 'Is there a way of tracking him down?'

'There might be...' Fen smeared some pâté on a chunk of bread. 'I'm sure I'll find some sort of reference to him in her papers.'

'The police didn't take any of them?'

'Not a sausage. They're so sure it's just a burglary, they didn't even go through her bag or desk or anything.'

'And what about the Bernheims?'

'Magda and Joseph?' Fen looked affronted. 'No, gosh no. Absolutely not. They loved Rose. And more than anyone else in the whole of Paris, they have absolutely no motive. She even told me that she'd found one of their paintings. They'd never get it back if they killed her now. Plus, if it had been one or both of them, then I think the paperwork would have been the first thing they'd take, not leave it to the gendarmes to, well, to ignore.'

'I see. We better speak to them all the same, to let them know at least. And Fen?'

'Yes?'

'I'm sorry about earlier. About arguing and about Rose and... well, Arthur would be really proud of you right now. I'm really proud of you.'

At that, he carried his own plate of bread and pâté and his glass of wine out of the kitchen and into the studio, while Fen wiped a tear away with the sleeve of her cardigan.

CHAPTER TWENTY-ONE

The next day brought it with it more rain and squally winds and Fen wondered if her old trench coat would suffice for the early-morning walk across the Pont des Arts to the offices of the Louvre. She and James had talked last night before he headed back to his hotel, and they had realised that Henri Renaud might not even know that Rose had been killed. Plus, due to their clandestine war work, he more than anyone would know who might want her dead.

Although the police had done a fair sweep of the apartment for clues, their insistence that it must 'just be a burglary gone wrong' had meant they hadn't taken away personal items such as Rose's carpetbag full of papers or her diary. Fen had found it open on the coffee table, untouched by the uninterested gendarmes, and had seen she was due to visit Henri today at the Louvre – or at least that's what she thought the big red HENRI encircled several times on today's page meant. She had been looking at it when a knock at the door, followed by Tipper's usual tirade, had startled her. That it was only James was a relief, and Fen let him in, while scooping up the squirming little dog before he tripped either of them up.

'How are you this morning?' James asked.

Fen sucked in her breath and exhaled, staring at the ceiling, trying to find the right words to describe her grief. How could she burden James, who she really didn't know terribly well, with her feelings of loss? First Arthur and now Rose, not to mention all the acquaintances and friends she and her fellow land girls had lost over the last few years. She rested her face against Tipper's neck before putting the dog down.

'Fine,' she said and smiled at James, who just nodded.

The knocking and Tipper's barking was enough to rouse Simone, who groggily opened her bedroom door. James had the decency to avert his eyes from her state of undress, and Simone closed it again, emerging a few moments later in a floor-length silk dressing gown. She rubbed the sleep out of her eyes and asked for some coffee, before dissolving into tears at the sight of the broken easel and stained floor.

'Come now, Simone.' Fen let her sob on her shoulder for a bit, while James fiddled around in the kitchen, finding the coffee pot and heating the water.

Fen always felt terribly awkward comforting people, especially such overtly emotional ones. Now was not the time for weeping and she said as much, in a gentler way, to Simone and settled her down on the chaise longue. It didn't help that Tipper kept jumping off her every time Fen tried to leave the small dog on Simone's lap, a warm little pup to snuggle would have been just the ticket. Still, once she was quite sure that Simone's sobs had eased, she tracked down James in the kitchen as he was filling up the coffee pot.

'She's a bit calmer now,' Fen said, finding three cups in the cupboard.

'It's been a shock for her.'

And me, Fen thought to herself, but just nodded. 'I'll go and see Henri this morning, as discussed, and let him know. Would you be able to keep an eye on Simone and possibly go door-to-door around the other apartments in case anyone saw or heard anything suspicious? I know the gendarmes did a quick whip around the building, but I still can't believe this was just a burglary. Maybe you could ask more, I don't know, *illuminating* questions rather than just the old "did you get burgled last night, too?".'

'Absolutely,' James agreed and Fen felt happier leaving the weepy Simone with him in charge.

After a quick slug of coffee, she collected up her coat and bag and headed out.

Fen was bracing herself to break the news to Henri that the woman he worked so closely with during the war was dead. By the time she arrived at the side door of the mighty Louvre, she was wet through and shivering. *It's as if the weather knows...* she thought to herself.

As Rose had done just a few days ago, Fen let herself in, wondering at the ease of it. *So much for saving the works from the Nazis, when anyone could just waltz in and steal them now...* With that in mind, she carefully closed the door behind her and retraced the steps she had taken to Henri Renaud's office.

'Come in!'

'Bonjour Monsieur Renaud,' Fen felt it necessary to be reasonably formal, given the circumstances.

'Ah, Miss Churche, hello.'

'I'm so sorry to disturb you, it's just I—'

'Madame Coillard sent you on a mission, eh? Too immersed in her paintbrushes to come herself? Or *rather you than her* in this rain, eh?'

He seemed so jovial and oblivious as he joked about Rose, it almost broke Fen's heart all over again to tell him of her terrible news. She sat herself down in one of the gold-edged fancy chairs the other side of his vast desk and recounted the recent, awful, events.

'Oh dear, oh dear indeed. Oh dear, dear, dear.' Henri was visibly moved and distracted himself by taking his glasses off and giving them a long and thoughtful polish as he muttered 'Oh dear' over and over again.

'I'm so sorry, Monsieur Renaud, I know you two were close.'

'We did some excellent work together.' He replaced his glasses onto his nose.

'The police think it was a burglary gone wrong, but I'm not so—'

'Oh yes, yes. Possibly possibly. She gave out that key of hers to every former pupil, lodger and art enthusiast.' As Henri spoke, Fen felt her own key to Rose's apartment in her pocket and had to admit that it had been given freely. But they were old friends…

'I don't know…'

'And I think I can count on one hand the times it's even been locked,' he continued, then he paused to think. 'I'll tell you who the police should be interviewing. That set of useless men who hang around in the bar at the end of the road!' Henri looked rather triumphant with his suggestion.

'Who do you mean?'

'Oh, I don't know their names… let me think… Louis something and Jacques…' he scratched his forehead as he tried to remember. 'The Arnault brothers, they'd be a good bet, too.'

'Gervais and Antoine?' Fen thought of James and Simone's slightly buffoonish friends. Then she remembered Gervais's boasting from a couple of evenings ago. *Of course Henri knew him.*

'Yes, yes. Fat little Gervais with his gap teeth and constant cheroot. He drove lorries for us in the war. Gervais "The Wrench" we called him. Antoine looks after my warehouse in St Denis, and I know he worries about his brother.'

'Gervais mentioned he drove lorries for you the other night…'

'Did he now? So much for confidentiality. But I suppose none of us has secrets any more. What's the point?'

'So what was he actually doing?'

'This place,' he waved his hand in the air, 'we knew it would be a target for the Nazi trophy hunters. Yes, they were interested in the "legitimate", or so they called it, stealing from the Jews, but they wanted the real masterpieces. The *Venus de Milo*, the *Mona Lisa*. We had to remove as much art as possible before the occupation. Countless masterpieces driven to châteaux around the country. The *Mona Lisa* was moved several times in an attempt to hide her from Herr Hitler.'

Fen sat back and took it all in. 'Rose said as much, but I didn't realise that the greatest treasures of the art world were left in the slightly grubby hands of a lorry driver like Gervais.'

'Indeed. All hands on deck at the time.'

Even though Fen hadn't exactly warmed to Gervais, something nagged at her. 'If he was deemed responsible enough only, what, a year or so ago—'

'Six years now. September 1939 we moved the *Mona Lisa*.'

'And he worked for you after that too?' Fen remembered now that Gervais had spoken about working for the Germans emptying Jewish apartments.

'Yes, he did. I needed someone I could trust to work with me and Rose on the moving of the artwork. You see,' he sat forward and addressed her more seriously, 'the way it worked was that Gervais would take the contents of the apartments to the warehouse where his brother worked.'

'You said it was your warehouse, yes?'

'I lease it, yes, for my own collection that won't fit into my gallery in the Palais du Jardins.' He sat back again. 'In any case, we needed a team we could trust. They would deliver the crates of artwork to the warehouse and unpack them. Then, using Rose's list and her encoded names, they would carefully mark up the paintings in some way – chalk on the back of the frames or a pencil on the back of the canvas – and then repack the paintings ready for delivery to the auctioneers or the Jeu de Paumes gallery.'

'I recognise that name.' Fen thought back to her life in Paris in the 1930s.

'As a good friend of Rose, so you should. She exhibited there alongside Matisse and Picasso, though perhaps that was after you left Paris? In any case, the ERR, the official looting squad of the Nazis, requisitioned it as the holding post for their plunder. Göring himself visited it, *ooof*, twenty times at least, to cherry-pick his favourite pieces for his and Hitler's collections, and of course those for the German nation.'

'Did you meet them, Göring and the ERR officers?'

'Many times, yes.'

'What were they like?' Fen knew her natural curiosity was dragging her off track, but she couldn't help but ask.

Henri took his glasses off again and gave them another rub with his handkerchief. 'Unimpressive, if you must know. Though intimidating, of course, as anyone is who holds the power of life and death over so many people.'

Fen took it all in. It really had been a daring and courageous plan. What had gone on afterwards, in the Jeu de Paumes gallery, was almost too tragic to contemplate. Stolen treasures picked over and judged merely on monetary value and racist ideals. No wonder Rose had tried so hard in her own way to make sure as much of it as possible could be returned to its rightful owners.

Rose... Fen brought her mind back to who might have killed her.

'So why,' Fen asked Henri once his glasses were back on and pushed up the bridge of his nose, 'do you think the Arnault brothers would rob and kill Rose? You both trusted them.'

'Ah, well... things had become a little strained between Rose and the Arnaults.' He paused. 'Gervais is what you might call the "enforcer" of the two, more clever with a wrench, if you catch my drift.'

'Hence the nickname,' Fen all but whispered, while Henri nodded.

'And his adeptness with that tool, in all senses, led him into the path of some nasty people. I think the Americans would call them "gangsters" or "the Mob".'

Fen frowned, she couldn't quite tally the buffoonish man she'd met the other night with this new image of him being a Machine Gun Kelly-style operator.

'Did he threaten Rose then?' Fen wondered how she had possibly got caught up in all of this.

Henri just shrugged and then laid his hands down on the desk, almost in resignation. 'I don't know, Miss Churche, but I do know that she had spoken to me only a few days ago about how she worried that Gervais would be a problem when it came to helping find the paintings. He was no longer trustworthy and had succumbed to a life of crime.'

'His brother too?' she asked.

'I do hope not, as he is my warehouse manager…'

Fen watched as he drummed his fingers on the desk for a moment, then he spoke again.

'The more I think about it, the more I believe Rose must have said something. Threatened to shop one or both of them in, if only to stop them from revealing…'

'Revealing what?' Fen was alert again and wondered what Henri could mean.

'Ah… I shouldn't have spoken so carelessly. Never speak ill of the dead and all that.'

'Please, Monsieur Renaud, if you know anything else about Rose that could help me find out who did this to her…' Fen begged and then waited as Henri made up his mind.

'You're right. There's no point in secrets now.' He sighed. 'Rose was a true and honest person. Her moral compass was unshakeable, but she did have that great talent for forging paintings.'

'Forging is a strong word…' Fen trailed off as Henri raised his hand. She let him continue.

'Forgery *is* a strong word, but what is the difference between a copy and a forgery? How you sell them, that is what. One is the honest homage to a famous painter, the other a cheap attempt at making money. She had an unbelievably good eye for copying. But only her art dealer, Michel Lazard, can tell you if she benefited more than she should have done from selling them.'

'Lazard… she told me about him.'

'Yes, yes. He's a friend of the Arnaults, you know? Antoine especially, I think. It's clear to me that somehow the Arnault brothers found out about Rose's paintings, perhaps they were even benefitting from Lazard without her knowledge? Believe me, somewhere between those two brothers and that two-bit dealer you'll find your murderer.'

Henri sat back in his chair with a sort of finality. As if his own words had sunk in, he now looked utterly desolate. His skin looked grey and he seemed about ten years older than he had when Fen had first met him, here in this office with Rose just a few days ago.

'To think,' he said thoughtfully, and quietly, 'I was going to surprise her with some good news yesterday, but I was caught up in my own gallery all afternoon.'

'What was the good news?' Fen asked.

'Just that I heard on the art world's grapevine that one of the paintings by Poussin stolen from Jacob Berenson was listed for auction in Westphalia, in Germany, this last week just gone. If I hadn't been on the telephone to London organising delivery of a rather good watercolour yesterday afternoon, I might have been able to stop it.' He took off his glasses again and rubbed his face in his hands.

Fen took it as her cue to leave, and she bid Henri goodbye with his endorsement to carefully look into the affairs of the Arnault brothers ringing in her ears and the address of his warehouse in the suburbs should she want to talk to Antoine.

Just as she was leaving, a thought occurred to her and she popped her head around the door to ask Henri. He was still looking dejected and only raised his head again when he heard her soft knock at the door.

'What is it, Miss Churche?'

'Just a thought really. But did you ever hear of a secret agent called The Chameleon?'

Henri stared at her and then shook his head. 'The Chameleon? I think you've confused real life with some American superhero comics. Now, please, I must make arrangements for some of the paintings in my warehouse. Goodbye, Miss Churche.'

Fen nodded and closed the door softly behind her, noting that Henri had not only provided some very good clues for her "two down" but during the conversation had also given himself an alibi for the time of the murder.

CHAPTER TWENTY-TWO

The rain had, thankfully, lessened to no more than a drizzle as Fen left the Louvre, but there was a definite chill to the air and she pulled her still damp collar up around her neck. She crossed the Seine and popped into a café near the École des Beaux-Arts. She couldn't quite bring herself to head back into the apartment yet, the image of Rose lying in a pool of blood still so real and visceral in her mind. The smell of brewing coffee and cigarette smoke helped bring her back to the present and she ordered a coffee from the waiter who was wiping glasses behind the bar.

Fen found herself a small table near the window and absent-mindedly pulled a paper napkin out from the dispenser on the table. She had started fiddling with it and curling its edges when an idea occurred to her. Reaching down to her bag, she drew out a pen and then started to write out a few words that stuck in her mind, sliding them together like a grid. There was something, she found, about seeing the words linked like this that helped her sort out the facts and clues in her head and how they might intersect in real life, too.

She had just finished writing out the final word in block capitals when the waiter brought her coffee over. Sitting back and sucking her pen, Fen then took a sip of her coffee. She stared at the grid, which looked like this:

The word, as much as the image itself, of PAINTBRUSH stuck in her mind. It was the brutality of it. It was so forceful, yet also silent. *Silent…* There would have been no sound of a pistol to alert the neighbours, but it also didn't feel like the weapon of choice for a premeditated murder. *A paintbrush…* It was so pertinent to the woman herself, too. Like a writer being killed with a pen, or a lorry driver being killed with a wrench.

Gervais 'The Wrench'… perhaps Henri had a point after all.

The rain started up again and, with little motivation to leave the café, Fen decided to order a late breakfast of simple baguette and jam and wait out the storm until it, hopefully, passed.

Pass it did and Fen followed the now familiar route back towards the large grey doors of Rose's apartment building. She turned the cast-iron handle and let herself into the communal hallway. The rank of mailboxes caught her eye, and before she headed up the stairs, she walked over to them and paused to look at the names.

'Aha. *Mde Coillard, Apt 5,*' she read out from the card slipped into the slot on the front of one of the boxes.

The box had a simple but effective lock, like that of a safety deposit box, and apart from the narrow slit at the top of the door, there was no way to get into it, or see what might be inside.

There must be a key upstairs somewhere, Fen thought to herself as she gave the mailbox's door one more rattle just to make sure, before she carried on up the stairs.

'Hello! Simone!' Fen called as she opened the front door. 'Oh hello, Tipper.'

The dog jumped up at her and she picked him up, and was rewarded with a quick few licks to her nose.

'Oh Tipper.'

Dog breath aside, she was relieved that the essence of Rose was still very much apparent in the apartment. However, the familiar smell of ylang-ylang and turpentine, with some cigarette smoke thrown in, was now tinged with the throat-burning smell of bleach.

As Fen walked with a squirming Tipper in her arms through the darkness of the hallway to the light-filled studio, she saw Simone on her hands and knees, scrubbing the wooden parquet floor, a bundle of dust sheets next to her that looked ready for the rubbish bin.

'Simone, oh dear. Here, sit up,' Fen put the little dog down and went over to the weeping girl.

'Someone had to do it,' she sniffled as she scrubbed, not even looking up from the floor. 'Oh... Rose.'

Mrs B would tell me to get a good strong brew on, Fen thought, remembering her old landlady. 'Simone, come and sit over here and I'll pop some tea on. You'll hurt yourself with all that bleach and no gloves on, gosh your poor hands. What's come over you?'

'I just couldn't bear it! How could you bear it?' Simone let herself be helped up by Fen and sank into one of the armchairs.

'The police cleaner had done a very good job, don't you think? Now, look at your hands, you silly thing.' Fen reached over and took Simone's red, sore-looking hands in hers. 'If only I had some decent hand cream. Here, let me pop the kettle on and then I'll raid Rose's room. I'm sure she wouldn't mind.'

When Fen returned, with a teapot of Lipton's finest and a tub of aqueous cream from Rose's dressing table, she sat down opposite Simone and started to pour.

'I'm sorry, it should be stronger really, but I'm too impatient to let it brew.'

'I don't mind, thank you. And for this.' Simone started rubbing the white cream into her hands.

Fen sipped her own tea and then the thought occurred to her about James.

'I'm so sorry, I thought I was leaving you in good hands with James here this morning. I would never have left you alone after, well, after last night, if I thought he wouldn't be on hand to… to stop you from getting upset.' Fen glanced over to where the bleach and scrubbing had left the old parquet floor in a terrible state.

'James was here for a bit, yes.' Simone shifted in her seat, then reached down for her own cup of tea. 'But he wanted to start talking to the other residents before they left for work or out for the day. Then he said he had some errands of his own to run. I'm afraid I was quite alone.' She sniffed and Fen fished around in her pocket for a hanky.

I'd hoped of better from him, she thought, sighing out a long breath as she handed over her handkerchief to sniffling Simone. She would have to have another word with him about leading the poor girl on; he really shouldn't just be present for the fun bits. But she did appreciate his help with canvassing the other apartments. Hopefully his interviews would turn up some useful clue, such as 'man seen running away clasping a wrench' or 'sound of newly tuned engine running outside'. She could but hope.

Simone started weeping again, but with tea and hanky administered, Fen wasn't sure of what else she could do. She took in a deep breath. 'This isn't what Rose would have wanted,' she said, leaning forward and gently wobbling one of Simone's angular knees.

'Why don't you go and get washed and brushed and I'll pack away all this bleach. Then we can have another pot of tea and work out what to do next.'

'Rose always said you had more of a practical head than an artistic one,' Simone said, through her sniffles.

'As much as I'd love to have been the next Michelangelo, I fear she was right, Simone.' Fen got up and squeezed the younger woman's shoulder as she walked past her. 'Give me a puzzle over a paintbrush any day of the week!'

CHAPTER TWENTY-THREE

The two women sat opposite each other on the armchairs in the studio room, which now reeked of bleach. Fen had helped Simone rinse off as much of the caustic solution as possible from the varnished wood, saving it from being permanently damaged. The dust sheets were bundled up and taken out to the rubbish bins at the back of the building and Fen had spent a quiet, contemplative hour packing away Rose's oil paints and cleaning her paintbrushes. She and Simone had made conversation throughout the rest of the morning rather sporadically, but now they were nibbling on some toast and butter that Fen had scratched together for a bit of lunch and talking more seriously about what they should do.

'It's not that I'm altogether happy here…' Simone cast her eyes over to where the body had lain. 'But it's like I said earlier, I just don't have anywhere else to go.'

'I understand. I suppose we need to speak to Rose's solicitor, but for now I can't see there being a problem with the both of us staying on while things are sorted out.' *And while I get to the bottom of all of this*, Fen thought to herself. 'Plus, someone needs to look after Tipper. The poor little chap will be grieving in his own way and I don't think we can just biff him off to the dogs' home just yet.'

'*Ooh la la*, no! I will have him. Little dogs like him are all the rage and I think Christian could make a wonderful little coat for him.'

Simone's flippancy made Fen smile. It was light relief to be talking fashion again.

'Of course,' Simone carried on, 'perhaps I will return to England with you and James?'

'Oh really? Have you both, well, discussed that? I'm not sure he wants to go back to London just yet.' *Or at least he hasn't mentioned it to me*, Fen thought. 'Has he said otherwise?'

'Not in so many words, but what is there in Paris for us both?' She shrugged. 'And I think James has a house or two in England. It could be very comfortable.'

'House or two?' Fen hadn't really thought what being *filthy rich* might actually mean.

Simone looked at Fen, examining her. Then she laughed. 'You mean you don't know?'

'I hadn't really thought about it. What don't I know exactly?' Fen was genuinely puzzled.

'James. Viscount Lancaster… His London house was bombed, I think, which is a shame, but the land itself – Knightsbridge perhaps, or Kensington – you must know these areas better than I do, well, it must still have value, you know? And the country house in Sussex is apparently vast.'

'How do you know all of this?' Fen was aware she didn't know much about James – finding out about his aristocratic connections had been a surprise enough the other night – but she did know he was a taciturn sort of chap and not one to spill the family secrets, or jewels, in idle conversation. Or was he seriously thinking Simone was the future Mrs Lancaster, or Lady Simone even, and he needed to show off to her?

At that moment, there was a loud rapping on the door of the apartment. The two women looked at each other and frowned.

'Who could that be?' Simone whispered, pulling her cardigan closer around her. 'You don't think it's the murderer, do you?'

Any chance the women had of pretending not to be there until the visitor went away was ruined by Tipper barking like crazy and scampering towards the door.

'I'm coming,' Fen called into the air, hoping the person in the vestibule could hear her. 'Who is it?' she called out when she was closer to the door.

'It's Joseph Bernheim,' the voice called back from the other side of the door.

Simone, who had followed Fen into the hallway made some excuse about being too unsightly to be seen and disappeared back into the studio and from there into her room, leaving Fen to unlock the door.

'Oh, Joseph, come in, come in.' She was pleased he was here, although she wasn't sure if she was looking forward to breaking the bad news about Rose's death to another of her friends on the same day.

As he entered the small hallway, Joseph took off his hat but hadn't got much further before Fen continued.

'It is lovely to see you, but I'm afraid I have something terrible to tell you.'

'I'm so used to the door being unlocked.' The frazzled man sat on the edge of the chaise longue, running his Homburg hat through his hands. 'Even after she… I mean, before the war when I would meet Magda here, we would just walk in.'

'I just thought for security…' Fen murmured as she poured him a cup of tea, the pot now refreshed several times and the loose leaves of the tea running slightly out of oomph.

'Of course, of course,' he nodded, 'and this happened… yesterday?'

'Yes. I remember Rose saying you were due to come and see her. What time was that?'

'Just after lunch, about two o'clock,' he paused and threaded his hat brim through his fingers again. 'But I was held up and never made it.'

'You may have stumbled on her killer if you had.' Fen then explained to Joseph, 'I overheard the police saying she had been killed in the early afternoon.'

Joseph sighed. 'I don't suppose you know what she had found out, do you? About our paintings, I mean.' Joseph looked keenly at Fen, who could only shake her head.

'I'm afraid not. Just that she thought she had tracked down one of them—'

'Ah, such bad luck!' Joseph tossed his hat across the chaise longue and hung his head down, with his hands hanging between his knees. 'So close yet so far.'

Fen held her tongue from saying something about Rose not meaning to get herself killed, but it was as if Joseph was reading her mind.

'Look at me, thinking only of myself and my paintings when our dear friend has died.' Joseph accepted the cup of weak tea from Fen and carried on. 'It's appalling of me. But it's Magda I feel so sorry for now. She was so looking forward to spending more time with wonderful Rose.'

Fen nodded and then turned to him again. 'Joseph, I wonder if I might be able to help?'

'Well, Magda will love to spend time with you, too.'

'Oh, well, yes, of course, me too. But I meant about your paintings.'

'Really?' Joseph looked at her keenly.

'I think her solicitor should possibly go through Rose's things first, but after that, well, we can have a jolly good go at trying to find the cipher and start decoding the list ourselves. Think about it, it was only Henri and Rose who knew about the list and her code. Rose was keen for them to be kept separate… and we know Henri had the list, so that suggests to me that the cipher is in *this* apartment somewhere.'

'You might be on to something there.' Joseph sucked his teeth, but looked brighter and reached across the chaise for his hat. 'Thank you, Fenella.'

'Don't thank me too soon, I have no idea who her solicitor is yet, but don't worry, I'll do whatever I can to help.'

Fen saw Joseph out and walked back into the studio, letting Tipper down as she entered the room.

Simone had reappeared and was painting her nails a wonderfully vibrant shade of red. She held the freshly glossy tips of her fingers up to Fen. 'Urgh, Tipper, *non... non*!' She tried to bat the frenetic little dog away with her elbow and Fen ended up picking him up and taking him back into the hallway.

'Slave to fashion, huh, Tipper? We better find those solicitor's details by ourselves,' Fen whispered into his ear as she carefully opened the door off the hallway that led into the box room. Squirmy as he was, holding the warm little body of the dog close to her was a lovely reassurance for Fen as she stood on the threshold of her murdered friend's bedroom. It was untouched since the police had been in to take fingerprints, and of course she'd had a look around too in the commotion to try to see if anything had been taken by the supposed thief.

The room was smaller than either hers or Simone's, but it was lit by another of the vast floor-to-ceiling windows that looked over the street at the front of the building. The light was marvellous, with a clarity to it that so often comes when rain has passed and the sun is gently suffused by scudding clouds. *Rose would have loved this light*, Fen thought. *No wonder she chose this smaller room over the other spare one.*

She caught sight of the upturned jewellery box on the small dressing table and a pang of grief stopped her in her tracks. Long strings of beads bled out over the side, while brooches littered the floor around the dressing table. Fen instinctively raised her hand to touch her own brooch, which had been stolen – but thankfully returned – in Burgundy. Having one's belongings turned over like this was such a violation…

Not as violating as death, she thought, shaking her head and dispelling the maudlin thoughts. 'We're more sensible than this, aren't we, Tipper,' Fen told the small dog as she wiped a tear away from her eye.

Tipper didn't answer but did poke his nose under the bed, nudging the floor-skimming quilt as he did so, and Fen followed his lead and started to look under there for anything that might point her in the direction of her friend's solicitor.

'Perhaps there was no will?' Simone's voice gave Fen a start and she looked up from rummaging under the bed to see the younger woman, resting her hip against the door jamb, her hands still splayed out in front of her as her nails dried.

'Perhaps.' Fen pushed a box of dried oil paint tubes back under the bed and sat back on her heels. 'But she was a woman who made lists, we know that much for sure, and it makes me suspect that, far from being the scatty artist, she was in fact a meticulous record keeper.'

'If you say so. Oh, one moment…' Simone flapped her hands to help dry the polish and disappeared out of view.

Fen had just sat herself down on the bed and spread out a box of paperwork on the counterpane when Simone reappeared holding a thin piece of paper carefully between her thumb and forefinger.

'It wasn't like we had a formal agreement or anything, but when I moved in, madame did want a reference from me sent to a Monsieur Blanquer…' She held out the piece of paper to Fen, who reached out and took it from her.

'Well, would you look at that! Thank you, Simone. Monsieur Blanquer, notary etcetera, etcetera. Paris 8659. Perfect.'

Simone smiled and left Fen to telephone and make the appointment with the solicitor.

CHAPTER TWENTY-FOUR

It was with more than a dash of good luck that Monsieur Blanquer's assistant was available to schedule in an appointment for eleven o'clock the following morning, and Fen made the arrangements on the telephone accordingly. She then put a call into Joseph Bernheim, catching another of his building's tenants on the communal telephone who promised to leave him the message that he should call round to Rose's apartment at around noon the next day. With those tasks done, Fen decided that a visit to one or other of the Arnault brothers was in order.

Gervais sounded like he might have the most to gain from killing Rose, if indeed she had threatened to turn him in to the police for his Mob connections, but Antoine seemed like the brother with the most brain cells, and perhaps he'd be able to shed some light on what shady business his brother Gervais was caught up in. And if Rose was caught up in it, too.

But the rain that had been on and off that morning had settled in properly for the afternoon and Fen didn't think her poor trench coat would keep her dry if it had to take another soaking. And as much as she had admired Rose's sense of style, she wasn't sure she could pull off wearing one of her flamboyant patchwork overcoats around town.

Instead, Fen settled down to write a letter home, telling her parents the sad news of their friend's death. She wiped away tears as they now fell onto the page, as persistent as the long drips that raced down the unshuttered windows of the apartment. She wondered if she should try to contact her brother too, still serving as the army gradually demobbed in North Africa, but she wasn't sure she had the emotional strength to write the words *Rose is dead* one more time.

Just as she was sealing the envelope to her parents, there was a knock at the door that sent Tipper into paroxysms of barking.

'Oh they're so beautiful! Such colours!' Fen could hear Simone, who had rushed to answer the door this time – obviously all thoughts of murderers coming back to stalk them gone from her mind – talking to James in the hallway.

Tipper scampered back into the studio and Fen scooped him up, smiling as he writhed in happiness at the attention. She put him down and he soon went back to licking the small pieces of toast, with a thin scraping of pâté on them, that Fen had been feeding him before James's arrival. They both looked up though as Simone led James into the room. It was hard to see Simone through the size of the bouquet she was holding.

'Look, Fenella, see what James has brought me!'

'It's just a little token, to brighten up the apartment somewhat. Afraid I had to drop a few francs in the local tailor, no sign of that shirt of mine turning up. And the florist was next door, so…' James said and then wrinkled his nose. 'Bloody hell, what is that smell?'

'Bleach,' Fen said as she quickly withdrew her fingers from Tipper's sharp little teeth.

'I had a whim,' Simone explained, cocking her head on one side. 'I could not bear the thought of dear Rose's blood being here, so I scrubbed and scrubbed.' She placed the bouquet on the chaise longue and showed James her hands. 'They are better now, thanks to Fen and her hand cream, but I will be in trouble at work tomorrow if they think I can't model like this.' She scooped the bouquet up again and took it into her bedroom. Fen watched her as she went, wondering if the flowers would make it back out to help brighten up the whole apartment, or just her room.

'And how are you?' James asked Fen as he took the seat opposite her.

'Oh, you know, coping.' Fen let Tipper lick some of the meat paste off her fingers. 'How did you get on with canvassing the other residents?'

'Ah, yes. Well, interesting bunch. Afraid I didn't get a chance to talk to them all, several unanswered doors and all that. The countess, though, she was a card. Dressed like an Edwardian *grande dame* and dripping in diamonds. I had to answer about forty questions about who I was and what I wanted before she opened the door even an inch. Eventually, she let me in and told me that she'd decided to wear all of her jewels as she felt safer with them on her, now that there's a burglar on the loose.'

'Oh dear, the police are definitely going down that route then, telling everyone that this was just a robbery gone wrong?'

'Seems so. She did say something interesting though.'

'Oh yes?' Fen's curiosity was piqued.

'Yes, she said every time someone comes to call on Rose, she can hear Tipper barking. She says it upsets her Persian cat. Funny snouty-nosed thing it is too. Called Tsarina. Anyway, I digress. She said that yesterday afternoon she only heard Tipper bark once at about two o'clock.'

Fen sat up and Tipper jumped off her lap. 'Once?'

'That's what she said. I didn't ask Tsarina.'

Fen ignored his joke. 'Once... Two o'clock was when Joseph Bernheim was meant to call...' Fen was lost in thought for a moment. 'So there was a visitor? Now, does that explain the burglary-gone-wrong idea? Or...'

'Or what?'

Fen brushed some of Tipper's hairs off her knees and dislodged a few crumbs from the toast too. She wasn't sure how James would take Henri's theory about the Arnault brothers, since he was on relatively friendly terms with them, so she took a deep breath and came right out with it. 'I spoke to Henri Renaud and he suggested it might be one, or both, I suppose, of the Arnault brothers.'

'Really? What have they got against Rose? I thought they all worked together?'

'He thinks Gervais might have fallen in with a bad lot and Rose might have forced his hand by threatening to shop him to the police.'

'A bad lot?' James furrowed his brow.

'You know, gangsters and the like.'

'Gangsters? What utter tosh!' James clapped his hands down on his knees. 'I don't think Gervais could fight his way out of a croissant, let alone get involved with some sort of mafiosi.'

'Henri called him Gervais "The Wrench"...'

This just made James laugh.

'We should at least check their alibis,' Fen suggested, and James, recovered from his laughing fit nodded, then shook his head.

'I just can't picture it... I suppose Henri had an alibi ready of his own?'

'Yes. And he offered it most readily. In his own gallery apparently, on the phone to London, asking about watercolours. I suppose we could check that out somehow if we think we need to.'

'No stone and all that. He shouldn't slander Gervais, or Antoine, come to think of it.' James shook his head. 'Just because a chap's not in a three-piece suit...'

'I know, I know. You weren't with them, yesterday afternoon, I mean? To provide an alibi?'

'No... but that's not to say they're—'

He was interrupted by Simone coming back into the studio, changed and dressed ready for a night out. She looked demurely elegant, dressed in black to honour Rose, yet the flashes of red at the end of her nails kept her looking more glamorous than grieving. She began clipping two large pearls to her ears and clasped a neat little bag under her elbow. She closed her bedroom door behind her before Fen could see if she'd found a vase for the flowers.

'Gosh, don't you look pretty,' Fen complimented Simone, relieved to have a change of subject – she hadn't liked the tension that had building between her and James in regards to the Arnault brothers. 'What super pearls.'

Simone finished clipping them onto her ears and smiled, meekly. 'They were a present from dear Rose.'

'How lucky the thief didn't raid our rooms,' Fen caught herself thinking out loud.

'Yes,' Simone agreed. 'Ready, James?'

'Yes.' He got up to leave, but then hovered by where Fen was still sitting, Tipper now gently snoring on her lap. 'I'll come with you tomorrow. To go and question Antoine and Gervais. I don't want you heading over to that part of town, and, well, especially not if Henri is correct.'

'Thank you, James.' Fen smiled up and him and then shooed him away. Personally she couldn't contemplate a night out, not so soon after Rose had died, but then people grieved in different ways. Perhaps Simone needed the distraction to help her cope with the shock. With this in mind, Fen tried her best to sound jolly. 'Now go and have fun, you two.'

Simone waved and was gone with barely a backward glance, while James hesitated just slightly before wishing Fen a good night. 'Just you and me then tonight, Tipper,' Fen said as she wandered through to the kitchen to see what else she could scrape together from Rose's rapidly diminishing cupboards. The day had taken its toll on her, emotionally at least, and while they were gallivanting she was happy to have a quiet and early night.

Before bed, though, that evening she did find the napkin she'd been writing on and carefully printed out two more words on the grid.

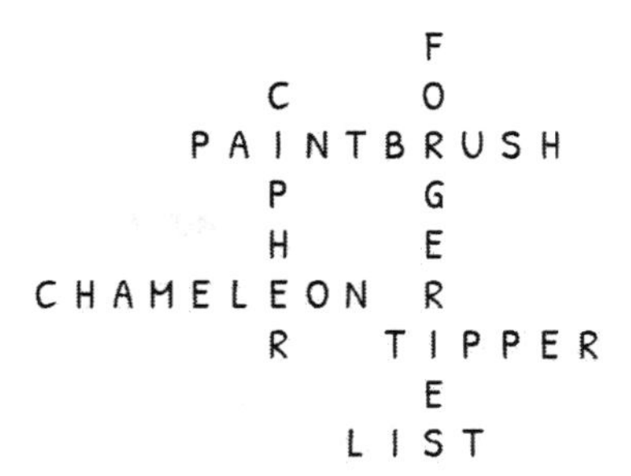

She wasn't sure why quite yet, but the little dog who was now curled up at the end of her bed kept coming to mind, and, of course, with the Arnaults possibly involved, it made her think of Rose's list of paintings and how they all had a hand in the scheme. Fen also wondered, as she wrote the words down, if someone had had a hand in something altogether less virtuous to do with all that artwork, and if that had led to Rose's death?

CHAPTER TWENTY-FIVE

Fen woke up with the napkin stuck between her cheek and the pillow. She peeled it away from her skin as she blinked her eyes open and then looked at the words again. There was definitely something ringing out at her about them... *Paintbrush, cipher, forgeries, chameleon, Tipper, list...* Why had those words stuck out to her in particular? She recited the words over again and then put the napkin to one side and slipped out of the blankets.

She had barely opened her bedroom door when she was met by a soft wet nose and a ball of fluffy energy and Fen leaned down and picked up Tipper.

'Good morning and goodbye Fen,' Simone called out from the hallway and Fen called back a goodbye as she carried Tipper to the kitchen, where she found some meat scraps for him for his breakfast.

'Looks like I'll have to sweet-talk the butcher this morning for you,' she said as she stroked the little dog between the ears as his muzzle was deep in his food bowl. Fen's own stomach rumbled and she added, 'And for me, too, I think.'

With thoughts of crispy bacon sandwiches and a proper roast leg of lamb milling around her head, she washed and dressed and then took Tipper out to the courtyard garden so he could uncross his legs. She was back up in the apartment and ready in good time for James's arrival. He knocked on the door at 8.30 a.m. sharp and was heralded by Tipper yapping.

'Calm down, fella,' James knelt down and played with the dog, winding it round in circles as it followed his hand.

'You're just winding him up, James,' Fen ticked him off as she led him through to the studio.

'You'd think he'd know me by now, wouldn't you?'

Fen laughed, not unkindly, but she teased him with the thought that perhaps Tipper knew exactly what he was doing, protecting the ladies of the house…

'I'll have you know that I left Simone chastely untouched and by this very front door by eleven o'clock last night.'

Fen chuckled again. 'I know! I heard you both not very chastely saying goodbye in the corridor!'

James blushed slightly and shrugged his shoulder and murmured something about the 'heat of the moment' and 'best intentions'.

'Anyway, you've already missed her, I'm afraid – she headed off at the crack of dawn to get to work.'

'Did Tipper alert you to that fact?' James crouched down and started playing with the miniature poodle again.

'No, Simone and I obviously pose no excitement whatsoever for the little beast.' Fen grinned indulgently at the dog, then sighed. 'And I'll have you know I was up and about in time to say goodbye to her. Sort of. Anyway, I suppose we better get this visit to Antoine over with. I have Monsieur Blanquer the solicitor arriving at eleven, so we better get a move on.'

The two of them took the bus to the north of the city, where the ancient Gothic cathedral of St Denis stood in what was now an area of small residential streets and industrial warehousing. Fen had studied the great cathedral church under Rose's supervision during her art lessons and knew all about the beautiful stained-glass windows that would apparently bring the congregation closer to the light of heaven.

It was a lovely thought, and no doubt the birthplace of what became the Gothic style of architecture, but St Denis held a darker secret too. The old barracks in the neighbourhood had been an internment camp during the war, for political prisoners and citizens of Allied countries caught in the crossfire of the occupation. Fen shivered a little as the bus dropped them close by to where thousands of innocent people had been sorted and labelled and sent on to perhaps even less desirable places.

The address of the warehouse was just around the corner and a few minutes later they stood in front of what looked like a large farm building, similar to the cinder-block winery they had both worked in in Burgundy last month. The blocks made up the first ten foot or so of external wall, and then corrugated metal took over. There were no windows, but there was a large grey door, which James pushed open.

Fen had expected to see a bustling workplace full of crates and stock, and she was more than a little surprised to find the cavernous space almost empty, save for a few packing cases stacked up in one corner and barrels of varying sizes along one wall. Electric lights hung from swooping wires, suspended from the cross-beams, and much like a simpler version of the Gare de Lyon, daylight came from vast skylights, each mottled with dirt. Clunking great chains on pulleys hung down from the highest girders and as Fen looked up at them, she could see dust motes hang in the air, gently floating in the stillness of the empty space.

Then, from nowhere, a crack of a pistol sent Fen to her knees.

Suddenly James had thrown his own body over hers, shielding her, turning the air blue with his language.

Crack!

Again, a report from a gun, echoing around the empty warehouse.

'Get down, Fen, stay down!' James all but pushed her to the dirty floor as he risked looking up. The sound of another shot ricocheting around the building had James swiftly ducking back down. This time it was followed by a metallic ping and the sound of breaking glass.

Fen raised her head. 'James,' she hissed. 'James!'

He looked at her and raised his eyebrows.

'I don't think they're shooting at us,' she whispered and he nodded, helping her up from the floor.

She was just about standing when a fourth shot echoed around them and James risked shouting out a warning to the shooter.

'They're a lousy shot if they are. Still… hallo there!' he shouted again and his voice was met with a shuffling and the sound of a bullet chamber being emptied.

'Who's there?' The man's voice echoed from the darkness at the back of the warehouse.

'Captain Lancaster—'

'And Fenella Churche!'

Their introductions were met with a belly laugh and gradually out from the murkiness of the far corner of the all-but-deserted warehouse a man's figure appeared.

'Thought I was taking potshots at you, eh?' Antoine Arnault laughed again, twirling the pistol around his forefinger as he walked.

'What *were* you doing?' Fen had just about brushed herself down and didn't feel the need for any more pleasantries. She did feel the need, however, to know why Antoine was walking towards them with a gun.

'Target practice,' he simply replied. When he was just a few feet away from them, he brandished the gun one last time and then tucked it into the back pocket of his overalls. He stuck out his hand for James to shake.

'In the dark?' James asked, taking the words out of Fen's mouth. He looked disturbed at Antoine's behaviour.

'Best place to practise.' Antoine smirked and eyed Fen up and down. 'Sorry if I shocked you. You've probably never heard a gun before, eh?'

Fen tried to disguise the shake in her hands by making a show of nonchalantly patting down her hair and adjusting her coat. And she'd heard guns before all right, just not like this.

'Unless it's pointed at a pheasant, no,' she replied quite tersely, as she crossed her arms, still trying to hide her shaking hands. She didn't like his overt style of machismo and was annoyed at herself for being a bit shaken up.

Luckily, Antoine laughed and ushered Fen and James towards an internal door that had a sign saying 'OFFICES' over it.

Fen had to remind herself that, as far as they knew, Antoine was still just the fun, if slightly buffoonish, man she'd met the other night, and, target practice with an old service revolver besides, it was only Henri that suspected him, or at least his brother, of being part of some sort of gang. Still, asking the right sort of questions to work out if he was or not wasn't going to be easy, especially with her heart beating like she'd just finished the Tour de France…

Antoine sat himself down behind an old wooden partner's desk and it reminded Fen of Henri Renaud's at the Louvre, just much, much smaller and far less imposingly ornate. 'Sit down, friends. Can I get you a drink? A coffee? Perhaps a little cognac?'

Fen could see James's eyebrow raising in interest, but quickly declined it herself – her hands had finally stopped shaking and she wasn't in the mood for early-morning drinking. Luckily, it seemed James wasn't either and he shook his head, too.

'How can I help you both?' Antoine asked, and James turned to face Fen. They had agreed, while on the bus on the way over, that Fen would do most of the talking and James's role would be to wrestle the conversation back to the jovial if Antoine started to get a bit tetchy. So Fen jumped in and started the ball rolling.

'Antoine, we're here with terribly bad news, I'm afraid…' Fen told him about Rose, and as she spoke she noted the colour drain from Antoine's face. He fidgeted as she went on and when she got to the part about finding Rose with the paintbrush piercing her neck, he jerked up from his chair, leaving it spinning on its central column and skidding across the floor on its castors.

'He couldn't have, he couldn't have…' he whispered to himself.

'Who couldn't have, Antoine? Do you know who might have done this to Madame Coillard?'

Antoine shot a glare at Fen, then softened his look as he received an equally ugly look from James. Antoine licked his lips as he worked out what to say.

'A burglar, you say?' Antoine asked and Fen wondered if he was stalling for time, or if he was purposefully avoiding answering her question.

'I'm only repeating what the gendarmes have said,' Fen told him. 'Personally, I think she was murdered for some other reason. Do you have an inkling who it might be?'

Antoine couldn't avoid answering the question a second time, so once back in his seat, he leaned forward and said, 'I don't know, I really don't know. But it sounds like something The Chameleon would have done in the war. Catching someone in their own home, unawares…' he mimicked stabbing someone and then leaned back, gently rocking on his chair.

'And I don't suppose you know who The Chameleon is, by any chance?' James asked, seeing that Fen was deep in thought.

'Lazard… lizard…' Fen tripped the words off the end of her tongue. Then she looked up at Antoine. 'Do you know Michel Lazard at all?'

'Of course, he's a colleague here in the warehouse. An art dealer of sorts. He had a certain niche, shall we say, in the art market. For the more, how would you put it, duplicated paintings.'

'He sells forgeries,' Fen said matter-of-factly, explaining it to James as much as answering Antoine.

'Ye…es.' Antoine hesitated. 'How did you know?'

'Rose told me.'

'Did she now?'

'And Henri Renaud knew about it too.'

'Ah, well, they say Monsieur Renaud has eyes and ears everywhere…'

'Can you introduce us to Lazard?' Fen asked outright, feeling emboldened by having James next to her.

'Sure, sure,' Antoine moved forward and shuffled some papers on his desk. 'I think he's away now down in the south, but I'll get a message to him.'

'Thank you, Antoine,' Fen said, wondering if perhaps he was being just a little too helpful. 'Henri Renaud also said that you and Rose had fallen out recently. About some sort of gang Gervais has got himself muddled up in.'

Antoine laughed. 'A gang! Gervais? Can you believe this?' He gestured towards Fen, looking at James.

James just shrugged one shoulder and the laughter left Antoine's face.

He continued, 'Look, if Henri Renaud has anything he wants to say to me or my brother, he should come here and say it to my face. I spend my life in this dump looking after his second-best paintings, and risked my life in the war to help him and Rose with their little scheme, not that I ever saw anything come my way because of it.' He rubbed his fingers together to indicate money changing hands.

'I should hope not,' Fen interjected. 'They weren't exactly making any money out of it either!'

'Ha, you say that, but…' He sat back again with his hands crossed over his chest.

'What do you mean?' Fen was genuinely puzzled.

Antoine merely drew his fingers across his lips, as if zippering. This made Fen shudder with frustration, but, luckily, James fulfilled his brief and took over the questioning.

'Antoine, my friend, we'll be out of your hair in two ticks. And hopefully see you at the Deux Magots tonight? A drink on me, at least.'

Antoine nodded and sat forward slightly.

Fen took the opportunity to question him again. 'Just one more question before we head back to the city. Were you and Gervais at the races a couple of days ago? Out in the Bois de Boulogne? I heard there was a fine filly who's worth keeping an eye on?'

Antoine looked at James and then laughed at Fen. 'Miss Churche, I'm glad that you were not in the Resistance with us. You are a terrible liar. If you want to know where I was at the time of Rose Coillard's murder, just ask me outright.'

'Well?'

'I was here. At work.' He got up from the chair, leaving it to spin again, and crossed the floor towards the office door, which he opened and called out into the warehouse, 'Guillaume! Guillaume!'

'What?' a disembodied voice called back.

'You know two days ago we had that shipment in, and you dropped that crate on my foot? What did I call you?'

There was a pause and then Guillaume, whoever he was, shouted back, 'You called me a stupid ass only fit for donkey's work, sir.'

'Quite right!' Antoine came back into the office, looking pleased with himself. 'There you go, instant corroboration that I was here that afternoon, being sentimental and caring to my underlings.'

Fen frowned. 'It's not exactly an alibi, is it. I mean, I didn't tell you what time in the afternoon she was killed and poor Guillaume out there might have been confused about dates or—'

'If you don't trust Guillaume, then you'll trust the manifests. I can show you the time-stamped delivery papers signed by me.' He went towards the filing cabinet. 'What time do you think she was killed?'

'Around two o'clock.'

Antoine pulled open a drawer and pulled out some carbon paper documents. 'Here,' he pointed at the bottom of the sheet. 'My signature and the time of delivery, 1.45 p.m.'

'Definitely not enough time to get from St Denis to St Germain, thank you, Antoine.' James pushed himself up from this chair. 'Come on, Fen, let's leave this poor man in peace. Drinks later, yes. On me?'

Antoine snorted but nodded and bid them goodbye.

'He's not wrong, you know…' James said to Fen with a wry smile as they closed the metal door of the warehouse behind them. 'You would have made a terrible spy.'

CHAPTER TWENTY-SIX

Fen and James spoke quietly to each other as they sat on the bus, the government posters stating that 'Careless Talk Costs Lives' still drilled into them. Who knew who was listening in, and just like the war, lives were possibly at stake here too.

'Do you think this Lazard chap is The Chameleon?' Fen whispered to James, following it up before he could answer with another theory. 'And do you think he might have killed Rose if she refused to paint more forgeries for him to sell?'

'Perhaps. You're leaping to a lot of conclusions though.'

'He and Rose were arguing just before she died. So, if he is in the south, as Antoine suggested, he almost certainly wasn't at the time of the murder.'

The pair of them mused over their theories as the bus pulled in alongside the stop on the Rue de Seine and they clattered down the stairs just in time, before the impatient driver took off again.

'Seems we need to take our lives in our hands almost every day here!' Fen gasped as she grabbed her hat from blowing off in a gust of wind.

'Good thing you have the solicitor coming next then,' James chuckled at her, sticking his hands in the deep pockets of his overcoat. 'You can make your own will.'

Fen and James had barely had time to get back into the apartment, greet a waggly tailed Tipper and put some hot water on to boil for a decent cup of tea, when the flat reedy sound of the front doorbell buzzed. Tipper was the first to dash to the door, yapping away, while Fen was quick on his heels, scooping him up and shushing him as she opened the door.

Monsieur Blanquer was a short, fat man with a black goatee beard and sharp blue eyes. Despite his portly nature, he was dressed smartly in a well-tailored three-piece suit, complete with pocket watch and the shiniest of black leather shoes. The morning light in the atrium bounced off his bald head, which was the first thing Fen saw as she greeted him. He passed his hat between his hands and reached one out to her. 'You must be Mademoiselle Churche?'

'And you Monsieur Blanquer, please come in.'

Tea was poured and pleasantries and condolences made. Monsieur Blanquer had indeed brought Rose's will with him and proceeded to read it out for Fen and James, in lieu of any of the actual beneficiaries being there.

'She left a strange sort of c...codicil,' he stammered, being a man who, although professional in the utmost, obviously found it hard to form the harder consonants. 'She insisted that whomsoever be in her apartment c...could act as an exec...utor.'

'How strange,' Fen shrugged but didn't argue as she was keen to hear who or what would benefit from her friend's death. She wouldn't have been surprised if a local dogs' home was about to become considerably better off.

Monsieur Blanquer opened up the folio-sized document and cleared his throat before starting.

'*My apartment on the Rue des Beaux-Arts I leave in its entirety to my g...good friend Henri Renaud, and request that he uses it either for himself or uses any monies forthc...coming from its sale or rental to further our war work vis-à-vis the restoration of artworks to the Jewish c...community. My paintings I donate to the École des Beaux-Arts for the further educ...cation of the students therein, and any other chattels I request to be divided among my friends, of whom I supply a list.*'

Blanquer flourished another piece of paper as he spoke, indicating that it was indeed the list of said friends.

'Thank you, monsieur,' Fen brought the will reading to a close and offered him another cup of tea. 'I think we should make Henri aware of the situation and talk to him about Simone, and me, moving out of this apartment. Monsieur, was there anything else that perhaps Madame Coillard had deposited with you? Another list of some sort, or a code or cipher at all?'

Blanquer shook his head, but then seemed to suddenly remember something and raised his finger. 'There was this… that is all.' He slipped his fingertips into the small pocket in his waistcoat and rummaged around behind his watch chain to extract a small key. 'The spare for the mailbox d…downstairs, I believe,' he said, handing it to her as he began collecting up all of his papers. 'You know where to find me, mademoiselle. If any bills or t…tabs need paying from the estate, then please send them through to me and I'll settle them. I will be c…contacting Monsieur Renaud, but if you wish to give him the happy news of his inheritance, I should not stand in your way.'

Fen took the key and thanked the solicitor, adding, 'I'm not sure it's particularly happy news. We'd all rather have Rose alive.'

'Indeed, indeed. But the fact remains, Monsieur Renaud is now the proud owner of this rather charming apartment.'

Which might well give him the perfect motive for murder, thought Fen as she showed Blanquer to the door. She made a mental note to check his alibi about buying those watercolours somehow.

While James washed the teacups, Fen trotted down the wide stone staircase to the communal hallway at the bottom. The key that Monsieur Blanquer had just given her fit like a dream as she turned it and used it to pull open the small metal door of the mailbox. A few flyers for theatrical nights and restaurant openings covered what looked like the real post: two brown, official envelopes and one handwritten one. Fen scooped them all up, closed and locked the mailbox and climbed back up to the fifth floor.

Once inside the apartment, she settled down in the saggy old armchair and let Tipper scramble up onto her lap and lick her nose a couple of times before he curled up in her lap.

Fen looked at the envelopes. 'I'm sorry, Rose,' she apologised into the ether, 'I know it's terribly rude to open someone else's post, but needs must.'

'If you're going to talk to yourself, at least do it with a cup of tea,' James said as he brought a fresh brew over to where Fen was sitting.

She smiled a thanks up to him as he moved over to the other armchair and sat himself down with the newspaper.

Fen went back to the post. The first was a bill from Rose's grocer – *seventy francs!* Fen was grateful that Blanquer had offered to settle any accounts from the estate. The second brown envelope was even more heart-stopping in its contents – four hundred francs to the art supplier.

'*Ooh la la*,' Fen sighed, thinking of how little she had left in her purse at the moment and placed the bill along with the one for the grocer.

The third envelope looked less official, it was on blue paper for a start and was altogether grubbier, as if it had been stepped on a few times or dropped in the coal scuttle. Fen opened it carefully and pulled out the handwritten note within.

As she read it, the hairs on the back of her neck rose and a shiver went down her spine. She raised the hand that had been idly petting Tipper to her mouth in shock and read it through again, just to make sure.

Madame Coillard,

Thought you could get away with it? I know what you're doing. Stealing from Jews and helping the Nazi scum. You'll pay for this, you mark my words. I know you're no better than a dirty thief. I'm watching you. Pay what I asked or I tell HR. NOW!

Fen couldn't believe what she had just read. She dropped the letter suddenly, her pragmatic mind suggesting that her fingerprints might contaminate this evidence, while her more emotional side wanted nothing from that letter to contaminate *her*. Tipper, roused by her sudden movement, jumped off her lap and then stood, looking at her, as if demanding an explanation for her behaviour.

'What is it, Fen?' James asked, lowering the newspaper from in front of his face.

Fen was speechless, but James followed her eyeline down to where the letter had floated gently to the floor. Then she picked up the envelope again, reminding herself that preserving the sender's fingerprints would be no use as countless postal workers must have touched it. It was only as she was staring at it, reading the handwritten address, that she realised that there was no stamp, no postmark. It had been hand-delivered.

CHAPTER TWENTY-SEVEN

'Whoever this is from,' Fen could feel herself shivering slightly as she held the letter between her forefinger and thumb, subconsciously distancing herself from its filthy contents, 'is more than likely our prime suspect now.'

James nodded. 'Lazard?'

Fen thought back to the words. *I know you're no better than a dirty thief*... 'If it was Lazard, wouldn't he blackmail her on her forging rather than collaborating or stealing?'

'True, it doesn't make a lot of sense. But then...'

'What?'

'Well, it doesn't make sense to us as we – you – very much believe that Rose was this wonderful person, an angel of the arts.'

'She was.' Fen put the letter down on the coffee table and braced herself for a mini war of words with her friend. 'And Henri said so too.'

'HR...' James pointed towards the letter, while Fen frowned at him. 'All I'm saying is that the blackmailer seems to think there's something even Henri didn't know about his dear friend.'

'No, no...' Fen shook her head. 'It just doesn't make sense. Forging, fine, I can get my head around that, though I still don't think she miss-sold any paintings on purpose. But it's a grey area morally and I think Rose was in need of a few extra francs. But stealing? No. And she definitely wouldn't collaborate. You saw her passion when she talked about her cipher and her list. She was desperate to help the Jewish families get what's rightfully theirs back. No, I'm sorry, James, but, whoever this blackmailer is, he or she has it quite wrong.'

Before James could play devil's advocate one more time, the doorbell buzzed and Tipper, who had curled up again in the warm armchair seat while Fen and James had been standing looking at the letter, jumped into action and yapped his way to the door.

Fen pulled her cardigan tight around her and left James mulling over the hateful letter.

'Oh, hello, Joseph.' She kissed him on both cheeks.

'Good day, Fenella.' Joseph Bernheim paused before he entered the apartment. 'You look upset, are you quite well?'

Fen wasn't sure if she was ready to share the secrets of the blackmailer's letter with anyone else yet, not even Joseph, so quickly thought on her feet and replied, 'Quite well, thank you. It's all just becoming more real, I suppose, the sense that Rose is gone forever.' It may have started out as a cover for her current upset, but Fen had to admit that as she said the words she felt them very keenly too.

'Gone, but not forgotten.' Joseph took a moment, then, as was his habit, started passing the brim of his hat through his fingertips as he spoke. 'When we realised that my parents hadn't made it, it didn't seem real at first. How could two such lively, musical and artistic people be silenced? But the days wear on and the grief thickens until you feel like you will drown in it. Then, very slowly, if you are lucky, it lifts, just very slightly, and you can catch a breath. You will find that happens too, I hope.'

'Thank you, Joseph.' Fen stood back and let him into the apartment. 'I don't suppose you've ever heard what became of them, yours and Magda's parents, I mean?'

'Just this morning…' Joseph shook his head, and reached his hand up to squeeze the bridge of his nose.

'Oh, I'm sorry, Joseph, I shouldn't have asked.'

'No, no. We mustn't skirt around this as if we're in polite society and what happened to them was merely unfortunate.' He took a deep breath and regained his composure. At that moment, Fen thought that she had never seen a braver man stand in front of her. He continued, 'Just this morning, we had confirmation from the Red Cross of what we believed to be the case anyway; that my parents are dead. Magda's we still have hope for, if there could be anything as beautiful as hope ever whispered in the same breath as those death camps.'

'I'm so sorry, Joseph,' Fen replied, touching him briefly on the arm.

'Thank you, Fenella. But now is not the time to dwell on my grief. No, now's the time to continue Rose's work, don't you think? I received your message. Has the solicitor been?'

Fen nodded and showed Joseph through to the studio room. She then heaved Rose's old carpetbag onto the coffee table along with the boxes of paperwork she'd found in the bedroom, glad that James had had the foresight to remove the blackmailer's letter before Joseph had sat down on the chaise longue.

'Here we go,' Fen sighed. 'Just about everything, I suppose, unless she has any loose floorboards around here.'

Joseph looked up at her as if she wasn't joking, and she bit her lip and shrugged.

'Well, let's start here anyway,' he said. 'And I hope you don't think me callous or opportunistic,' he said as he started pulling out some of Rose's personal belongings, including a spare paintbrush, some throat lozenges and a fabric tape measure, 'but it's because I feel that she was on the brink of finding something out about my family's artworks that I want to keep going. Not let the trail go cold, as they say in the American films.'

'We understand, of course, Joseph,' Fen replied as she picked up the tape measure and wrapped it around her fingers, threading it through each digit as she watched Joseph now meticulously lay out the paperwork that had been languishing at the bottom of the bag, some of it stuck to a half-sucked boiled sweet.

'Here we go,' he said as he placed the bag back on the floor and started to read through the papers.

'I know she had the original list back from Henri,' Fen felt rather differently saying Henri's name now, since he was mentioned, if only by his initials, in that ghastly letter. 'Although I don't know how far she'd got in decoding it.'

'Let's see, shall we…'

The three of them looked over the papers and slowly it became apparent that Rose had started to transcribe the original list, although none of the coding had had the benefit of her cipher – it was still unintelligible.

Fen noticed the colour pale from Joseph's face, though, as he ran his finger down the list of the artworks.

'What is it, Joseph?'

'These descriptions… Rose has stopped transcribing her list here, at these paintings.'

'Why was she transcribing the list at all?' James asked, 'If Henri had given her the original?'

'I suppose just because there was only one copy and perhaps Rose wanted a more work-a-day one for her own scribbles,' Fen answered and then turned back to Joseph. 'What have you noticed?'

'She's stopped copying the list at my family's artworks.' Joseph sat back and rubbed his hand across his brow. 'Look, this Degas that they describe, the ballerina at the barre, that was… is one of ours. And the Cezanne of the bowl of fruit against a grey background, that was always in mother's salon.'

'Perhaps she was interrupted?' James ventured.

'Or maybe these handwritten scribbles in the original have something to do with it.' Fen pointed at a neatly written addition in the margin of the original list. 'Anyone good with their German?'

'Let me see.' James took the list and held it close to his face. 'This is a note to say that the painting was to be sent to auction, and the Cezanne too. Rather than go back to Germany, I assume.'

'Henri said that was what they did to the "degenerate" art that was worth money but didn't align to the Nazi ideals. But the Degas and Cezanne, they aren't that sort of painting.'

'Was there any sign of the cipher in the bag?' James asked, while Joseph stared at the inscriptions alongside his family's paintings. 'With Joseph knowing that those paintings are his, there should be an encrypted BERNHEIM somewhere near them. It could be the key to cracking the cipher, if we had any idea what sort of cipher it is.'

Fen pulled out a length of string, some receipts from the grocer and a few more slightly grubby boiled sweets from the bag, but then shrugged. 'Nothing I can see that looks like a secret code book.'

'Hmm. Joseph, are you sure those are your paintings listed?' James asked.

'Of course I am!'

'We believe you of course,' Fen shot James a look. 'But can we prove they're yours without the code? I mean, if Rose was right and the Americans are starting to find whole caverns of the stolen artworks, then perhaps we could show this list to the authorities and use Joseph's own testament that these are his?'

The three of them thought about this possibility for a moment. It was Joseph that broke the silence.

'We have no proof though. The code is the proof. My family's apartment was stripped, we escaped with what we could carry and, in hindsight, perhaps the receipts from the galleries would have been more useful than my pyjamas, but there you go.' He seemed to physically deflate, but carried on, albeit in a much quieter voice. 'Now everything is lost and we have no way of proving those paintings ever hung on my parents' walls.'

'I'm so sorry, Joseph. We will find that cipher and we will crack this code,' Fen reassured him, and herself. She couldn't have him face the horrible truth about his parents' deaths *and* think that all hope of finding their stolen artwork was lost on the same day. 'If those two paintings went to auction, there's a good chance they're still here in France. It might be easier to get them back.'

'I don't think any of this will be easy.' Joseph wiped his brow again. 'But I do appreciate your help.'

CHAPTER TWENTY-EIGHT

A quick forage through Rose's kitchen cupboards later and James and Fen had found something to stave off the stomach rumbles. It was gone 3 p.m. by the time they had finished, and Fen decided that she should go and tell Henri the news of his inheritance. James thought it an opportune moment to head back to his hotel, so it was Fen alone who had donned her hat and coat again and headed out into the streets of Paris.

By now Fen knew her way through the labyrinthine corridors of the Louvre palace rather well. She was still astounded, though, that the little door at the side of the vast building was never kept locked. Using people like Gervais to cart their treasures around the châteaux of France to save them from the Nazis was one thing; just letting someone walk out with them via the back door was quite another.

Fen fantasised for just one moment about nonchalantly walking out of the museum with her own stolen masterpiece… a Vermeer perhaps or a small Byzantine icon? Either would look super above the mantelpiece in Father's study. The notion made her smile, but then she frowned. How easy it was to imagine these things… how easy would it actually be to follow through on an idea like this? And take your opportunity when it was presented?

Fen still felt uncomfortable doubting the integrity of her friend, but she had to get to the bottom of who killed her and she felt that Henri, despite needing to know about his inheritance, might be able to shed some light on her questions. But how much should she reveal to Rose's partner? The worry being that if Rose was being blackmailed, was Henri being targeted too?

Sadly for Fen, her trip to the Louvre was a waste of time. The secretary who sat in the office next to Henri's informed her that it wasn't his day to be in the gallery and that he was no doubt at his own premises. The secretary handed Fen a note of the address and wished her good day.

Luckily, the address of Henri's gallery, the eponymous Galerie Renaud, was in the arcades of the Jardin du Palais Royale, only a few hundred yards from the Louvre.

Fen walked the route confidently and navigated her way through the colonnaded gardens, remembering her history lesson on how the arcades had been some of the first in Paris to have glazed windows, to help the emerging middle class of the eighteenth century to window-shop. The area had always been associated with luxury goods, and a high-end private art gallery like Henri's fitted right in with the feel of the area.

Fen, like many Parisiennes before her, couldn't help but be attracted by the expensive wares in the windows and wondered how these shops had kept their doors open during the occupation. James's words about his new friends and some of their black-market dealings echoed in her mind. Before she could ponder too long on the provenance of a rather lovely pair of red leather gloves, Fen saw the shopfront she was looking for. Like the others in the arcade, the Galerie Renaud had one large deep-silled window with a door next to it. In the window, there were various watercolours, framed in thin gold frames and hung, suspended in the air, by wires.

Fen took a deep breath and pushed the door open.

'Ah Fenella,' Henri greeted her from behind a desk at the back of the gallery. 'I must say it is a pleasure to see you. You remind me of my dear friend, even if you have decided not to carry on the tradition of those flamboyant turbans of hers.'

Fen smiled, Henri's stab at humour had hit the spot and relaxed her somewhat. 'I don't think they'd look so chic on Midhurst's High Street. We're more tweed skirt than silk turban there, I'm afraid.'

'True, true. Come, sit yourself down. What can I do for you?' Henri gestured to a chair in front of his desk. Unlike the ones in his Louvre office, these were modern and far less fussy. In fact, the whole gallery, even though it was situated in an old building, had a real air of modernity to it. The walls were painted white and the paintings were mostly very contemporary: works by the Fauves, Cubists and abstract artists hung from thin chains and made striking statements against the stark white of the walls.

Fen glanced around and then addressed the matter at hand. 'Monsieur Renaud, Henri… I come bearing news in a way. About Rose, actually. You see, I hope you don't mind, but I called her solicitor, a Monsieur Blanquer, who was able to come over to the apartment pretty smartish and let me know the contents of her will.'

'Ah…' Henri pressed his hands together and rested his chin against his fingers for a moment. Then he said something that surprised Fen a little. 'The apartment that is now mine, I take it.'

'Oh. You knew?'

'As I said before, Rose and I had no secrets, well, until recently it seems. When you lived like we did, on a knife-edge, you have to absolutely trust the other person. We decided, during the war and at the height of our work, that we would bequeath each other our estates. It was the ultimate sign of faith in each other. Of course, it helped that neither Rose or I have any immediate family.'

'I see. Well, there you go. I'm sure Monsieur Blanquer will be in touch officially, but, Henri, may I ask you a small favour?'

'Of course, dear girl, what is it?'

'It's not so much for me, I can be on the next train out of here, if I must, although I do want to find out what happened to Rose… but me aside, would you allow Simone to carry on living in the apartment? I know she hasn't much in the way of family left and, from what she's said, they never had more than a bean to rub together anyway...'

Henri pressed his chin to his hands again, so that he could have been mistaken for praying as much as thinking. He barely took a moment's contemplation, however, before replying, 'I see, I see. Yes, she must stay on. A young woman like that cannot be ousted onto the streets. I shall speak to Blanquer and arrange an agreement with her, some sort of rental contract. Dear Rose, she was always so kind and I feel like I should do my best to honour her – in all aspects of her work.'

Fen smiled in relief. She would be able to tell Simone the good news this evening at least now. And from what Henri was saying about Rose, how kind and generous she was, well, it sounded like she really couldn't have been implicated in what the blackmailer had written about. Fen made a hasty decision to talk to Henri about it. 'One more thing, while I'm here. Henri, I have to admit something to you.'

'Taking that hideous carpetbag of hers home with you after all, dear girl?'

Fen smiled again, and carried on, reassured that Henri's good humour would help them both to come to terms with what she was about to say. So she told him about finding the letter from the blackmailer as he sat there, his hands pressed against his chin again in his prayer-like pose. He listened carefully as Fen described not only the contents of the letter but the envelope in which it had arrived.

'So, you see,' Fen finished explaining, 'I just couldn't equate it in my head with the woman I knew. And I wondered, assuming you're the "HR" the author is referring to, if you knew anything about it?'

'I'm afraid I did, yes. But I can tell you absolutely that it is unfounded lies. As I said, Rose and I had no secrets, but I must own up to keeping this little one from you last time we spoke.'

Fen frowned a little in consternation, but didn't interrupt Henri.

'You see, she came to me when she received a similar letter a week or so ago. I advised her we should both do the same: ignore them.'

'You received one too?'

'Yes, about a week ago and again today in fact.' He sat upright and then pulled one of the desk drawers open. From it, he retrieved an envelope that looked identical to the one that Fen had found in Rose's mailbox. It was slightly grubby and had a handwritten address on the front. Most notably, it had also been hand-delivered as there was no stamp or franking mark on it at all. Henri carried on talking, 'It's nothing but a work of fiction from a racketeer who thinks he can extract a fast buck from us.'

'I get the impression you have an idea who it's from?'

'I'm afraid I have my suspicions.' He paused. 'As I said last time we spoke, Rose had had dealings with the Arnault brothers. The oily, grubby marks on the envelope confirms it in my mind. Are these not the greasy fingerprints of a mechanic? I would wager my life that the author of these letters is Gervais "The Wrench" Arnault.'

Fen frowned in thought. She had so wanted the blackmailer to be The Chameleon, even if that hadn't really made a lot of sense. But there was no doubting Henri's logic and deduction – the letter he had shown her, and the one she had back in the apartment, bore signs of grease and oil. And she really didn't think Gervais 'The Wrench' Arnault was also the master of disguise and double agenting that The Chameleon purported to be.

'Thank you, Henri, and again for letting Simone and me stay on. I'll let her know the news.' Fen got up to leave.

'Farewell and take care, dear girl. Perhaps as a thank you to me you can both start to clear away Rose's belongings? Send them to the Red Cross or whatever, I don't think I'll find a use for her dresses and beads. Or indeed that damned list any more.'

'The list? You really want us to just throw it away?' Fen asked, her obvious confusion showing.

'My dear, what use is it now? I don't have the cipher for Rose's code. Without it, the list is useless. Our Jewish friends might be able to spot their paintings from the descriptions, but without the cipher there is no proof. Antoine and Gervais, under Rose's instruction, labelled each painting with that code of hers. What is the point of the list if we can't decode it?'

'So you're just going to give up? After all you risked?'

'I don't see what else I can do?'

Fen thought for a moment. 'Do you know how I can contact Michel Lazard?'

'Rose's art dealer? Yes, why?'

'I just think that he's a missing cog in the wheel. Someone I'd like to speak to, see if he knew if Rose had any enemies.' *Or if he was one of them…* Fen thought to herself.

'I'm not sure what use Lazard would be to you, to be honest, Fenella. He is good for two things in this world, and two things only. One is selling almost any picture you give him, and the second is that he will try to charm the stockings off almost every woman he encounters, with varied results.'

'I thought you barely knew him?'

'I really don't. But the man has a certain reputation… Look, why don't you join me at a drinks reception tonight, at the Louvre. It's a sort of benefit for the wealthy patrons to see that the art they fundraise for so generously has been restored to the museum. You won't look out of place in one of Rose's fabulous outfits. Do come, it will be something to cheer you up.'

'If by fabulous you mean outrageous,' Fen bit her lower lip. Rose had been such a massive personality she'd been able to pull off velvet turbans and floor-length patchwork coats with aplomb. Fen wasn't sure if there would really be anything appropriate for her to wear and she wasn't even sure if she was in the mood for a grand gala. Henri could obviously read these thoughts as they played across her face.

'I'm sure you'll find something as chic as you, my dear,' he said, and then added, 'and it really would be such a shame for you to miss tonight. Rose was invited, you know, and I think if she could look down on us now and perhaps flick some ash from her cigarette at us…' he paused, gauging Fen's smile perhaps. 'Well, I think she would tell you to come.'

Fen looked up at the ceiling and considered the idea. The thought of a party was indeed rather exciting and if nothing else it would give her another chance to double-check with Henri that he really did intend for her and Simone to destroy the list Rose had made. She sighed and then smiled at Henri.

'Until tonight then.'

'Wonderful, wonderful,' Henri clapped her on the back as Fen took her leave and left the gallery. She decided that it would do her pocketbook no good at all to linger in the arcade, plus she was in no mood now for shopping, real or of the window variety. Instead she was still running the question of Henri and the list over and over in her mind. Was he really going to give up so easily on his and Rose's mission? *If the cipher is so important*, she thought, *I really must try to find it.*

Fen was just leaving the colonnade when a flash of colour caught her eye on the other side of the courtyard. She paused and looked, waiting for the chance to see it again. It might have been the speed at which the person was moving, or perhaps Fen was just on edge after the events of the last few days, but something told her to wait and see what it was that had captured her attention.

She moved slowly along the colonnade until she was hidden behind one of the columns, and was almost instantly rewarded by seeing the colourful fabric again. This time she could make out what it was: a boating blazer. Paired with summery cream slacks, as if the wearer was dressed for a regatta on a riviera rather than an autumnal day in the city. Fen had seen that jacket before, its old-school stripes giving the game away immediately. This man, darting between the columns the other side of the courtyard was the same man she'd seen Rose arguing with just before she was killed.

'Lazard…' Fen whispered to herself, holding onto the rough stone of the column, letting its width conceal her in case he turned around. Watching from her spot, she tracked him as he half ran, half walked along the street until he slipped inside one of the galleries and out of sight.

Fen emerged from behind her hiding place and nodded a confirmation to herself. The gallery she had just seen him enter was none other than Galerie Renaud.

CHAPTER TWENTY-NINE

'Well, that is as it should be,' Simone replied to Fen as she helped herself to a glass of wine from a bottle in the kitchen. She had just come in from the atelier and Fen had told her about Henri Renaud's kind offer to let her stay on. 'Henri Renaud doesn't need this apartment anyway.'

'Well, no, I don't suppose he does, not straight away at any rate, but it's very generous of him. We could have been out on the street tomorrow if he wanted.'

'Oh, I don't think it would ever have come to that.'

Well no, not with your eye on James's two houses, Fen thought, then chastised herself for thinking so cruelly about Simone's intentions.

'And I am really quite at home here,' Simone leaned against the kitchen countertop. 'Despite the horrors of what happened, of course,' she added, although it sounded rather like an afterthought.

Fen just nodded and took a glass of wine into the studio. She had an hour or two to spare before she needed to be back at the Louvre. She'd laid out three potential outfits that she'd found in Rose's wardrobe, her own being completely deficient in anything fancy enough. Fen had felt terrible going through Rose's clothes, but Henri had given her permission to, nay, even asked if she could start clearing out the clothing, and she thought Rose would have given her blessing, too. Now she just hoped that Simone wouldn't be too preoccupied getting her own outfit perfected for her evening in with James and would be able to help her decide what to wear and add a few stitches here and there if need be.

*

'I just love this silk,' Simone exclaimed as she unwound one of the orange silk turbans. 'I'm sure with a stitch here and there we can turn this into a super off-the-shoulder top to go with one of those flouncy skirts.'

'You might have to sew me into it,' Fen glanced down at her watch, 'I'm not sure we have time to do a proper fitting.'

'Don't you worry! I have more skill than you'd think at working up a costume like this. Let's just say I made a lot of my own clothes during the war out of a lot less than this, and each one the perfect disguise!'

'Disguise?'

Simone laughed. 'Disguise, costume, uniform… whatever the Resistance needed from me, I could make for them and you know how I feel about fashion? It just changes you from one person into quite the other,' she clicked her fingers. 'See, turn around… *Ooh la la*, you are now a patroness of the arts in your silk blouse and chinoiserie skirt. *Bellissimo*!'

Fen had to laugh too, Simone's own joy at her work was so infectious.

'Can I see in a mirror? Do you have one in your room?' Fen made towards Simone's bedroom door when the younger woman clasped her arm.

'I think Rose has the best long glass. Let's go to her room.'

Fen followed her in and stood in front of the mirror. She barely recognised herself. Without her land girl overalls or sensible woollen skirts and blouses, she was, as Simone said, *quite a different person*. Simone had taken in one of Rose's skirts, this one in a pattern that resembled the wallpapers of smart country houses decorated in the chinoiserie style. A burnt orange colour in the skirt was picked up by the silk of the top that Simone had styled by wrapping the turban fabric around Fen's waist and layering it up until it crisscrossed over her chest and then wrapped around the very top of her arms to form a piece that was perfect for an evening reception.

'I love it! Thank you, Simone.'

'My pleasure. Now you have to be careful not to unravel until you get home.' Simone laughed again and left Fen staring at herself in the mirror.

Unravelling before she left the apartment might be the first challenge, but still, the overall effect of the outfit was fabulous, just as Henri had suggested, and she felt, for first time in ages, like the belle of the ball.

Belle she might be, but she still had half an hour to spare before she had to leave. Fen knew James would be over soon to spend some quiet time with Simone, and she would have to update him on what Henri had said, and more importantly about whom she had seen going into his gallery. But there were some other people she wanted to update too, and Fen sat herself down, carefully in order not to break a stitch, in one of the armchairs, to write a letter to Mrs B, Dilys and her dear friend Kitty.

Rue des Beaux-Arts, Paris
October 1945

Dear Mrs B, Kitty and Dilys,

It's hard to put pen to paper when the news you have to share is rather sad, and not only that but utterly horrifying. Since I last wrote, events have taken a terrible turn and my dear friend Rose has been murdered. James and I found her body here in this apartment, and although the police are ruling it as a bungled robbery (as some jewellery and artwork have gone missing), I fear there might be a more sinister force at work.

She was killed with one of her own paintbrushes, dastardly though that thought is, but it strikes me that it was a violent and desperate act, and there would have been many other ways for a mere burglar to have incapacitated her if they so wished. Also, this apartment is on the fifth floor and although Rose was living comfortably, there are many more wealthy people in the building (including a Russian countess dripping in diamonds apparently!).

And, the piece of evidence that really makes me think this isn't a burglary gone awry is that I have recently discovered that Rose was being blackmailed, I think misguidedly, as thankfully her good friend, and heir, Henri agrees she was an absolute angel. So, me being me, I've decided that I'll have to work out who did it!

Sorry for my rambling, and Kitty, I would love to send you another clue to work on – did you get the last one? I was watching paint dry – but I don't think I'm in the right frame of mind to think one up now. I will approach this mystery like a crossword instead… and in order to find out who killed Rose (let's call her my one across), I'll have to find the answer to my three down… simply put, who blackmailed her!

Very best, etc., etc.,
Fen xx

Fen put the pen down and rested her eyes for a bit. Whether it was the effect of a little too much wine or whether she was just exhausted from the last few days' goings-on, she felt like she could hit the hay and sleep for a week, rather than go out and have to be polite and the veritable life and soul.

She looked over to where Tipper was curled up on the chaise longue. 'You've got the right idea, lad,' she said quietly, not wanting to wake him up.

She carefully slid the large tome of Art History that she'd been using as a 'desk' down the side of the armchair and flicked the letter onto the coffee table so the ink wouldn't run. As she pushed herself up from the armchair, her hand came in to contact with something that had slipped down between the cushions. She fished around and caught it, and pulled it up from where it had been hiding.

'Oh, Rose…' Her voice, or maybe the sound of his mistress's name, woke Tipper up and he looked alertly at the long pearl necklace that Fen had pulled out. 'What is this doing here?' She held the string of pearls up and dangled them, letting them catch the warm, golden light of the electric light bulbs. 'She must have lost them,' Fen told Tipper, who was now more interested in chewing his own tail. She felt tears approaching at the sight of this familiar piece of Rose. 'I wonder if…' she said briskly, trying to pull herself together.

She brought the necklace up to her mouth and rubbed one or two of the beads against her teeth. Their grainy texture told her all she needed to know, but when she let them spool into her hand and clasped it shut over the pearls, they warmed to her touch almost instantly – she was sure then, they were real pearls all right. Poor Rose, Fen would have loved to have surprised *her* with this treasure, but now there was no one to return them to.

'They say you're never cold with a pearl necklace on,' Simone said as she walked into the room. 'Where did you find them?'

'Just here,' Fen pointed to the chair, 'I suppose Rose must have lost them, else the thief would have taken them from her jewellery box.'

'What a thing to miss…' Simone stared at them. 'You should put them on, they'd set off that outfit beautifully.'

'Oh no, I mustn't. I mean, they belong to Henri now.'

'Well, you can ask his permission when you see him later.' Simone shrugged and then responded to the buzz of the doorbell, leaving Fen to save the silk of her skirt from an overenthusiastic Tipper, who was running round in circles by her feet before dashing off to greet James too.

'You look smashing Fen,' James stood back and admired his friend as he came into the studio. 'Arthur would—' he stopped when Fen held up her hand.

'Not tonight, James, I'm just about holding it together, stitch by stitch almost literally. I don't think I can cope with thinking about… well, anyway, thank you,' she said, remembering her manners. She took a deep breath. 'Tonight should be interesting. I'll try to get some more information out of Henri at the very least.'

'More information?' James moved over to where Rose had always kept brandy in some decanters and poured himself a glass. 'What's happening tonight then?'

'Henri has invited me to a reception at the Louvre. A fundraising do to lure in some more wealthy patrons, or thank them for their donations or some such. The thing is, I had a rather interesting chat with him earlier, followed by an even more interesting stroke of luck.'

James put down the decanter and empty glass. 'Right, well you can tell me all about it on the way to the Louvre.'

'But you're meant to be having dinner here with Simone?'

'And let you walk all by yourself to the museum? Simone can keep the kippers warm,' he winked at her and picked up his coat. He helped Fen into one of Rose's less voluminous velvet housecoats and then called out to Simone, who had the grace to only look a little peeved. She air-kissed them both goodbye and moments later Fen and James were walking side by side down the Rue de Seine to the Louvre.

'So, you see, Henri had received a blackmail letter, too,' Fen said, as they walked between the pools of light cast by the street lamps, the ground glistening after a brief rain shower that afternoon.

'Crikey. Same wording.'

'He didn't show me, but it sounded like it. He said they'd both received one last week and Rose had come to him with hers, all in a pother about it. He'd reassured her that it must just be some charlatan trying his luck, but he had his suspicions.'

'Oh yes?'

'Gervais "The Wrench" Arnault.'

James was quiet for a moment, then said, 'Henri certainly has it in for the Arnault brothers. First he sends us off to talk to Antoine and now Gervais is heading for the noose.'

'Perhaps for good reason,' Fen said thoughtfully. 'Both the letter we found and the one Henri received were covered in grease and oil. Straight from a mechanic's garage perhaps?'

James stayed pensively quiet and they walked, both lost in their own thoughts for a few moments longer. As they crossed the Pont des Arts, James reminded Fen that she had said that she'd seen something else of interest.

'Oh yes, so when I was leaving Henri's gallery, something caught my eye, well, some*one* to be more accurate.'

'Who?'

'Lazard, complete with Saint Tropez-style striped blazer and slacks on. And it's odd—'

'Because that sounds more like something you'd see at Henley Regatta rather than Paris in the autumn?' James interrupted her.

'Well yes, that… and that Henri had just been telling me that he really only knew Lazard by reputation, not personally very well at all.'

James huffed out a laugh. 'Well, be careful in there tonight. I'm sure Henri is more than open to helping you find Rose's killer, but don't forget, there is still a murderer on the loose.'

'I know.' Fen looked at James and then over to where she could see a red carpet, lit each side by large candle flares, that led into the main entrance of the gallery. 'Though I think I should be more worried about this outfit staying stitched together than getting myself into trouble. Wish me luck!'

'Good luck, Fen.' With that, James leaned down and kissed her on the forehead and then was gone, leaving Fen to walk the red carpet into the Louvre museum on her own.

CHAPTER THIRTY

The Louvre, it turned out, was the most perfect place for a party. 'I suppose it was a royal palace,' Fen had mused to herself as she'd accepted a glass of something that she thought might have been champagne, although she wasn't sure.

She had decided to wait for Henri just inside the main entrance, and as she stood with her back to a large marble pillar, she could not only take in the marvellous architecture around her, but also watch the other guests as they spilled into the gallery from the chill night outside. Fen could quite imagine herself at a ball at the court of Louis XIV, except that, like her, the ball dresses of the women around her had that air of 'make do and mend' and the white tie and tails of the gentlemen had the whiff of mothballs and cedar wood.

But there were smiles on people's faces and they embraced and air-kissed each other. She caught snippets of conversation – mentions of names such as Elsie de Wolfe and various countesses and how this felt like the pre-war parties. Fen sipped her champagne and watched as the crowds mingled and moved, couples introducing singles, men and women flirting and laughing, jewellery that might not have been aired for five years or more glittering under the electric chandeliers that illuminated the gallery.

'Fenella!' Henri's voice cut through the crowd and Fen looked around to see him moving towards her.

'Good evening, Henri.' Fen air-kissed him on both cheeks, as it seemed the correct thing to do in this company.

'Glad to see you enjoying the fizz,' he nodded at the glass. 'We had it safely stored at a château in the Loire, much like our precious artwork! Ah,' he gripped Fen's hand and held her at arm's length, giving her an appraising look, 'you remind me of Rose in so many ways. How did you find such a unique dress?'

Fen cocked her head on one side and smiled at Henri. 'I'm not entirely sure if you're teasing me or not… you know this is one of Rose's turbans?' She pointed to her chest and shook her head. 'With a lot of help from Simone and her needles!'

'She is a woman of many skills indeed.' Henri nodded in admiration as Fen gave him a little twirl. Henri clapped his hands together once in appreciation. 'Magnifique! Now, I want to introduce you to some folk and I caught sight of them lounging on the grand staircase. Come, let's go and find them.'

With that, he led her through the other guests to where a set of glamorous partygoers were looking rather louche, draping themselves against the stone balustrades of the staircase.

'Fenella, can I introduce Christian and Catherine Dior, brother and sister, and the equally talented Pierre Balmain.'

'We've already met,' Christian held out his hand to Fen, who shook it enthusiastically, while Pierre nodded and smiled, just as he had done from his drawing board when Fen had met them at Atelier Lelong. 'But I don't think Catherine was there that day, was she?'

'No.' Fen stretched out her hand to the rather stern-looking woman. 'Lovely to meet you, Catherine. I'm friends with Simone Mercier, in fact we're lodging together since… well, since recently.'

Catherine smiled, and in so doing her whole aspect changed and she went from looking terribly serious to really quite playful. She shook Fen's outstretched hand and Fen remembered what Simone had said about how badly Catherine had been treated by the Gestapo for her work with the Resistance. It was a relief for Fen to meet her and see that, although still gauntly thin, she looked dazzling tonight, dressed in a full black silk skirt and cream silk blouse with a starched, upright collar. Her hair was styled in a neat chignon, but loose flyaway strands created a halo around her head.

'Come and join us, mademoiselle,' she made room for Fen on the step next to her. 'We are discussing hemlines and haute couture and other such things of earth-shattering importance.'

Christian laughed at his sister and Fen sat down, entranced by the company of such glamorous people. *If only Kitty were here…* she thought as Henri suggested a round of drinks and went off in search of the wine waiter.

'It's good to meet you. Simone has told us all about you.' Catherine said.

'Nothing too terrible, I hope.'

'Oh no, she is rather enamoured, though perhaps more so with your handsome friend? She is always popping out from the atelier to see him. Are they not here tonight?'

'I'm afraid Henri only invited me. I must admit, until now, I didn't realise that Henri knew Simone all that well. Anyway, I don't suppose Simone will mind too much; she and James found some gramophone records to play and are no doubt enjoying each other's company.'

'*Ooh la la*, yes. *Lady* Simone…' Catherine lit a cigarette and laughed as she exhaled the first plume of smoke.

'She told you then?'

'Told us? Does she ever stop!'

They all laughed, though it did make Fen wonder again if Simone liked James for the right reasons. *Lady Simone…* Fen couldn't shake the feeling that there was some ulterior motive to her marrying her way into the aristocracy. Or James's branch of it at least. She shook the thought from her mind, tonight was not the night to dwell on such things.

'Speaking of gramophones,' Christian stood up and brushed down his tuxedo, 'anyone fancy a dance? Pierre, you can see what the well-to-do of Paris are wearing and get inspiration for that new collection of yours.' He winked at his friend while holding his hand out to Fen, who gratefully took it to help her off the step with some semblance of elegance.

Pierre laughed and then jokingly held his forefinger to his lips, shushing his friend.

Christian had that same playful look about him as his sister had done just moments before and whispered to Fen as he led her to where guests were dancing to the music of a swing band, 'He's leaving Lelong, you see, starting his own atelier.'

'Gosh, good for him.' Fen glanced behind her and saw that Pierre was leading Catherine Dior to the dance floor just behind them. Then, before she could think of anything more clever to say, Christian's hand was lightly placed on the small of her back and she was swept onto the dance floor, the music of the band and the swishing of silk skirts taking her mind off all her recent sadness and reminding her that there was life to be lived still, now the war was over.

By the time the band stopped, Fen's cheeks were flushed and almost ached from laughing. Christian had been giving her a running commentary on all the other ladies' outfits as they'd twirled and swayed, from admiring the cut of a gown to accusing one doughty older lady of not being in possession of all of her own hair.

'It's so obviously a hairpiece,' he'd whispered, and Fen had craned her neck to see whom he was talking about.

'Oh I don't know,' Fen had cheekily replied, 'it's hard to tell under that tiara…'

'Monsieur Renaud will have that off her and into his fundraising pot before you can say "Mona Lisa", if she's not careful.'

Fen laughed. 'I didn't realise you all know Henri Renaud so well?'

'He's is one of our patrons.' Christian wiped his brow with a silk handkerchief, which Fen noticed was in the same pretty pattern as the scarves Simone had given her and Magda just days ago.

'Patrons?' His sister Catherine appeared next to them, on the arm of Pierre Balmain, and raised an eyebrow at her brother. 'Let's say we all knew each other well during the war.'

'I see.' Fen nodded. 'Did you help with the…' Fen waved one arm in the air, cautious not to rip a seam, '… evacuation of the Louvre then?'

'No, but we helped with the evacuation of some of our friends. Tailors, seamstresses, fabric merchants… so many Jewish families are involved with the fashion trade. We had to do what we could.'

'I understand.'

'Henri was a good source of information, what with his *dealings*,' Catherine emphasised the last word, 'with the German "art historians".' They all laughed at her reference to the Nazi officers. *Philistines*, Rose had called them. 'He knew when raids were due to happen as he was needed at those apartments or galleries to value their art. Your friend Rose, too. I'm sorry… what happened to her has us all shocked.'

'Thank you,' Fen all but whispered, brushing her hands over the corset Simone had stitched out of one of Rose's flamboyant turbans.

'Anyway,' Christian slapped his hands on his thighs, lightening the mood, 'Henri did us a favour at the end of the war too and sent Simone to the atelier as an apprentice. And she's got a good eye, I'll tell you that.'

'And the perfect model, too,' Pierre chipped in, finally joining the conversation.

Fen let them all chat together, nodding and smiling at their anecdotes and gossip. Her mind wandered away from their conversation for a moment or two when a familiar fox fur caught her eye on the other side of the dance floor.

Adrienne Tambour! She of the forged Dutch still life. Fen kept an eye on her, although it was hard with other guests, flushed from dancing and wine, getting in the way. She didn't particularly want a confrontation with someone who so recently had had cause to quarrel with Rose… but the thought did cross her mind that that might be exactly *why* she should see if Madame Tambour could be persuaded to talk and let slip if she had an alibi… or not.

CHAPTER THIRTY-ONE

Just as Fen was plucking up the courage to cross the room and speak to Adrienne Tambour, Henri came back, leading a simpering wine waiter behind him.

'Ah, here you all are. Enjoying the music, I see, wonderful.' They all refreshed their glasses and Henri courteously pulled Fen away from the chic fashionistas. 'I must introduce you to the director of the board. He's a fine fellow and, dare I say, another of us grieving for our lost friend.'

Fen could just imagine Rose here, holding court with the Diors or nattering with the aged countesses. 'She must have touched a lot of hearts round here.'

'And quite a few canvases,' Henri said wryly, as he steered Fen through the groups of guests enjoying themselves.

She tried to keep an eye on where Madame Tambour was, and saw her talking to the bewigged older lady with the tiara. With thoughts of alibis in her mind, Fen pulled at Henri's sleeve to slow him down so she could ask him something.

'When I left you earlier, was it Michel Lazard I saw entering your gallery?'

Henri frowned. 'Yes. A coincidence indeed. He had the cheek to ask me if I wanted to buy some art of very dubious provenance. He should know better. I sent him away with a flea in his ear. Now, please, no mention of that charlatan as I introduce you to Claude and Berenice.'

Henri ushered Fen in front of him and she was soon shaking hands with an older crowd.

'*Enchanté*, mademoiselle,' the man named Claude kissed her hand instead of shaking it and then caught Fen unawares as he spun her around on the spot. Fen silently thanked Christian for the spin round the dance floor a little while ago; aside from being jolly good fun, it had prepared her for this sort of thing. 'I see you have brought me another dancer, eh, Renaud?' Claude laughed and turned back to his previous conversation.

'Ignore him, *chérie*,' Henri squeezed Fen's shoulder and then turned himself to engage in conversation with a very aristocratic-looking lady who was dripping in diamonds. Fen was just wondering how many carats there must be on her fingers alone when another hand was stuck in front of her to shake.

'Good evening, mademoiselle.' The man was tall but portly, a chin or two's extra weight filling out his pale face. His blond hair was swept over to one side and his eyebrows, being blond too, didn't do much to break up the monotony of his vast forehead. He wasn't a good-looking man, but he had a certain presence and his voice, even in those few words of introduction, held Fen's attention.

'Good evening,' she replied and let him kiss her hand. 'My name's Fenella Churche, Fen.'

'Fen Churche… like the station in London?' The man laughed and Fen nodded, trying not to let the old joke get to her. The man carried on with his own introduction. 'Don't worry, I have a humorous name also. Valentine Valreas, at your service. Val Val!' He laughed and Fen smiled too, genuinely amused.

'Monsieur Valreas…' Fen let the name register. 'I recognise your name, where might I have heard it?'

'Perhaps you are a local of a small town in Provence?' He raised an eyebrow and Fen shook her head. 'Or a lover of fine art who comes to my auction house – both of which are called Valreas!' He laughed again and then accepted another couple of glasses of champagne from a passing waiter. He passed one to Fen.

'Thank you.' Fen took a sip. 'And yes, that's it, Monsieur Valreas, I've heard of you in connection to selling art.'

'Please, call me Valentine. And tell me, how do you come to be at this fine institution tonight? Are you a collector, as I have my card here somewhere...'

'I'm a guest, a very lucky one,' Fen raised her glass to Valentine, who had started to look through his evening jacket pockets for a business card. 'Monsieur Renaud invited me tonight. I fear he has taken pity on me as our mutual, and very dear, friend Rose Coillard was... well, she died very recently.' Fen saw as she spoke the countenance of the man's face change. He stopped looking through his pockets and went from being exceptionally jovial to having the proverbial face like thunder just as she had mentioned Rose's name. 'Monsieur?'

'Ah, Rose Coillard.' He spat her name out as if she were a dirty word. 'You know that woman had the gall to come and see me, just the other day? Oh, some excuse or other, but I sent her packing. "Do not darken my door again with your fakes and forgeries, Madame!" I said to her.'

Fen was gobsmacked by Valentine's words. 'Surely... I mean, Rose never meant to sell her paintings as—'

'Didn't she?' Valentine downed his champagne in one swig and smacked his lips. Luckily, this calmed him somewhat. 'I'm sorry, of course, for her death. She was murdered, they say?'

'Yes, most violently.'

'Well, I am sorry that you have lost your friend. But Paris will not mourn the passing of *Le Faussaire*, I tell you that.'

'Was she...' Fen still couldn't believe that Rose had been the infamous forger, but she decided that Valentine wasn't the man to have this reasoned debate with at this moment. After a brief hesitation, Fen carried on, '... so very awful?' She could feel herself on the brink of tears. Here she was in these sublime surroundings, drinking champagne with Paris's high society, a society Rose was very much part of, and yet in this gilded room were two upstanding people, Valentine Valreas and Adrienne Tambour, who were adamant that Rose was nothing more than a tuppenny forger. Perhaps Rose Coillard wasn't the person Fen had thought she was after all?

Luckily Valentine pressed a hand to Fen's arm, and although his fingers felt like warm sausages, she was pleased of the comfort. Perhaps he was going to tell her that he had made a mistake.

His voice softened. 'No. She was not awful, as you say. But her paintings have caused quite the ruckus. There is not a dealer now between here and Marseille who is not cursing her name in case one of their precious, and valuable, pieces is a fake.'

At that, Valentine Valreas nodded a goodbye to Fen and left her as he merged back into the group of patrons and philanthropists, gallery owners and Louvre staff, who were all orbiting around Henri and his friends.

Valentine's words, and sentiments, had knocked the wind out of Fen's sails and her heart was no longer in the party. Noticing that the Dior siblings and Pierre Balmain had already gone, on to another more fashionable party perhaps, she decided to slip out, too. She whispered her goodbyes and thanks to Henri and crept out of the back of the room and into the vast atrium of the grandest art gallery in Europe.

There was no queue for the cloakroom and moments later she was back out into the chill of the autumnal night. An owl hooted from somewhere in the Tuileries and Fen sought out a bench on which to sit so that she could loosen the buckles on the velvet T-bar shoes she'd found in Rose's closet. They'd matched perfectly with the cobbled-together outfit, but only now as she sat down did she realise quite how much they'd been pinching all evening. The relief was exquisite and she let her back rest against the bench as she massaged her blistered feet.

While I'm here… she thought to herself, allowing herself a few minutes' more rest, *and before I forget…*

Fen reached into the small evening bag she had brought with her and pulled out the table napkin from the café on which she'd started to create a crossword-like grid. She found a pencil from an old dance card at the bottom of the bag and quickly jotted down a few more words as she thought of them. Why these words in particular struck her she didn't know, but she kept writing until the grid looked like this:

```
                    F
            C       O
        P A I N T B R U S H
            P       G
            H       E
C H A M E L E O N   R       A U C T I O N
            R     T I P P E R
                    E       T
                L I S T     D
                            E       W
                        B L A C K M A I L
                            L       R
                          D E G E N E R A T E
                            R       H
                                    O
                                    U
                                    S
                                    E
```

Fen carefully folded the now quite tatty napkin, popped it back into her bag and put her shoes back on.

'You're meant to be able to solve your own puzzles,' she grumbled to herself as she limped out of the Louvre's main courtyard, and only made it twenty yards or so before she slipped the shoes off again, deciding that barefoot through the chilly streets of Paris was preferable to the pain. 'No shoes and no clues,' she sighed as she made her way back, the words of the grid tumbling like a waterfall through her mind. Somewhere in that grid was the answer, she was sure of it.

Fen made it home without stepping on anything too painful or foul, and appreciated Simone's help in carefully unstitching her from the bodice she had created earlier that evening. Tipper was less than helpful, trying everything he could to get Fen's attention until she picked him up and held him. She was rewarded by quite a few licks to the face while Simone worked around them both.

'He's still missing Rose, I think.' Simone said, trying to pat the dog, who burrowed his way further into the nook of Fen's elbow. '*Tch*, silly pooch. Oh, James says he'll meet you in the Café Chat Noir tomorrow morning at nine,' Simone told her as she unravelled the orange silk of the former turban.

'Did you have a nice evening together?' Fen could sense there was something at play here, Simone wasn't her usual confident and opinionated self and she hadn't asked Fen about the party at the Louvre at all.

'James is a gentleman,' was all Simone would say and from that Fen inferred that James hadn't perhaps played into the younger woman's waiting arms as much as she would have liked.

Fen changed the subject. 'I met your friend Catherine, tonight. She must have been so brave…'

Simone brightened. 'She was. Did they ask after me? I don't know why Henri didn't invite me, too,' she said with a little huff.

'I didn't realise you were all so close. Henri with the Diors and Balmain, too.'

'He's been kind to me,' Simone said and gave Fen a gentle push away, the bodice now completely undone and spooled on the parquet floor of the studio. 'Time for bed. Don't forget your date with James in the morning.'

'No, rightio. And thank you, Simone. Goodnight.'

CHAPTER THIRTY-TWO

Fen awoke the next day with a clear head but still no idea as to why Rose was murdered, or who had done it. She did notice that the bells of Saint Sulpice were ringing out, welcoming worshippers on this fine Sunday morning, and her own watch confirmed it; it was 8 a.m. already.

The apartment was quiet and still now. Perhaps Simone had gone to church? Fen ticked herself off for not finding the local Anglican one. What would Mrs B and Rev Smallpiece say? What with one thing or another, it had been weeks since she'd been. She said a few prayers next to her bed and then dressed and fussed over Tipper, who had made his bed for the night in the crumpled silk of the old turban.

'I'm sure that's a dreadful waste on such a hound as you, young sir,' Fen tutted while stroking his head. 'But enjoy it while you can. Got to dash. It's back to the dog basket for you though later!'

She checked the mailbox at the bottom of the apartment building's staircase as she left and, to her joy, there was a letter addressed to her in it.

'Kitty!' Fen exclaimed out loud, recognising the handwriting on the front of the envelope. She glanced at the large clock that hung above the mailboxes, however, and saw she was running late for her appointment with James. 'Later…' she whispered and tucked the letter into her trench coat's pocket, tapping it and holding her hand over it protectively as she walked along the few streets to get to the café.

*

'You look well,' James said as he stood and pulled out a chair for Fen in the café. 'Not such a raucous night as it might have been in Elsie de Wolfe's day?'

'Elsie de who? I heard that name mentioned several times last night.'

James laughed. 'De Wolfe. Society hostess with the mostest before the war.'

'I suppose you would know all about that, *Viscount Lancaster…*' Fen cocked an eyebrow at her friend, who laughed in return. 'Speaking of which, thank you for inviting me to breakfast via Simone. I'm not sure she's wholly thrilled at our little *date* though.' Fen blushed a bit as she said those last few words. 'Not that it is, by any stretch of the imagination, a date, as it were.'

James just smiled at her and raised his hand to call the waiter. 'Simone's a charming young woman, but, well, I'm feeling more and more like a lion tamer every day,' he joked as the waiter approached. 'Breakfast? Coffee?'

'Oh yes, rather. I felt tickety-boo first thing, but perhaps I did have one too many glasses of fizz last night.' She rested her forehead in her hand. 'I'm getting away with it at the moment, but something to take the edge off wouldn't hurt.'

'Another drink?'

'No, James! I meant just a coffee. And maybe an omelette…'

James chuckled and ordered them both a simple herbed omelette and a coffee each.

'Well,' he sighed. 'This is very civilised.'

'As was last night, it really was a super do. The gallery is simply divine by night. And I met Christian and Pierre from Simone's atelier again and Christian's sister Catherine. They were a really fun bunch and Christian took me for a couple of turns around the dance floor. I hadn't realised Henri Renaud knew them all so well. Apparently *he* was responsible for getting Simone the job there after the war.'

A couple of coffees appeared between them and Fen took a sip before carrying on.

'And, most importantly, I spoke to Henri about Michel Lazard. He couldn't exactly deny that he had seen him, but he was very quick to tell me that he hadn't been expecting him and he'd sent him packing pretty pronto. I really must try to find him and ask him what it was all about.'

'Good luck with that one.' James started fiddling with the cutlery on the table, obviously hungry.

'Then there was a perfectly pleasant man, though very strange-looking, called Valentine Valreas, who's an auctioneer. He almost bit my ear off when I said I was friendly with Rose, as if she were the Devil himself… or, worse than that even by his standards, Le Faussaire!'

'Motive?' James looked up at Fen. 'And why didn't he like her?'

'I have a feeling it's Lazard that's the root cause, but the crux of it is, those "copies" of Rose's really were starting to get her into a bit of hot water.'

'An angry auctioneer, a dodgy dealer, an armed Arnault brother…'

'An Henri with an inheritance and maybe a blackmailer with a bludgeon… I know, I know… the list of suspects is becoming impossibly endless! And I'm trying to approach the whole mystery like a crossword – you know, keeping an eye out for indicators and clues – but I'm pretty stumped.' Fen sat back with her coffee and sighed. 'So what's all this about you being a lion tamer?'

'Ah,' James said as the omelettes arrived and he tucked in straight away. After a quick chew and swallow, he continued talking. 'It's Simone. She's a great girl and all that, stunning and obviously very elegant, but, boy, is she headstrong.'

'You're not about to come over all misogynistic now, are you? Women are allowed to know their own minds. It is 1945 after all, not 1845.'

'I know, I know,' he waved his fork in the air, then skewered another bite of omelette. He popped it in his mouth and swallowed quickly. 'And I think it's a wonderful thing to know your own mind. Lord knows we've all been pushed and pulled and told what to do for so long by the powers that be… it's just she really knows what she wants and she doesn't mind telling me. *All the time*.'

Fen analysed his words as she chewed. 'Rather forward in coming forward as it were, you mean?' James nodded and Fen carried on. 'Well, when a girl wants to be the future Lady Lancaster, can you blame her?'

'Well, I don't think Lady Simone will be happening any time soon, but yes, that's what she's got her eye on and it's rather unattractive. Or am I being a spoon?'

'A spoon?'

'Yes, a fool, a fusspot. Perhaps an old bachelor like me shouldn't be so choosy. So what? She wants a title, I have a title. Maybe it's a fair trade to get a nice girl by my side?'

'Title, yes. And don't forget the land, houses, probably a rather spiffing motorcar…' Fen teased, but in saying it did wonder if James, who in her mind wasn't that old at all, was selling himself a little short, and she said as much.

'Do you think she really only sees me as a meal ticket?' James replied, before eating some more of his breakfast.

'No.' Fen acquiesced, and then thought about it before carrying on. 'But I think she's a girl who saw great poverty in her youth and doesn't want to experience it again. She may well hitch her cart to you, James, but it doesn't mean she doesn't like you, too.'

'Hmm.' James cleared his plate and sat back. 'True, true. Still, it was all a bit much last night and I ended up leaving rather early to get back to my hotel. But enough of the nattering, are you finished eating? Let's go and see Gervais, shall we, and at least clear that mess up before I make another one with Simone.'

CHAPTER THIRTY-THREE

Fen and James walked down the Rue de Seine, in the opposite direction to the river and towards the Église de Saint-Germain-des-Prés. Parisians in their Sunday best nodded to them as they walked along and seeing them so neatly turned out made Fen pause in front of one of the shop windows to quickly check that her hastily done victory rolls were still in place and her lipstick was just so. *I probably won't be troubling the catwalks of Paris's fashion houses*, she thought to herself, *but I'll do*.

The side streets around the church were older in style and without the grand Haussman architecture it felt more like they were in a rural town, such as the one in Burgundy they'd recently come from. The roads were narrow and turned suddenly around blind corners, so much so that it was hard to imagine the great boulevards only a hundred or so yards away.

James guided them both through the labyrinth and arrived at an archway that was barred by double doors. Unlike the ones that led into Rose's apartment building, these were curved to match the stone arch above them and had a single small door cut into one of them. It was this door that James pounded with his fist to announce their arrival.

'That's odd,' James remarked. 'I passed Gervais on the road last night as I was leaving your apartment and he said he'd be in this morning. There's a car he's working on for some Italian chap; he said he'd be under the bonnet all day and sprucing up the paintwork. "Working all hours on a Sunday, for an Italian!" he'd moaned.'

'An Italian chap? Perhaps Henri was right about gangsters?'

Fen didn't mind the pause too much. She and James had been idly chatting as they'd walked to the garage and she hadn't had the chance to think properly about what questions she might pose Gervais. Blurting out 'are you a blackmailer?' probably wasn't going to cut the mustard, but it was what she so desperately wanted to know.

James pounded on the door again and called out Gervais's name.

'This is very odd,' he finally conceded. It looked as though he was about to try ramming the door with his shoulder, until Fen reached over and turned the handle on the smaller cut-out door. It opened with ease and she raised an eyebrow at James. 'Fine, fine,' he muttered, but his eyes suggested that he saw the funny side to the situation too.

Once inside, with the door softly clicked behind them, Fen realised that the arch would have originally led to the stables of a coaching inn or similar, but now the familiar smell of engine grease and fuel suggested that this was a garage for motorcars. It reminded her of the tractor shed on Mrs B's farm, damp and earthy but spiced with the smell of petrol and oil.

James found a light switch and Fen's eyes confirmed what her nose had guessed. It was a fully functioning mechanic's set-up, with metal shelves of gasoline cans, spare parts and boxes of fuses and spanners, wrenches and wires. There was a pit in the floor, and above it a hydraulic ramp, upon which was a smart black car that looked new and in excellent condition, except for the spray of bullet holes that peppered the paintwork.

Fen pointed at them and James nodded, he'd seen them too. Behind the car there were piles of tyres and beyond them more double doors. The smell of white spirit and oil also reminded Fen of Rose's apartment and she was just about to point out that fact, as well as comment on the rather interesting addition to the car's paintwork, when James gave a cry of shock.

'Fen, stand back.' He placed his hands on her shoulders and tried to turn her around to face the car again, but it was too late. There, in a small office area, which was crudely made from old window frames atop cinder blocks, was Gervais. Despite James's efforts, Fen had already seen the pool of congealed blood on the floor by where his shattered head had fallen and above it the splatter of red across the wall, crudely vandalising the pictures of showgirls from the Moulin Rouge that were adorning it.

Fen held her hand up to her mouth and stood there silently. She knew she had to collect her thoughts pretty darned quick if she was going to be of any use to James, but the sight of the body, its blood and other unspeakable matter was truly shocking.

'We should call the p...police,' James stuttered slightly, but his voice strengthened as he asked, 'Who would do this? This is... well, this is an *execution*.'

Fen shuddered and wanted very much to stop looking at the body of Gervais crumpled onto the floor, his knees bent beneath him as if he had been shot in a firing line. *Just like Arthur...*

She covered her eyes with her hands and shook her head to try and dislodge the image in her head. 'James, this can't be a coincidence, it just can't be.'

'I only saw him... He seemed so full of life...' James's sentence just faded away.

'James, I'm so sorry.' Fen turned away, finally, from the dead body and looked at her friend. They both stood there in silence for a few moments more, taking in the fact that another body was now lying in front of them.

'So, you don't think this is a coincidence?' James was the first to speak, his voice steadier now.

Fen took a deep breath. 'No. How can it be?'

'Well, in that we only have Henri's word that Gervais was blackmailing Rose.' James looked up at the shiny black car on the ramp. 'Perhaps it's a gang thing after all and that Italian chap didn't like the look of the bill for the paint repairs?'

'James, be serious.'

'I am. It's far more likely that Gervais had got himself involved with some sort of criminal gang than started blackmailing Rose, don't you think?'

'I understand what you're saying, but… two bodies, one so soon after the other? Both connected to the Louvre and artworks in some way, even if Gervais wasn't blackmailing Rose.' Fen thought for a second. 'And, personally, I'm inclined to believe Henri and say that he was. Look, James, this is going to sound terribly callous, but once you've phoned the police, we should spend the time before they arrive searching this place for clues.'

'No three down then yet?'

'Well, he was it – so no, not any more. But we might at least find something that could tell us who did this to him.'

'Fine. I'll call, and you can start with those drawers.' James nodded to a filing cabinet in the office, which thankfully hadn't been splashed with any blood from Gervais's grizzly end.

Fen thought the desk might yield some clues, too, as to what Gervais might have been up to, but she felt understandably squeamish about disturbing the remains of what lay on top of the papers there. One piece of paper, partially hidden under a telephone exchange directory, caught her eye though. Fen waited for James to finish his telephone call and pointed it out to him.

James had a cursory glance at the manifest, holding it between finger and thumb in his left hand.

'Do you see what I see?' Fen asked him.

'A lot of crates of paintings going to the Jeu de Paumes?'

'And to Valreas & Co auctioneers, by the looks of it.' Fen thought back to meeting Valentine Valreas at the party the night before. He had known Rose, too, and was perhaps another connection between the murders.

James handed back the manifest to Fen. 'Well, Henri and Rose told us that the Nazis liked to auction off the art the Führer didn't want back in Germany, so your new friend Valentine must have been the auctioneer they used.'

Fen frowned and looked at the papers. 'It's something else. I don't know, maybe what *isn't* here is as important as what is.'

'What do you mean?'

Fen shook her head. 'I don't know, something Joseph said about the codes being the proof. This list doesn't have any of Rose's code on it. And look, the paintings are listed… a Cezanne, a Degas… It's terrible, isn't it. Those poor families, robbed and then murdered most likely. No wonder Rose and Henri were doing their utmost to restore what they could to the rightful owners, or their heirs at least. Could this have been what Gervais was blackmailing them for?'

James shrugged his shoulders. He slipped the manifest into a plain envelope he found in the filing cabinet and the two of them carried on their search.

The garage was filthy, but that hadn't surprised Fen much and, in fact, rooting around the spare parts and cans of oil and lubricant had been a good distraction from the two rather gruesome murders that had happened so close together. *All this one needs is a whiff of ylang-ylang*, Fen thought to herself as she recoiled from a particularly potent jar of turpentine.

'Ah,' James was still at the filing cabinet, coping better it seemed with searching the area closest to the dead body.

'What is it?' Fen asked, hoping she wouldn't have to come too close to see.

'More lists. Manifests, itineraries, that sort of thing. Hmmm.' James picked up a document and read it through before reading it aloud to Fen. 'Invoice to Monsieur M. Lazard, for transporting three crates of paintings to Valreas & Co Auctioneers, Paris.'

'He knew Lazard, of course,' Fen stated. 'Antoine told us that.'

'And by the looks of some of these chits, he knew the Germans just as well, and Henri Renaud, too. Here, look at this invoice: for transporting one marble bust and three oil paintings to Strasbourg – five hundred francs.'

'Crikey, that's a tidy sum. He certainly had his finger in quite a few pies.' Fen looked up at the black motorcar with its decoration of bullet holes. 'Do you think these were done at the same time?'

James looked up from the filing cabinet and across to the car. He thought about it. 'No. It looks like Gervais was killed with a single gunshot to the forehead. That's a machine gun, like you see in the films.'

'James…' Something clicked into place in her head and Fen suddenly pointed to the papers James was holding. 'I think we might have our answer.'

'About who killed him?'

'No, as to whether he was the blackmailer. Look at the piece of paper you're holding. It's the same colour as the letter Rose received – blue! And that one has his handwriting on it, does it?'

James looked at the handwritten note towards the bottom of the bundle of paperwork he was holding. He was quiet for a while.

'It's his handwriting all right,' he said quietly, and exhaled. Then he looked at Fen. 'Looks like you might have been right about him being the blackmailer after all.'

By the time the police arrived, Fen and James had decided they had unearthed all they could about Gervais – they'd found inventories and itineraries, logbooks and manifests… basically all the paperwork you'd expect from a lorry driver-turned-mechanic. Before they'd even had a chance to show what they'd found, including the manifests, to the gendarmes, the officer in charge had declared this a murder between underworld gangs and questioned James intently about what he might know regarding Gervais' various contacts and where they could find his brother.

Fen decided at that point that their own findings would only muddy the waters and slipped the envelope containing the manifests, the example of Gervais's handwriting and the invoice to Michel Lazard into her bag.

After what seemed like hours of waiting around and questioning, the police finally allowed them to leave. Having to wait so long for them to finish questioning James did have one advantage though. As he was stating time and again that he was nothing to do with Gervais's underworld dealings and just a new friend, Fen had eavesdropped on the police surgeon's dictation to his assistant.

Turns out they hadn't stumbled on a recently deceased body at all, and poor Gervais had been lying in his own blood in the cold, dark, stench of the garage since eleven o'clock the night before.

'Now don't think I'm trying to encourage you into bad habits,' James said as they finally ducked through the small door out into the daylight, 'but I think I need a strong drink.'

'I'm not going to argue there.' Fen pulled her lightweight trench coat around her, suddenly quite chilled from the cool of the garage and most likely from the shock of finding another dead body. She shivered and then had to admit that the warmth of James's arm, which had slipped around her shoulders, was not unwelcome at all.

CHAPTER THIRTY-FOUR

'I can't help but think that finding mention of all those paintings in those manifests in Gervais's garage means the murders are linked, don't you?' Fen said between mouthfuls. The pair of them had decamped to the café at the end of the road and a strong drink had turned into lunch. Fen had been untowardly delighted when she'd seen that *coq au vin* was on the menu and ordered it. James had followed suit, and asked for a portion of potato *tartiflette* too, which had arrived, hot and steaming, in a heavy black cast-iron dish.

'They were so different though. In their modus operandi,' James argued. 'One a paintbrush to the neck and the other an execution-style gunshot to the head. And you couldn't get more different people than Madame Coillard with her eccentricities, and salt-of-the-earth, lorry-driving Gervais.'

'Yes… true… but those itineraries and manifests – all to do with art. I mean, that has to be a connection. Plus, we know they knew each other and the murders happened so soon after one another.' Fen spoke, but she also watched as her hand still trembled as she reached for the carafe of wine. James must have noticed it too and got to the wine first, taking the carafe and pouring some into her glass. 'Thanks, James.' Fen sipped it and thought again about what they'd just discovered. She cleared the final few pieces of chicken from her plate, still grateful to be eating such succulent meat after the austerity of the war, and sat back.

'I agree, there's a connection all right,' James said, sitting back too and then reaching forward for his own glass of wine. He cradled it in his hand and swirled the red liquid around. 'So Gervais was blackmailing Rose, and Henri.'

'I think I'm thinking what you're thinking.' Fen looked at James. 'If Gervais was the blackmailer, was he Rose's murderer too?'

'Not quite,' James corrected her. 'Gervais may have been the blackmailer, and he may even have murdered Rose, though I doubt it. No, the pressing question now is... who killed Gervais?'

Fen took a sip of her wine and then looked James in the eye. 'And is Henri next?'

After the lunch had been chased down by a brandy, on James's part at least, the pair of them set off in the direction of Rose's apartment.

'It'll always feel like *Rose's* apartment,' Fen mused as they walked along. 'I can't think of it yet as Henri's.'

'While her belongings are there, I suppose it must feel like she's still very present,' James agreed.

'That reminds me, Henri asked me if I could start clearing out her clothes. I don't suppose you have anything better to do this afternoon, do you? I can't see Henri wanting to inherit a section of colourful turbans and housecoats along with his property.'

'As long as I don't have to rifle through any knicker drawers, then yes. Though I feel as if I should try and find some of Gervais's friends in the bars and tell them about his, well... his murder.'

'Yes of course. Some of them might know something about who could have done it. See if they know of anyone who wasn't in the bar at ten o'clock last night.'

'I wouldn't hold out any hope. Snitches aren't looked upon fondly these days.'

They walked on in silence until they arrived at the large double doors of Rose's apartment building. Fen turned to James. 'Good luck. It never gets any easier, does it. Giving bad news, I mean.'

'Especially not to family. I don't suppose anyone has told Antoine yet.'

Unless he did it…? The thought flashed through Fen's mind, as suddenly as those gunshots had rung out in the warehouse the day before, but she kept quiet. There was no reason for Antoine to murder his brother, and he had an alibi for Rose's death, too. Fen waved goodbye to James and headed up the cantilevered staircase to the apartment.

A few hours later and Fen and Simone were hard at it, clearing out Rose's bedroom. Simone had greeted Fen's idea of going through Rose's belongings with a squeal of excitement.

'I don't think there'll be much of any value there, the thief saw to that,' Fen said, rather guardedly, hoping that a lack of spoils wouldn't put Simone off helping her.

'Who is to say what is valuable to whom? She had some amazing dresses and I don't think Henri would be interested in them! Or the men's clothing she had either.'

'Men's clothing?' Fen raised an eyebrow.

'For her models. You know, a cloth cap, a pair of trousers… in case someone needed props for their portrait.'

'Explains this tricorn hat, I suppose!' Fen laughed as she pulled the dusty, felt-brimmed thing out from under the bed.

Together they set about sorting and tidying, placing various items in piles either for refugee charities or to sell. Fen kept a little pile of the best pieces separate, hoping that Magda might like them, and she hoped Henri wouldn't mind if she took one of Rose's feathered hatpins home for her mother as a small memento.

Simone was the most animated Fen had ever seen her, as she dramatically pulled long satin gowns and velvet housecoats out of the wardrobe and large tea chest at the bottom of Rose's bed.

'These fabrics are so beautiful! Oh, Christian and Catherine would love these!'

'You should take them to them. I think Rose would like to think that her dresses were inspiration for the designers of tomorrow.'

'And you're right, Henri wouldn't be interested at all. He was never one for commenting on what we wore.'

Fen wanted to question her more when Tipper suddenly started barking and emerged from under a pile of feather boas and scarves and dashed towards the door.

'That'll be James then,' Simone said matter-of-factly and put the silk blouse down that she was folding and went to go and answer it.

Fen could hear the door click open and the yapping finally cease.

'What ho!' James popped his head around the door. 'Captain Lancaster reporting for knicker-drawer duty.'

CHAPTER THIRTY-FIVE

The sun was starting to set on what had been a rather long and emotional day for Fen. From finding Gervais dead this morning to spending the afternoon clearing out Rose's clothes, well, it had left Fen far from fancying hitting the cold streets to go and meet up with Magda, who had telephoned just after James had left and asked Fen if she could make the time to see her.

Fen could hear the scream of a hungry or tired baby in the background, which she knew wasn't Magda's, plus shouts and general hollering, so Fen had assumed she was making the call from a municipal box in the hallway of her building. Although Fen's feet still ached from squeezing them into Rose's velvet high heels last night and she was desperate for a bath and bed, she had agreed. However hard done by Fen was feeling today, she had to remind herself that Magda and Joseph's plight was far worse. At least if she went to see Magda tonight, she could take the bundle of clothes she'd set aside for her too; they might not be Atelier Lelong scarves or haute couture, but sometimes just something new was a treat.

Before heading out, Fen decided to run a bath, and enjoyed filling the deep steel tub up more than a few inches, which had always been the approved etiquette during the war. She decided to throw in some of Rose's lavender-scented bath salts too – it wasn't as if Henri was going to use them – and just before she undressed, she remembered the letter from Kitty that she'd picked up from the mailbox this morning. She fetched it from her coat pocket and eagerly opened the envelope before slipping into the hot bath.

Mrs B's kitchen table, Midhurst,
Tiresome West Sussex,
October 1945

Darling Fen!

We are sitting here round the kitchen table with mugs of tea in our hands puzzling over your clues. Dilly got there first on the TRAIN one, swot, but I got PAINT, though really that was too easy.

I can't believe you got to go to a real fashion house – how simply divine! I'm dying to hear more – please come home soon… and if some of those scarves accidentally fall into your luggage, promise I won't tell!

We tuned into the wireless the other day and you'll never guess what we heard? Josephine Baker singing just like you wrote about. I closed my eyes and imagined I was in a dark, smoky nightclub with you, wearing red lipstick and drinking hard liquor – then Mrs B stoked the fire (it's perishingly cold here, you know) and the parlour was full of smoke, so in that way at least I didn't have to imagine too hard. I'm sure you were with much more glamorous people than I was though: Mrs B has taken to wearing three cardigans and two pairs of thick stockings – Parisian fashion this is not!

Fen laughed at Kitty's letter and could well imagine the scene in the old farmhouse. Kitty carried on with some local news and signed off.

Fen read the whole letter through again and then let it drop to the dry floor beside the bath as the steam filled her nose and the warm water soothed her tired muscles. She was just about to doze off when the buzz of the doorbell, and Tipper's accompanying barking, roused her.

Fen listened as Simone answered the door and realised it was only James, returning from a brief freshen-up at his hotel to take Simone out. She got more of a shock when Simone breezily stepped into the bathroom, much to Fen's embarrassment, to say a quick goodbye.

'Oh, no need to cover up,' Simone had said, sitting on the edge of the bath, 'it's not like I don't see naked models all the time in the fitting room at Lelong.'

'Ah, yes, well…' Fen sat up a bit in the bath and grabbed a pink flannel to cover her slightly. 'Anyway, have a lovely time tonight. Where are you two off to?'

Simone clapped her hands together once and held them in the prayer position, closing her eyes with excitement and anticipation as she replied, 'The Ritz! A show and The Ritz! I've never been and I hear it's where Madame Coco Chanel lived during the occupation, and I am obsessed by her designs.'

'Gosh, lucky you.' Fen hated to admit that she was rather jealous.

'I think tonight could be the night,' Simone said, winking conspiratorially and getting up from the edge of the bath to look in the mirror above the basin. It was steamed up, so she wiped her hand across it and Fen watched as she pouted her rouged lips into it.

'For…?'

'For a proposal! I mean, I don't see the point in waiting until we are old, well, until I am old – he is already very old.'

'He's only… well, I don't know how old James is actually.'

'Thirty-six apparently. Ancient.'

Fen, who was twenty-eight, wondered if she was regarded as 'ancient', too. Simone's next statement cleared that up though.

'You should find someone to take you out, you know? You're not getting any younger and I know you're sad about Arthur, but life goes on.' Simone pouted again and dabbed a finger to the corner of her mouth. 'Got to fly now, lover boy is waiting!' She winked and blew a kiss to Fen, then left in a flounce of skirts and confidence and Fen was alone once more, thinking about Arthur as the water around her started to cool.

A little while later and Fen had bucked herself up and dressed ready for heading out into the chilly evening. Simone had looked stunning in a dress that must have come straight from the atelier, while Fen settled for her woollen trousers and trench coat. As much as she'd loved dressing up for the Louvre last night, and would adore to be wined and dined at The Ritz too, she was relieved to be slipping into her sensible lace-up shoes for the walk over to the Marais tonight. As a nod to her and Magda's trip to the atelier, though, and just to jazz things up a little, Fen fixed the Lelong scarf from Simone around her neck and tied it in a jaunty bow.

She set her hair in victory rolls and carefully pinned a rather natty red beret she had found in Rose's cupboard to her head. 'Lipstick…' she mumbled to herself as she delved around in her handbag looking for her favourite Revlon shade.

Once pouted and puckered, she looked in the hallway mirror before she left the apartment. She may not have been dressed to the nines, but she looked relatively *Parisienne* and that made her smile. *The Ritz though… lucky Simone.* Perhaps James had decided to become a lion tamer after all.

Fen shook her head and brought herself back to the present. 'You're lucky to be alive and in the city you love, old girl,' she said to herself. Being envious over something as trifling as going to The Ritz really wasn't becoming.

With a deep breath, she picked up the clothes she'd put aside for Magda, opened the apartment door and headed out, determined not to let some petty jealousy ruin her evening.

As she walked out of the building and onto the street, the cool air of the autumnal night embraced Fen and she shivered. But the slight chill in the air only made her walk that little bit faster and soon enough she was crossing the river and heading north towards the Marais. By the time she was past the Louvre and almost at the gardens and arcades of the Palais Royale, she was starting to tire. The walk across the city was longer than she had remembered and she really should have tried to catch a bus.

Her pace slowed and she was about to pause to reassess the whole sanity of this evening's adventure when a familiar face caught her eye. It was Henri Renaud, and like her he was wrapped up in a coat and hat. She was about to wave at him when she noticed he was carrying a large package, different to hers, a painting perhaps? It was tied up tightly with brown paper and string but Fen could see it was rectangular and quite slim. A convenient break in the old palace's colonnades shielded her as she saw him cross towards the other side of the road.

'Why are you carrying paintings around in the dark?' Fen whispered to herself, thinking of those lists of stolen artworks that never made it to Germany. She watched as he continued south towards the Louvre and the river.

Fen knew that following him would take her in completely the wrong direction and she'd be letting poor Magda down awfully.

'But,' she whispered to herself as she crossed the road too, to follow Henri, 'this might just be the three down I've been looking for.'

Fen followed Henri until they reached the Place du Carrousel, one of the road junctions outside the Louvre. She chided herself, *What could be less suspicious than an art dealer, nay, a curator, carrying artwork back to his place of work?*

She was about to hang back just in case she was spotted, as she hadn't come up with an excuse at all about why she might be in the neighbourhood. But then Henri didn't take any of the paths that led across the square to the great art gallery and instead he carried on walking south, crossing the river at the wide and cobbled Pont Carrousel.

A light drizzle started to fall and Fen wiped the moisture off her face as she followed on behind him, glad that she knew these streets fairly well, not just from the last few days of holidaying here, but from her childhood too. Her brother had once threatened to throw her over this bridge when she'd naughtily flicked one of his toy soldiers into the Seine. Her claims that the little fellow wanted to be a sub-mariner hadn't cut the mustard and sibling relations had hit rather a low point.

Fen wished that she could stop and dwell on these sorts of childish reminiscences, but she felt pulled, almost magnetically, to keep following Henri. The drizzle was getting heavier and Fen could feel the splash of water off the pavement chill her ankles and calves. If she had been wearing Nylons, she'd be cursing the state they'd be getting into, but as it was, it was her woollen trousers that were taking a soaking from the now rather damp pavements.

Where are you heading to? she wondered as Henri took a sudden left-hand turn off the Quai Voltaire away from the river. She kept back a pace or two as Henri slowed. They were passing more art galleries, much like his and the ones on the Rue des Beaux-Arts where Rose's apartment was. In actual fact, with all her criss-crossing of the river tonight, she was now only a few streets away from the École des Beaux-Arts and her temporary home in Paris.

Henri veered left into another narrow road, but by the time Fen had trotted along the pavement for the last few yards before the turning, and then subtly poked her head around the corner, he was gone. There was no sign of him at all. Instead, she found herself staring at the entrance to the elegant Hotel de Lille. It was a double-fronted building, with a large door in between windows; one on the left-hand side and two to the right. Fen sheltered under one of the canopies out front as the rain had become persistently heavier.

The Hotel de Lille... why did its name ring a bell? Fen puzzled it over, knowing that she'd heard talk of it recently, while also trying to peer into one of the windows to see if it was where Henri had ended up.

The inside of the window had started to mist up, and Fen could barely make out the internal layout of the reception area of the hotel. She peered closer and caught movement inside and wondered if it might be Henri and if this was her chance to see what he was up to with the painting-shaped parcel. She took a deep breath and decided to go for it – she'd come this far and there was no point standing out in the rain wondering who or what was going on inside. If Henri caught her following him she'd just have to think on her feet.

Fen pushed the hotel's door open and cringed slightly as the bell above it gave a little tinkle, like entering a boutique. She quickly took in the scene. There was a desk in front of her and to the left, with a few sofas in front of it and a well-dressed receptionist sitting behind it, and disappearing up the staircase behind the desk, Fen caught sight of the tail of Henri's overcoat.

'Dash it all.' Fen stood, dripping wet. She pulled off her beret and then looked apologetically at the receptionist as water dripped off it, and the parcel of clothes for Magda, onto the patterned tiles of the vestibule.

Fen turned to leave, she couldn't very well follow Henri up the stairs without a very good reason to give both him and the receptionist, and was just about to pull the beret firmly back onto her very damp and frizzy curls when she saw two people she could have sworn should be the other side of Paris.

James and Simone were sitting on a velvet sofa in the bar area of the hotel, half shielded from view by a higher bar table and the stools around it. Simone's cheek was leaning into one of James's hands as he stroked her hair with the other.

Fen flushed and gave an involuntary gasp, which had the unfortunate effect of alerting James to her presence.

He looked up from where he was about to kiss Simone and then narrowed his eyes and withdrew from her. 'Fen?'

'Oh gosh, so terribly sorry. Had no idea, can't think what I'm doing here now. Must dash. Cheerio, carry on, etcetera!' Fen could feel the blush in her cheeks reddening as she wedged the hat down onto her head. She was out of the door and running through the rain before you could say 'caught in the act' and once again thanked her former self for knowing the route back to the Rue des Beaux-Arts so she could at least get home and dry quickly, if not ever shake off the embarrassment of catching James and Simone smooching in the bar of what must have been – she remembered why she knew it now – *his* hotel.

CHAPTER THIRTY-SIX

Fen woke the next morning still feeling as embarrassed as she had been the night before. She slipped her hand up from under the eiderdown and touched her own cheek and wondered if the heat she felt was pure shame or if running around in the rain had brought on a fever.

She thought back to last night and how she'd left James and Simone in a flurry of apologies and blushing and had run out onto the street. Fen couldn't be sure, but she thought she might have heard her name being shouted down the road behind her, but she had absolutely not been about to turn round and have *that* conversation with James. The one where he would ask her what the blazes she thought she was doing spying on him and then she'd have had to bluster her way through some sort of explanation that would eventually result in her having to admit that she was jealous of the time he was spending with Simone.

For that, she realised, was a little to do with all of this. Not because she had any sort of feelings other than platonic ones for James himself; she was still in mourning for her Arthur, after all – but because she had liked having a friend and James reminded her of Arthur in some ways. They looked completely different and there was no way that Arthur had been hiding a title and various country houses under his hat, but they were both intelligent, decent men who had bravely fought for their country.

She had imagined this trip to Paris would be the two of them spending afternoons walking along the Seine, reminiscing about Arthur, and James telling her more about him and the work they'd done in secret in the war. She hadn't imagined herself to be sitting up in bed, alone in an apartment where a dear old friend of hers had recently been murdered, passing the time of day talking to a small, yappy dog.

'Oh and Magda,' she winced as she remembered that not only had she interrupted James and Simone in a clinch, but she had let down her old friend, too.

As soon as she opened her bedroom door, Tipper nosed his way in, and by the time she'd put in a call to Magda's building and left a message to let her know that she'd visit her that very morning, the little dog had nestled himself in her still warm sheets.

Fen slipped back in under the eiderdown and reached over to her bedside cabinet where the slightly torn and grubby napkin containing her grid was sitting. She stared at it and jotted down another couple of words that sprung to mind, so that a little while later, it looked like this:

```
                    F
            C       O
        P A I N T B R U S H
            P       G
    M       H       E
C H A M E L E O N   R       A U C T I O N
    N       R     T I P P E R
    I               E       T
    F           L I S T     D
    E                       E       W
    S                   B L A C K M A I L
    T                       L       R
                          D E G E N E R A T E
                            R       H
                                    O
                                  G U N S H O T
                                    S
                                    E
```

Once dressed, Fen carefully folded the napkin up and slipped it into the pocket of her trench coat. She felt that somehow these murders were linked to some, if not all, of those words, and that connecting them in a grid could perhaps help her see how they might intersect in real life. But did the degenerate art have any relation to the warehouse or Tipper to the forgeries? It was a puzzle all right, and one she was scared of not being able to solve.

'I wish I could solve these too,' she grunted, pulling a brush through her unruly curls. The drizzle and rain last night had sent her neatly rolled hair into wayward tendrils and there wasn't much else Fen could do except tie the Atelier Lelong scarf over the lot of it. 'There, fixed,' she said as she knotted it under her chin and dabbed some lipstick on.

There was no sign of Simone in the apartment – perhaps she'd never come home last night? And if not, had James indeed popped the question? Fen was about to leave when Tipper nuzzled his little nose into her ankle.

'Fancy a walk too, old chap?' Fen asked and at the 'w' word, his tail started wagging at such a pace she wondered if he might take off. 'All right, all right, steady on,' Fen laughed and hooked his lead up to his collar, picked up her handbag and the parcel of clothes she'd put together for Magda and started out towards the Marais. 'You shall be my accessory today, Tipper, and please,' she knelt down and held his little fluffy head in her hands, 'if I start to follow totally innocent strangers around the place, stop me!'

Fen knew the way to the road where the Bernheims were lodging and as she and Tipper neared the down-at-heel neighbourhood, she thought again about how much as a family they had lost. Rose had reminded Fen about the Bernheims' former apartment near the Champs-Élysées, with its artwork and Persian carpets, its rooms flooded with light from elegant windows twice the size of her own. Fen remembered evenings when crystal chandeliers did a merry job of illuminating their many soirées and parties. Magda and Joseph's wedding had been one of those glittering affairs and Fen thought back to that first taste of champagne and the weight of the lead crystal glass in her hand.

That night, the apartment had glowed with wealth and opulence, the marble finishes and polished wood reflecting all that glorious light onto the masterpieces on the walls. And now Joseph and Magda were reduced to living in a small tenement in the Marais district. Hundreds of years ago, Fen remembered from her history lessons, the Marais, and the grand Place des Vosges within it, had been the centre for French and Parisian nobility. But it had fallen into disrepair after the revolution in the eighteenth century and had become the home instead to shopkeepers and refugees, among them many Jews. Over the years, the Marais had become the Jewish quarter and because of this it was constantly raided during the occupation, with apartments and shops either locked-up, empty and disused, or with extended families crammed into inhumanely small spaces for them all. Fen shuddered to think where their occupants might be now.

She looked down at the piece of paper she had brought with her on which the Bernheims' address was written and walked the last few streets towards it. The building itself wasn't dissimilar to Rose's, but instead of one apartment per floor, there were three or four, and the communal staircase of this one was dirty with children and animals playing listlessly on it.

Fen picked Tipper up as she climbed towards the second floor, where the Bernheims lived. She jumped a few times as voices shouted out of nowhere and it took Fen a moment to realise that it was just because so many people were now living cheek by jowl. Refugees and displaced families were squeezed into tiny apartments; voices raised and shouting at each other, babies crying and the wireless playing jazz music while dogs barked at each other through the thin walls of the building.

Tipper buried his head into her armpit as she stepped over a pile of old newspapers and cardboard, and Fen herself had to keep her nerve as she saw something dart suspiciously quickly across the landing in front of her, its little tail the last thing that caught her eye as it disappeared into a hole in the skirting board.

Fen knocked at the door and Magda soon appeared, unchaining the lock and letting her in.

'Magda, hello.'

'Fen, come on in.'

The Bernheims' apartment might have been small, but it was immaculate inside. The door opened into a narrow hallway that dissected the apartment in half. Magda led Fen through to a room on the right that was the bed-sitting room, the double bed the couple shared was neatly made up but semi-hidden behind an upholstered fabric screen. The rest of the room consisted of just enough space for a small table and chairs and two armchairs. There was a wireless on the table and a small cupboard for their crockery and linens.

'I'm so sorry about last night…' Fen started, aware now more than ever of how frightfully she'd behaved. *And Magda didn't even know the half of it.*

'Oh please, don't worry.' Magda pointed to one of the chairs and Fen sat down.

'I can explain… I think.'

'I assumed you had a better offer.' Magda reached down and received a few licks from Tipper.

'No, it was nothing like that. I was on my way over and I spotted Henri Renaud, oh I don't know, it sounds even sillier now that I say it out loud, but he was acting furtively, if you know what I mean.'

'Fenella dear, I think maybe the stress of Rose's murder is getting to you. Henri is our friend, he was helping Rose.'

'I know… And I'm sorry, again. Can I at least give you this as an apology?' Fen handed over the parcel of Rose's clothes and explained that Henri had asked her to clear out the closet. 'I thought you'd look lovely in some of these tea dresses, though I dare say they might be a little out of date.'

'Thank you, Fen.' Magda turned to where they had a small gas burner and a kettle. 'Tea? Or whatever approximates for it these days.' She gave a nervous laugh as she lit the stove. Fen wondered if she really was forgiven for last night; Magda didn't seem herself at all and had barely acknowledged the hand-me-downs. Fen hoped she hadn't offended her, adding insult to injury on top of standing her up last night.

As they waited for the kettle to boil, Magda didn't chat away as she might have done and Fen watched as she ran a tea towel through her fingers, then folded it and unfolded it again and again. Fen pulled Tipper up onto her lap and made a few throwaway comments about her walk over until finally Magda had made the tea and sat down on the other armchair herself.

'Magda, is there something wrong?' Fen decided to just ask.

'Well, you see…' Magda started and then chewed her cheek as she thought. Finally, she spoke again and said something that Fen wasn't expecting to hear at all. 'You see, Fen, well, I'm afraid it's about Rose. I have a confession to make.'

CHAPTER THIRTY-SEVEN

Magda sat back and took a sip of her tea. 'Please don't be cross.'

Fen, who had for just the most fleeting of moments, feared the worst, let out a sigh. 'Of course I'm not cross. In fact, it clears up something that's been troubling me. Ever since James said that the countess downstairs, or at least her pampered puss, had heard Tipper bark just the once that afternoon, I'd wondered who it might be.'

'I'm afraid it *was* Joseph. He'd kept his appointment, you see, and let himself in. He said Tipper here,' Magda leaned forward and stroked the dog's head, which made Tipper jump up and scramble off Fen's lap and onto Magda's, much to her joy, 'well, he said Tipper was beside himself and going crazy, barking and chasing his tail, weren't you, poppet?'

'So Joseph was the first to find Rose. Oh, Magda, I do feel sorry for him. I know how it feels, really I do.' Fen thought back to when she asked him about it. 'Why didn't he tell me though, he said he'd missed his appointment with Rose, that he was never there that day at all.'

Magda concentrated on stroking the very top of Tipper's head, then looked up at Fen. 'Well, of course, he didn't know what to do. He feels rightly ashamed at his cowardice in not reporting it there and then, or in trusting you with the truth, but you see, when you've heard stories like the ones we've heard…' Magda tailed off and Fen reached over and touched her on the knee.

'No one would have thought he'd done it, surely?' asked Fen.

'The police might have suspected him…' Magda looked pale and Fen realised that even voicing these concerns was paining her.

'They didn't suspect us…' Fen trailed off, realised that wasn't exactly reassuring. There was no reason why any Jewish person should trust the authorities after the horrors their people had been through. Fen rethought her words. 'I mean, there is absolutely no way that Joseph could be suspected of killing Rose. She was helping him, he had no motive whatsoever. Please don't distress yourself with it, Magda, but thank you for trusting me with it. I won't tell the police. Those dunderheads think it's all a burglary gone wrong anyway.'

'And you don't?' Magda seemed visibly calmer after Fen's reassurances.

'No. And not just because of the rich countess downstairs, dripping in diamonds, mind, who seems to have mysteriously escaped the burglars. No, it was something Antoine Arnault said when we spoke to him. That the murder seemed like something The Chameleon would have done.'

Magda shuddered when Fen spoke the double agent's code name.

'The Chameleon… I would spit on the floor, if I hadn't spent days scrubbing it clean.'

'How did you know it was him who betrayed Joseph's and your parents?'

'Just whispers… but then that was all there ever was with those networks anyway. We made plans in whispers, we escaped in whispers, but Mama and Papa and Jacques and Selena…' her voice faded as she said their names and Fen waited as she mouthed a quick prayer for her dead parents and in-laws. 'They were ready to go and were expecting an agent to pick them up and transport them to the docks, where a boat was ready to take them out of the city and from there to the coast. But the lorry that turned up, it wasn't the Resistance. It drove them to the Gestapo headquarters and we never saw them again.'

'I'm so sorry, Magda.' Fen, who was usually so awkward when it came to comforting people, was led by her heart and reached out a hand to Magda. 'I'm so sorry.'

'Rose wrote to us, did you know? In New York. She tracked us down and told us she was working on something on our behalf. It gave us hope when we were at our very lowest.' Magda paused, then continued quietly, 'Joseph would have *died* rather than see that dear woman hurt. Her friendship saved our lives in more ways than one.'

'I will find out who did this to her,' Fen said, more confidently than she felt. Her three downs were disappearing by the minute, but she knew she had to solve this murder, for all their sakes.

She stayed and chatted to Magda for a while longer, bringing the conversation back to more jolly subjects, such as autumn fashions and speculation as to whether James and Simone would wed. Then Fen took her leave with a meaningful kiss on each cheek and carried Tipper back down the crowded and noisy staircase and out to the street where the lime trees swayed in the autumn breeze.

The last twenty-four hours had certainly been illuminating, but Fen, for all the three acrosses and six downs she was being given, was still no closer to working out who had killed Rose Coillard.

CHAPTER THIRTY-EIGHT

Fen walked slowly back along the Seine from the Marais district and the Bernheims' tiny apartment there. Tipper obediently padded along beside her, sniffing at whatever the pavement had to offer as she walked along the quayside. Her mind was alight with theories and ideas and she tried to make sense of what she had just found out. She spotted an empty bench that overlooked the river and beyond it the Île de la Cité and its most famous landmark, the cathedral church of Notre Dame.

She had to tug Tipper away from a particularly interesting pile of leaves, but he came easily enough and jumped up on her lap. As she sat, she mulled over what Magda had said to her. The Chameleon had betrayed her family at the eleventh hour with devastating and tragic consequences. And yet Rose had been in touch with the younger Bernheims all the while they were in New York. Could Rose have known who The Chameleon was? Perhaps that was the reason for her argument with Lazard on the embankment?

And poor Joseph, finding Rose just as she'd been killed and feeling like he couldn't trust a soul, save his own wife, with the discovery. At least it narrowed down the time of the murder and married up with what James had found out from the countess about Tipper's barking.

Fen fished around in her pocket and pulled out the tatty napkin on which she'd written out her grid. She pulled a pen out of her pocket, too, and instead of writing any more words onto the grid, she circled the word TIPPER.

As if he knew he was being thought about, the little dog pulled at his lead and Fen called him back. 'Tipper, I wish you could talk,' she said as she slipped the napkin back in her pocket. 'But I suppose I'll have to crack this on my own. Come on then, the cathedral bell says it's almost lunchtime. Since I didn't spend all *my* money on going to The Ritz last night, how about I treat us both to some steak?'

The occupation had damaged much of Paris's ways of life, but Fen was relieved to see that the kiosks selling street art and rather dubious 'antiques' were still very much in action along the riverbank. They sold everything from second-hand books and sheet music to bric-a-brac and portraits. Fen had always loved browsing them as a girl and had more often than not found something to spend a few bob on. She walked along now, keeping Tipper to heel as much as possible and idly looked at the wares on sale as she decided on where might be decent for lunch.

One stall along the quayside was selling paintings in various styles. She wasn't quite in the market for the less salubrious etchings of Salome, taken it seemed from a book or portfolio, or the ultra-modern abstract pieces, but then something caught her eye. It was a small painting in oils, beautiful in its pastel colours and Impressionist in style. It depicted a pink blossom tree, its swirling branches created by just a few dashes of powder-pink paint. Fen looked away, then turned back to look at it again. *That was it…* she was sure of it. It was the painting by Delance that, until a few days ago, had hung in Rose's studio. *How did it get here?*

'Excuse me, monsieur,' Fen called the kiosk owner over to her, slightly shaking with indignation and not entirely sure how to broach the subject of the painting's provenance.

The salesman stepped forward and eyed up Fen, and she realised that for once, with her hair tied back in a designer scarf and what looked like her very *à la mode* dog at her side, she might have been mistaken for one of Paris's more wealthy citizens.

'*Oui, mademoiselle?*'

Fen took a deep breath. 'Can you tell me a bit about this painting?'

'It's pretty enough, isn't it? Very nice work for a lady like yourself. Tell you what, I'll give you a good price for it.'

Fen shrugged in the most Gallic way she could muster. 'Could you tell me who it's by?'

'Ooof, now you're asking.' The salesman unhooked the painting from the back of his kiosk and held it up to the daylight. 'Not much of a signature there, it might be hidden behind this backing paper, shame to unseal it to look. Anyway, it's about how it makes you feel, isn't it. Can't get het up about names and such. It's yours for two thousand francs.'

'I don't have that sort of money, and anyway—'

'Eighteen hundred then?' he cajoled.

'Is it by Delance? It looks very similar to another of his works, you see.'

'Like I said, what's in a name, eh? Fifteen hundred? Best and final.' He stuck his hand out to shake on it.

'I'm sorry, no.' Fen backed off away from the hard sell she was receiving but couldn't help but overhear the slightly offensive muttering coming from the vendor as she walked away. 'How rude,' she said to Tipper, who growled a little in reply. When she was quite out of earshot of the kiosk, she spoke to the dog again. 'And how despicable! Rose's painting turning up at a street kiosk like that… Ooh, if I get my hands on whoever sold it…'

Without much to say in return, Tipper just wagged his tail and carried on sniffing everyone and everything he came across, while Fen pondered the consequences of her find. She had to bottle up her instinct to walk right back up to that cretinous man and reclaim the painting on behalf of Rose's estate, stolen as it was; but with no proof on her, she'd just as easily be accused of theft herself. Plus, she didn't want to admit it, but the police might have been right after all… Fencing a painting to a street dealer was much more like something a burglar would do, and not exactly the modus operandi of a murderer.

CHAPTER THIRTY-NINE

Walking all the way to the Marais district and back had been a long enough jaunt for Fen, but it had been positively exhausting for little Tipper, who now insisted on being carried. Fen picked him up and shifted her handbag along her arm so that he could sit comfortably for the last few hundred yards or so. She herself was glad of the exercise, having treated herself to a steak in one of the quayside cafés after her encounter with the kiosk vendor.

Fen opened the large door to the apartment building and fished around in her bag for the spare key Blanquer had given her for the mailbox. She let Tipper slip down and he sniffed around by her feet. The key opened the mailbox up again easily and Fen was almost surprised to see a few more letters addressed to Rose in there. News obviously wasn't travelling that quickly.

She picked them out and gave them a cursory glance. More bills it seemed. Then her heart leapt – a letter addressed to her from England! She pocketed them all and scooped up Tipper before climbing the staircase up to the fifth floor, a new lightness to her step.

Once settled with a hot tea infusion beside her, Fen opened up the letter from home.

Mrs B's kitchen table, Midhurst,
Boring old West Sussex,
October 1945

Dearest Fen,

We got your last letter and all feel terribly sad for you. Poor Rose! With a paintbrush, you say? And blackmail… and a countess dripping in diamonds… lumme, you have had a time of it. No wonder you didn't feel like setting us any more clues. Dilly and I agree with you though, it all definitely sounds suspicious.

Speaking of Dil, she's been and found out some bits and bobs from the library about Arthur's pal James Lancaster. He's proper posh, I mean I hope you've been doffing your cap at his nibs! Larks aside, though, I can see why Arthur wanted you to look out for him. The library in Midhurst had the papers and Dil saw an obituary for not only his father (a Lord Lancaster!) and mother, but an older brother as well and, gosh, this is the saddest, James's fiancée too. He was due to marry the Right Hon Lady Arabella St John. She died in the Blitz with his parents, and his brother, Oliver, was taken in Dunkirk. Sounds like he might need a shoulder to cry on, Fen.

Must dash, Mrs B is still cracking the whip at us. Winter beet is ready to harvest and grumpy old Mr Travers' calves are being weaned, so we've offered (kicked in the seat of our pants more like!) to help.

Cheerio, dear friend, and please come back soon.
Much love from us all,
Kitty xxx

Kitty's letter was a breath of wonderful fresh air – Fen could just imagine her chatty young friend scribbling it among the scones and jam of the farmhouse kitchen table – but it also caused her a pang of sadness too. Poor James. Not only had he lost his family, but, like her, his fiancée, too. *Why hadn't he said?*

Fen folded the letter up, not knowing quite what to do with all the information within it. She was just pondering how best to offer some sort of support to James when Tipper started barking at the door.

'What is it, kiddo?' Fen asked as she pushed herself up and headed towards the hallway. 'Honestly, shush would you? It's not like you haven't had the most outrageous lunch for a little dog. What more can I do for you?'

Fen opened the door, still talking to Tipper, and James answered for him.

'You could stop following him everywhere and spying on him for a start,' he said, but as Fen looked up, she could see a smile playing around the corners of his mouth.

'Oh James, come on in. Yes, I have some explaining to do…'

'It's not that I mind you popping up so unexpectedly when I'm in, let's say, a private moment.'

'Oh, don't remind me!' Fen briefly covered her eyes with her hands and hoped she wasn't blushing too much.

'But if you could do it next time looking less like something dragged from the bottom of the English Channel.'

'How rude!' Fen sat herself down on one of the armchairs and gestured towards the saggier one for James.

He laughed at her. He was in such a good mood she didn't feel it was right just now to bring up the terrible loss of his family. Maybe he had got over Lady Arabella and had some exciting news of his own regarding Simone?

'Tell me, though, what were you doing in my hotel reception last night? Looking like the Kraken?' His eyes twinkled.

'Honestly, James, I wasn't that bad! And anyway, why weren't you at The Ritz like you said you would be?'

'Maître-d' lost our booking. Simone was terribly disappointed, but I've got us a table there next week.'

'Ironed out your worries about her then? Decided not to be a… a "spoon", was it?' Fen wondered if the thought of Lady Arabella had been behind James's reticence with his new girlfriend the other night, and not so much Simone's pushy behaviour.

'Still lion-taming, but she says someone like her would be good for me. Anyway, stop trying to change the subject, Fen,' he cocked his head on one side, and Fen was pleased to see him back to a more playful version of himself.

'I know, I do owe you an explanation. And I'm sorry I interrupted your little *tête-à-tête*. But, you see, the thing is, I was there because I was following Henri Renaud.'

'I see,' James sat forward, his elbows on his knees and his fingers making a steeple in front of him. 'But what were you doing following Monsieur Renaud in the first place.'

'It was terribly badly behaved of me, and I had to grovel to poor Magda this morning, but you see I caught sight of him on my way over to visit her last night, and I saw he was carrying a package that looked very much like a painting wrapped up in brown paper and tied with string.'

'Hmm, highly suspicious for an art dealer.'

'Sarcasm is the lowest form of wit, James.' Fen tutted and sat back in the chair. 'It was long after gallery opening hours. Perhaps that's why I thought it so odd.'

'And did Magda forgive you?' James asked, more seriously now.

'Yes, the darling, she did. And she told me something very interesting. Joseph was here, in this apartment, just after Rose had died. He found her body before we did.'

'What?' James looked startled and shifted in his chair.

'He let himself in, he was due an appointment anyway and you know she never locked the door. He said Tipper barked like billy-o, but he couldn't bring himself to call the police.'

'Why on earth not? If he had, it would have spared you the—'

Fen raised a hand to shush him. 'Don't worry about me. And you have to understand, the authorities haven't exactly been just and fair to Joseph and his family these last few years. And before you start pondering, no, he wouldn't have killed her. He had no motive and was rather shaken up, by all accounts.'

'Agreed,' James rubbed his chin. 'And it explains Tsarina, and the countess, hearing Tipper bark.'

'Yes, but it doesn't explain why Tipper *didn't* bark.'

'I thought we just agreed that he did?'

'At Joseph, yes…' They both looked at the little dog who was curled up in a ball, snoring gently on the chaise longue. Fen thought for a moment and then shook her head, '… But not at the murderer.'

CHAPTER FORTY

Fen and James sat in silence for a few more moments, both watching Tipper's chest rise and fall, dreaming small doggy dreams.

'She couldn't have killed herself, could she?' James volunteered, acting out stabbing himself in the neck.

'I don't think so. She had so much to live for – a mission. And anyway, she couldn't have then stolen her own jewels and paintings? Oh, speaking of which, James, you'll never guess what I saw on the way back from Magda's!'

James raised his eyebrows and Fen carried on.

'In one of those shabby street kiosks…' she pointed to the empty patch of the wall where the Delance had once hung. 'Rose's favourite painting.'

'Really?' James sat forward, interested.

'Really. And the dealer wanted fifteen hundred francs for it! I was spitting feathers.'

'Did you ask him where he got it from?'

James's question embarrassed Fen and she blushed. 'No, I mean, I asked if it was by Delance and he gave me some spiel about not caring about names, but then I, no… well, I was just a bit too angry to really think straight.'

'Fen, don't worry. We can go back and ask him. No one's expecting you to be a super sleuth. But still, it's another three down for you perhaps?'

Just as James had leaned over and briefly touched Fen's knee to reassure her, the peace in the apartment was shattered by a clattering sound at the front door. Moments later, Simone appeared in the studio in complete disarray, her beautiful silk skirt torn and ripped, her hands scratched and bloodied as she clasped her blouse to her, as there were no buttons in place any more to wear it properly.

James drew his hand back from Fen and pushed himself up from the old saggy armchair. He was by Simone's side in an instant and helped her back to the chaise longue. Fen too had jumped out of her seat and moved out of the way for the pair of them to get through. Tipper, who hadn't been fazed when Simone had first appeared, was now yapping in excitement, picking up on the atmosphere in the room.

'Dear God,' James released his arm from Simone as she sat down on the chaise. 'Are you all right? What happened to you?'

'I was attacked… I was mobbed… by—'

'By who? Who did this?'

James's interruption didn't stop Simone from repeating over and over, 'I was attacked…'

Fen found a shawl on the back of the armchair and handed it to the girl. 'Here, Simone, take this.' The younger woman was still in a trance-like state of shock. 'James, here, you put it around her so the poor thing can let go of her blouse. And I'll go and make tea.'

'Lots of sugar,' James added.

'Yes, of course. And a shot of brandy, I think.'

By the time the kettle started to whistle, Fen noticed that Simone had progressed from shocked mumblings to full-on tears. She couldn't begrudge her the waterworks, it sounded and looked like she'd had a rough old afternoon.

She filled the silver teapot, using whatever tea she could find in one of the caddies in the kitchen. *Lapsang souchong, perhaps…* The smokiness of the brew brought back memories suddenly of being in this apartment before… Before Rose was murdered, before she was embroiled once again in finding out what happened to someone she cared about. Not to mention poor Gervais too.

'Here you are,' she brought the tea and three cups into the studio room.

Simone was now huddled up in James's arms, a pose Fen was becoming more and more familiar with.

Fen let the tea brew for a few moments longer before saying *sotto voce* to James, 'Anything?'

James shook his head, and then carefully pushed Simone away from him slightly so that she could accept Fen's proffered cup of tea.

'Simone, dear, can you bring yourself to tell us yet?'

'Yes, I think so.' She pursed her lips and blew across the teacup to cool it slightly. 'It's not too sweet, is it? I mustn't have too much sugar,' she said.

'It's quite sweet, dear, but you need it right now.' Fen urged her to drink while thinking, *Now is not the time to worry about your waistline.* 'So, can you tell us what happened to you? I know it's hard, but you're safe now.'

'Oh it was horrible, horrible. Today was meant to be so fun, you know? A fashion shoot on the Right Bank of the river, just me and Carmella from accounts, who is very beautiful – not versatile like me, you know, but very thin and her bone structure is… Anyway…' She cautiously sipped the hot tea and then carried on, 'We were posing for the photographer, you know how the light is so good in the afternoon and the autumn leaves are so, how would you say, *romantique*.' She playfully twiddled a hand in the air to mimic the falling leaves, before becoming serious again. 'Then the shouts started, then there were catcalls and shrieks and then there was a mob of them…'

'Bloody ruffians, how dare they attack two women just doing their job. I mean, talk about lowest of the low. If I find those men—'

'They weren't men…' As Simone said those words, it was Fen and James's turn to fall into a shocked silence. 'It was women. All women.'

'What do you mean?' James was flabbergasted.

'I think she means that it wasn't an attack like we might think, but more of a… protest?' Fen eked out the last word, testing the water.

'A protest against what?' James asked.

'Against the clothes.' Fen turned to Simone. 'Isn't that right? You mentioned something like this happening to you before. Up near Montmartre?'

Simone just nodded and raised a handkerchief to her eye. 'It's just jealousy, they're just jealous.'

'Sadly,' Fen sat back in her chair, relieved to have cracked one small puzzle at least, 'I don't think it's *just* jealousy. I'm sorry, Simone, and please don't take this the wrong way, or think that I agree with them, but it's rather pushing their buttons, isn't it?'

'Whose buttons? What have buttons got to do with it?' James was still confused. He just couldn't get his head around the fact that women could be so violent.

'You know, psychological buttons. These women, these *Parisiennes*, have been through so much during the occupation. Rationing, shortages of food, clothes, life's essentials. There's a feeling that too much of a good thing is just too much, full stop.'

'But I am the future!' Simone rebuffed Fen's words. 'The war is over and we should look to tomorrow, you know?'

'I know, I know. And perhaps you're right and maybe it is mostly jealousy from the other women. But—'

'No. No "but".' Simone seemed to be more in a huff now than scared or upset. 'This is my life and I shall wear what I like. Catherine didn't risk her life and end up in Ravensbrück for us all to wear sackcloth for the rest of time. You'll both see, Christian will start his own atelier and the clothes will be fabulous and luxurious and I shall be wearing them.' She sounded nothing less than triumphant and all Fen could do was nod and sip her tea and let the young woman, ably supported by James's strong arms and words of reassurance, settle down.

A little while later Fen stirred the pot of bean cassoulet on the stove as James rested his back against the wall of the galley-style kitchen. She had picked up some simple cooking tips from her hostess in Burgundy a few weeks ago, and although that sojourn had ended in a murderer being brought to justice, it had also left Fen with a new appreciation for simple French cooking.

After she had drawn Simone a nice steaming bath to help her forget the trauma of being set upon, she had sent James out to see if he could find a grocer still open to pick up some items she could cobble a supper together from. James had returned with some canned goods and half a pound of good herby sausages from the local butcher who was just closing up for the day.

'I either caught him at the right time or wrong time, depending on your viewpoint,' he had reported back to Fen.

'Meaning?'

'Good in that I got a very keen price on the bangers and he threw in those lardons too. Bad in that they were practically the only things left, so sorry if you fancied gammon or lamb tonight instead.'

Fen had laughed and taken the waxed paper parcel of meat from James. 'This will do very well, James, thank you.'

So she had started to cook and soon enough Simone had emerged from the bathroom and got herself dressed. She was in the studio room and Fen could imagine that James felt slightly torn as to which room he should be in. Fen was about to put him out of his misery and claim he was getting under her feet in the kitchen when he brought up the subject of the painting again.

'How much did you say that street vendor was charging for the Delance?' he asked.

'Two thousand francs at first. That's about three pounds! He came down to fifteen hundred as I kept telling him I wasn't interested.'

'He might have given it to you for nothing if you'd kept playing that game,' James joked, but Fen just shook her head at him.

Simone appeared around the kitchen door, a pretty shawl draped around her slim frame, covering the peasant-style blouse she had dressed in, along with a simple floor-length skirt, after her bath.

'What are you two talking about in here?'

'That painting of Rose's,' James explained, 'The little Impressionist one. Fen's found it for sale on the Right Bank of the river.'

'Oh really?' Simone looked interested.

'I'm pretty sure, yes. This apartment was like a second home to me when I was younger, I'm sure I'd recognise those swirls and colours anywhere.'

'How macabre, to find something of Rose's so soon after…' Simone couldn't finish her sentence. Her eyes filled with tears and she dabbed the corner of one with the edge of her shawl. 'Was it expensive? Could we afford to buy it back, do you think?'

'Out of my reach, sadly.' Fen sighed and stirred the pot.

'I could buy it for you…' James pushed himself off the wall and stood up straight.

'Oh, James, that really is awfully kind, but I couldn't possibly accept—'

'Ah, well, I meant Simone… sorry, Fen.' James looked a bit awkward and pushed his fingers through his sandy-blond hair a couple of times. He smiled apologetically to Fen and shrugged, then turned back to Simone. 'If you'd like it?'

'You would do that for me?' Simone looked at him, her eyes still glistening with tears and her hands clasped up to her chest.

Fen accidentally dropped the wooden spoon on the floor. 'Oops, sorry.' She nudged James out of the way as she picked it up and carried it over to the sink.

'Well, there we go,' James seemed pleased with himself, the awkwardness of just a moment ago gone. 'We can go there tomorrow morning if the fine weather holds. That would cheer you up, wouldn't it?'

Both James and Fen were a little shocked when Simone stammered and started to cry. 'Oh, no… no… I can't go back. I mean, in that direction. The memories of this afternoon…' She clutched the shawl around her some more and shivered. 'Please don't make me cross the river by that quayside. It's too embarrassing to think that those men, those kiosk vendors, might have seen me so… so vulnerable.' She shuddered.

James reached a hand over to her shoulder to reassure her. 'Of course, of course. I'll take Fen, she can show me which one it is…' James followed Simone into the studio, comforting her as he went.

Fen rinsed the wooden spoon off in the sink and let out another sigh. She would have loved to have bought that painting, but at least if James bought it for Simone it would be back in its rightful home, in this apartment. For the time being anyway.

Supper was delightful and the sausages really were a treat and so unlike the wartime 'bangers' that had popped and spurted in Mrs B's greasy frying pan. The meat content in some sausages from as far back as the Great War had been so low and the water content so high that the sausages often exploded if left too long to sizzle over a high heat, hence the term 'banger'. These sausages, however, were more like the ones from Toulouse, filled with pork meat and bulked up with herbs and spices. They were delicious, but that didn't stop Simone from picking at her plate. Fen couldn't bear waste so was pleased when James stuck his fork in Simone's untouched sausage and devoured it in two or three bites.

Simone herself didn't even notice, and although Fen and James had tried to keep the conversation light and their spirits as high as possible in the recent circumstances, it was only when James started talking about the previous evening that she fully entered into the conversation.

'And it wasn't just *you* that surprised us last night,' he said, nudging Simone, who was staring at the floor where Rose's body had lain.

'Hmm, no that's right.'

'Oh really? Do tell, and I hope they weren't as sopping wet as I was.'

'Well,' Simone seemed more with it now and gave Fen her full attention, 'oddly enough, it was Michel Lazard. You know that art dealer of Rose's.'

'That is bizarre,' Fen agreed, and as James and Simone talked about the other people they'd seen in the hotel bar, Fen thought how interesting it was that Simone had seen Lazard in the very same place that Henri had led her to. 'Did you see Henri Renaud, just before I came in?'

'No, Fenella, but then, before you charged in last night, we only had eyes for each other.'

'Right. Quite so. Of course.' Fen felt a bit flustered and busied herself picking up the plates so that she could remove herself from the lovebirds and have some space to think in the kitchen. Something wasn't adding up, that was for sure. It was as if she was being given all the clues she could wish for, but all mixed up. What could it mean, Henri Renaud possibly meeting Michel Lazard in private at a hotel? What had Henri been carrying and why did he lie to her so often about his relationship with the art dealer he himself said was a charlatan?

CHAPTER FORTY-ONE

The next day was bright if a little blustery, which meant that James and Fen's plan of visiting the quayside art dealer could go ahead. Simone had insisted the night before that even if the thought of heading towards the Right Bank hadn't given her the shivers, she should really head back to the atelier for a debrief on the disastrous photo shoot. Expensive clothes had been ruined and no doubt the police would be called. So it had been agreed, as James had bid the ladies farewell that night, that he would call for Fen the next day and the two of them would head over the river and buy back the painting that had been stolen from Rose.

'I suppose,' Fen said as she tightened the fashionable scarf around her neck a little more to keep off the chill wind as she and James crossed the Pont des Arts, 'we could just tell the gendarmes that we've located some stolen artwork and it could help them trace the murderer?'

'We could… but then it would be confiscated as evidence and end up locked in some police station for evermore, or worse, end up in the undeserving hands of some crooked police inspector.'

'Well, when you put it like that…' Fen was unsure if James really believed what he was saying, or if he was just talking himself into thinking he was doing the right thing. It was admirable that he wanted to buy a piece of Rose's estate back for Simone, even if Fen was secretly rather jealous that she couldn't afford it herself.

'Tell you what is interesting though,' James cut across her thoughts.

'Oh yes?'

'When I got back to my hotel last night, guess who I saw in the reception area?'

'Henri Renaud again?' Fen glanced across at James as the wind caught both of their hair in a mad twirling dance.

'Bingo. He didn't notice me, even though he was sitting by the bar with another man.'

'Who?'

'That Lazard chap. They were talking about a meeting at four o'clock this afternoon.'

'A handover perhaps?' Fen remembered the brown paper-covered parcel she'd seen Henri carrying.

'The man is an art dealer, after all.'

'Yes… not one that Henri *usually* deals with though…' Fen was deep in thought still when they arrived at the kiosk where she had spotted Rose's painting. James nudged her back into the present and she pointed it out to him.

'I recognise it, you're right,' he agreed with her, but kept his voice down in case the dealer could hear. 'What price did he offer it to you at yesterday?'

'Fifteen hundred by the time he really wanted me to clear off.'

'Mademoiselle,' the art dealer appeared from behind his stand, his voice making them both jump, 'have you come to buy this time?'

James interceded and started negotiations, which they were surprised to find out started much higher than Fen had assumed.

'Well,' the dealer argued. 'There's been more interest in it since I last saw you, mademoiselle, and look, you are back with your young gentleman to buy it for you, too.'

'What tosh,' Fen harrumphed as James haggled him down from an overinflated three thousand francs, finally handing over two thousand francs for the painting. 'You should have held out, James. I swear he was just stringing you a line.'

'I don't mind. Rather him than me standing out here in all weathers selling tat. A few extra francs is no skin off my nose but might pay his rent for a few more weeks.'

Fen felt slightly chastised and walked a few steps ahead as James waited for the dealer to wrap the painting up in brown paper and string. James's generosity paid off too as the dealer, when handing over the package, slipped James a few postcards.

'These are rather, er, risqué, thank you,' James stammered as he poked the postcards into his coat pocket.

'Always popular with my gentleman customers,' the vendor winked, and Fen shook her head as James blushed slightly. Then she remembered the other reason for their visit and turned back to join James and the kiosk owner.

'Just out of interest, from whom did you buy that painting? Have you had it long?'

'*Eh, la...*' the vendor took his cap off and scratched his head. 'A day, two days perhaps.'

'And your supplier?' Fen wondered if she'd used the right word. It had been hard not to say 'fence'. But the vendor must have read between the lines and turned his back on Fen and James and started to pull down the shutters of his stall. Fen was about to ask him again when he turned around and spoke to them.

'It was a young man, I think, it was hard to see.'

'How can you be sure it wasn't stolen from someone?' Fen couldn't help it, the thought of all the stolen art, sold just like this but on a greater scale. The buyers not questioning where their new purchases had come from. With the Germans doing the thieving for you, how easy it must have been to get your hands on paintings you had only ever dreamed of owning...

'I must close now, the painting is yours, thank you for your custom.' The street vendor turned his back on them, saying the words quickly and mechanically and not answering Fen's question at all, and continued locking up his stall. Fen wanted to quiz him and opened her mouth to ask him the question again but before she could speak she felt James's hand on her arm.

'Fen,' he whispered to her. 'It doesn't matter now. *We* know where the painting is from, no point pushing him. I don't think we'd get much more out of him anyway.'

Fen looked at where the two-bit art dealer was shaking the padlock on his shuttered stall, checking it was locked, and then half ran, half skipped off down the quayside before they could ask any more questions.

They were almost halfway back across the Seine when Fen, who had been mulling things over as they'd walked, spoke.

'James, would you do me a favour?'

'Of course.'

'Could you bring Simone to Henri's gallery this afternoon, at four o'clock.'

James stopped on the bridge and looked at Fen. 'I could…'

'And could you possibly find Antoine Arnault and bring him there too?'

'Fen…' There was a tone of warning in James's voice.

'Trust me, I think I know what I'm doing. I need to check one more thing, and then I'll meet you there.'

'Be careful, Fen, whatever it is you think you know, there is one thing that's certain. There's a murderer out there who's killed two people already—'

'And I don't want to be the third, believe me. That's why I need you all there. Galerie Renaud, at four o'clock.' She caught James's eye and he nodded at her.

'Me, Simone and Antoine Arnault.'

'Yes. And I'll make a few phone calls too.'

They neared the end of the bridge and James took his leave. 'Be careful, Fen.'

'I'm not the one who's taming lions, James.' She winked at him. 'Four o'clock, don't be late!'

CHAPTER FORTY-TWO

Bronzed and curled leaves decorated the pavement as Fen crossed Paris, darting under the shelter of a café awning every now and again to avoid a downpour. She didn't mind, however, as she was pleased with a certain piece of information she had picked up. A written testimony no less, that was now securely in her trench coat pocket. Alibi or not, she was surer than ever over the guilt of one particular person.

She was thinking it through in her mind as she approached the Marais district and found the entrance to Joseph and Magda's apartment building. Fen climbed the staircase, picking her way between children playing games. She made her excuses each time and squeezed past, until she was at the Bernheims' door. Before she knocked, she took a few breaths and looked at her grid again. 'Tipper… and the blackmail… of course, the warehouse would be vital… those auctions… and who says they're degenerate…'

More confident now in her own mind, she knocked on the Bernheims' door.

A few moments of quick explanation later and all three of them were on their way back down the staircase, picking their feet carefully over complicated games constructed of string and sticks, and apologising to languid youths, driven inside due to the rain and wind.

'Are you sure Monsieur Renaud won't mind us suddenly appearing without an appointment?' Magda had worried as they walked briskly from the Marais towards the Palais du Jardin and Galerie Renaud.

'He's helping you find your artwork, isn't he?' Fen replied, asking the question semi-rhetorically. Henri had told her in no uncertain terms that he could no longer help the Bernheims, but they didn't know that, not yet.

The rain had really started to fall when the Bernheims and Fen reached the shelter of the colonnade of the Palais du Jardin. Fen felt a pang of guilt bringing the couple to an area of Paris that was once so accessible to them, but now the fancy goods in the shop windows were temptation far beyond what they could afford. *Never mind, almost there…* Galerie Renaud was in sight.

'Are you sure it's open, Fenella?' Magda asked, seeing the blackout blinds drawn down across the main window and the glass of the door.

'Let's see, shall we?' Fen pushed the door open, and the tinkling of the bell made the two men, deep in conversation either side of the desk, turn their heads to face the incomers.

'Fenella, and the Bernheims, what a surprise.' Henri stood to greet them.

The other man turned to face the other way, and Fen noticed his hands rub up and down his thighs; he was agitated, that was for sure.

'Monsieur Lazard here was just about to leave.' Henri gestured for Michel Lazard to stand, and without looking Fen or the Bernheims in the eye, he started to move towards them to get to the door.

'Actually, Henri, I was wondering if we might have a word with both of you. Monsieur Lazard, I don't think you know me, but I'm a great friend of Rose Coillard… and here to tell everyone who murdered her.'

'Well, it wasn't me!' Lazard looked even more nervous, a sweaty sheen appearing on his forehead.

'Mademoiselle, please, manners,' Henri looked stern and Fen wondered if his tolerance of her scheme would last long enough for her to reveal the murderer.

'I'm so sorry, Henri, please excuse me,' she hammed it up. 'Speaking of manners, would there be a chair at least for Madame Bernheim? I can stand, although… Ah, hello, chaps.' Fen ushered the Bernheims further into the gallery as James, Simone and Antoine Arnault appeared at the door. 'Bang on time, well done.'

'Mademoiselle Churche, please explain yourself to me!' Henri, having fetched a chair for Magda, was now looking more and more put out. 'What are you all doing here?'

Fen looked him in the eye and said, 'They're all here, Henri, to uncover the truth.'

'Safety in numbers, eh, Fen?' James whispered as he moved behind her. With all eight of them now squeezed into the relatively small space, it wasn't claustrophobic as such, but there was a frisson in the air. Henri was sitting now behind his desk and Michel Lazard had moved his chair around so that he was sitting at more of an angle. Magda was seated too, opposite Lazard, and Joseph was standing behind her, his hands gently laid on her shoulders.

Fen stood close to Michel Lazard and could now take in at close quarters his slicked-back hair, very much like that of a matinee idol, and his thin moustache, which was neatly twizzled into pointed ends. He could definitely pass as a young man in a certain light… Next to Fen stood James, who had moved in protectively from the corner of the gallery, with Simone hovering behind him, looking every inch the naïve innocent. Antoine Arnault was the final player in the tableau, his bald head illuminated by the gallery lighting, and he completed the semicircle around the desk by standing between Simone and the Bernheims.

'Will you explain yourself now, Fenella?' Henri asked, taking his glasses off and giving them a long and drawn-out wipe with his handkerchief.

'Yes. Bear with me, as there's a bit to get through, but I'm pretty sure that one of us here in this room murdered my dear friend Rose and Antoine's brother, Gervais.'

'Gervais Arnault was caught up in all sort of underground dealings,' protested Henri. 'He was nicknamed "The Wrench", for heaven's sake. How can you link the two murders?'

Fen noticed Antoine shifting his weight from foot to foot. Perhaps he didn't like hearing his brother slandered, or perhaps the allegation stung as it was all too true. 'They were linked. Rose was being blackmailed by Gervais.' As Fen spoke, there was a murmur through the room.

'Why was this Gervais fellow blackmailing Rose?' Joseph Bernheim asked, while Fen fished around in her pocket and retrieved the now very scruffy napkin on which she'd been writing out her crossword-style grid.

'Henri might want to answer that,' Fen replied, 'as Gervais was blackmailing him too.'

Henri replaced his glasses and then opened his desk drawer. 'It's true, I was being blackmailed. But there was nothing in it. Here, the note is the same as the one you said Rose received.'

Henri passed it to Fen, who quickly scanned it, noting that it was written on the same blue writing paper as they found in the garage.

Henri continued, 'You see, Gervais, was after a quick buck or two, I should imagine. He was speculating. Who knows how many other dignitaries he was sending these notes to? One in ten might yield him a franc or so to cover a guilty conscience, but not me. And I told Rose to ignore it too.'

Fen nodded, then turned to the other art dealer in the room. 'Someone does have a guilty conscience, though, isn't that right, Monsieur Lazard?'

Michel Lazard looked up at Fen as if she'd just struck him. 'Me? I didn't kill Rose! And I barely knew Gervais. *I* wasn't being blackmailed!'

'No, but you were getting Rose into considerable trouble, selling her beautiful homages as forgeries. I saw you both arguing on the Pont des Arts the day before she was murdered. Did she threaten to turn you in to the authorities?'

'On the Ponts des Arts? Ah, no, no, no. Arguing? No, you see, Rose and I had a wonderful business relationship and what you saw would have just been a healthy debate.'

'A healthy debate?' Fen couldn't help but dislike the man, cause as he was of most of Rose's troubles before she died.

'Yes…' he drew the word out and then licked his lips as he was thinking. 'It's true that she was cross with me for perhaps over-marketing her paintings, but we reached an agreement. And, mademoiselle, I can assure you, I would not kill her!' Lazard had started to sweat a little and he quickly wiped his forehead with a spotted handkerchief.

'I know,' Fen grudgingly had to agree with him. 'To you, she was the goose that laid the golden eggs. Killing her would be the death of your own very lucrative business.'

Lazard looked relieved and slumped back in his chair.

'Mademoiselle Churche,' Antoine interrupted. 'Why have you dragged me here? I had no motive either! One of the dead was my own brother!'

'And don't you want to know who killed him?'

'Of course, I—'

'Unless the method, a single gunshot wound, at night in his dark garage, rings any bells with you?'

'The potshots in the warehouse…' James chimed in.

'Exactly. We know you have your own weapon and we know you can shoot a target in the dark, and we also know that you and your brother were involved with Rose's scheme during the war.'

'Why would I kill my own brother?' Antoine was getting quite irate and the words were all but spat out at Fen and the gathered suspects. 'We worked as a team, we risked our lives storing those paintings in Henri's warehouse, we risked them even more chalking up Rose's code on the back of them. You've got a screw loose, you have. Hey, and don't forget, I have an alibi for Rose's murder, you know that. I was in the warehouse on the other side of town when she was killed.'

'Antoine, you're right,' Fen said, noticing that James had already clasped a hand on the warehouse manager's shoulder, whether to stop him from fleeing or to calm him down she didn't know.

'I'm just a warehouse manager, I've got nothing to do with these murders.' Antoine shrugged his shoulders and James let go of his grasp on him.

'I'm sorry, Antoine,' Fen said, as calmly and in as measured a way as possible, 'but what happened in that warehouse during the war has *everything* to do with Rose's murder, and your brother's, and here's why…'

CHAPTER FORTY-THREE

'Before I came here, before I collected Joseph and Magda from the Marais, I visited Valentine Valreas at his auction house to the north of the city.'

There was an audible groan from Lazard.

'Yes, you're not his favourite person, Monsieur Lazard, but that's not why I went or what I need to tell you all. When I met him at the party you very kindly invited me to, Henri, he was as cross as two sticks when I mentioned Rose's name. But he did say something that occurred to me later. He mentioned that he had "sent her packing, never to darken his door again with her fakes", but also that she had come on some sort of errand, an "excuse" he called it. I went to visit him to ask what that excuse was, and he told me.'

'Are we nearly done with this, Fenella?' Henri asked, shuffling some of the papers on his desk. 'I really would like you all to leave now.'

'In some ways, I'm only just getting started – sorry, Henri. But you might like to take a look at this.' Fen reached into her pocket and pulled out the signed testimony from Valreas. 'He is willing to testify that you, Henri Renaud, came to him to ask a favour.'

'And what was that?' James asked, trying to peer over Fen's shoulder and read the statement.

'Apparently, Henri here asked Valentine to "sell" at auction several paintings for him, paintings that had been stolen from the Jewish families.'

Henri sighed and gave Fen a withering look. 'As I have explained before, the Germans weren't interested in what they called the degenerate art, so they wanted many of the paintings sold and the funds sent back to Berlin for their war effort. I was merely carrying out orders, despicable as they were. You think Rose would have got away with her coded list if I hadn't been so good at seemingly going along with Herr Müller and his team?'

'I know all of that. Except that paintings by Degas, Cezanne and Gainsborough certainly weren't classed as "degenerate", were they? They should have gone straight to Berlin or the new Führermuseum that was being talked of, or dare I say it, to the Eagle's Nest itself.'

'Gainsborough…' Joseph said and whispered something to Magda. Fen caught his eye and nodded to him.

'Well, perhaps I made the odd mistake…' Henri stared at Fen.

'There was no mistake.' Fen fixed Henri with a steely glare. 'Valentine Valreas is willing to go on record to say that not only did you ask him to consign those paintings to auction, but you asked him to rig the sale so that you bought them back at far below their market rate. To all intents and purposes, they were fake lots. Once you had bought them back, for peanuts, you could sell them, or keep them. Your theft had been legitimised, without anyone knowing and certainly without incurring the wrath of the Germans.'

'You mean our paintings were never sent to Germany?' Joseph asked.

'I think some of them were, I'm sorry to say. But Henri traded on the fact that the overseeing Nazi officers here in Paris couldn't tell a Cezanne from a Christmas card and would do no more than glance at a list of paintings, bowing down to Henri's superior knowledge, and rubber-stamp the list. Rose herself said they were remarkably trusting at times.'

'This is preposterous!' Henri stood up and thumped his fist on the desk.

'Sadly, it's not. Valentine Valreas also put a call into Claude Leflavre for me.' Fen took her eyes off Henri and explained to the rest of the room, 'He's one of the patrons of the Louvre who Henri introduced me to.' She looked back at Henri, who was looking exceedingly uncomfortable. 'He confirmed that he was very happy with the Degas you sold him. "You've brought me another dancer", do you remember Claude saying that to me when I met him at the Louvre? He was alluding, of course, to Degas's favourite subject matter of ballerinas, and one of the paintings you'd stolen and then sold to him, no doubt for a small fortune.'

'Where's the proof, eh? He said this, they said that... you could be spinning lies!' Henri looked agitated.

'Henri, the game is up,' Fen said, as gently as she could, aware Henri could make another, more deadly, sudden move. 'Rose discovered that you had stolen paintings from your own warehouse and, under the noses of the Nazis as well as her and the Arnault brothers, sold them. But she only guessed at it once she'd received the list back from you and started decoding it. She had stopped at the Bernheim Cezanne and it must have looked very strange to her, someone who did know her artists, to see written in German next to it "for auction". She knew full well that that sort of painting would have been on the next train out of town.'

Fen glanced down at her grid and then continued, 'When she told you about the blackmail letter and you showed her you had one too, far from reassuring her that it was just a speculative shot in the dark, she realised the blackmailer was only speculating between you two. They had narrowed it down to Henri or Rose as the only two who would have been able to manipulate the list like that, and were just trying to flush out the right person. And she sure as hell knew that she wasn't responsible for stealing from the Jewish families. I think she confronted you with all of this, and you killed her.'

'What rot! I told you that on the day of the murder I was here, on the telephone, negotiating with a dealer in London about some watercolours.'

'Impossible to check...' James whispered to Fen, 'unless you did?'

'I haven't checked up on your alibi, no. But I don't buy it. And here's why. You also claimed never to have heard of The Chameleon, even though you were in the Resistance. Plus, as a trusted friend of Rose's, Tipper wouldn't bark at you coming to the door, and we know Tipper only barked once that afternoon.'

'At me.' Joseph nodded.

'The evidence of Tsarina...' James concurred.

'Exactly. The countess's Persian cat only noticed Tipper barking when Joseph came to visit, and that was *after* Rose was murdered. You've told me before that you knew that she never locked her front door and you also knew that someone as principled as Rose would never let you get away with the thefts of those artworks.'

'As I said,' Henri tried to look nonplussed as he shuffled more papers around his desk, 'I was on the telephone at two o'clock.'

'How did you know she was killed at two o'clock?' Fen asked Henri, and every other pair of eyes in the room followed her gaze as she looked at the accused. 'Henri...' Fen held his gaze. 'Are you The Chameleon?'

In an instant, Henri was standing. 'I have alibis, I made sure of it...'

'You've made sure of it?' Then Fen followed up more gently, aware that Henri was unravelling in front of them, 'You killed them, didn't you, Henri? Rose and Gervais?'

'For the paintings, do you see? The paintings...' Henri looked crazed all of a sudden 'I had to have them. They couldn't go to *Germany*, to those *philistines*. Gainsborough and Cezanne, Degas and Matisse! Masterpieces! Do you know what Müller said, the imbecile? "Pretty little things, aren't they?" Pretty? How could we let them have them? They'd treat them like wallpaper! But Rose would never understand, oh she would want those paintings back for the Jews, but they're mine now, you see… and she was so close to finding out… she had to die…'

He turned to look at Fen and suddenly she realised. 'Henri—'

'I didn't kill them, not by my own hand, but—'

All of a sudden, darkness enveloped them, the bright, picture-illuminating lights had been turned off and barely any daylight could make it through the blackout blinds. There were shocked gasps and then Fen saw Henri's face illuminated by a single, bright torch beam. Then darkness again and the room reverberated with a volley of gunshots.

CHAPTER FORTY-FOUR

Pandemonium reigned for what seemed like minutes, though it must have only been a second or so. Fen tried to get her bearings in the dark, while nursing her eardrum that must have been only inches away from the crack of the pistol shots that had rung out among them. Trust Henri to have drawn his blackout blinds before his meeting with Lazard – the privacy they had afforded them then was now cloaking the gallery in darkness.

Ears ringing, but eyes growing more accustomed to the dark, she felt her way along the wall, feeling the cool of the painted plaster under her fingers until she found a light switch. Click. The room was illuminated again and the scene that met her was one of utter horror. Henri had been gunned down where he had stood, his blood, and who knew what else, spread across the pristine white of the gallery wall behind him.

Lazard was on his knees, collapsed to the floor from his chair, but alive and unhurt, while Antoine was clutching his ears. He must have been inches from the shooter too. James was on the floor, but gradually coming up to standing. Fen offered him her hand and he was just about upright, shaking his head as if to dislodge something from his ears too, when Fen heard Joseph Bernheim shout out.

'Magda! Where is she?'

'Simone...' James looked around. Both of the women were gone and Fen realised that the chill breeze that was blowing a few damp autumn leaves into the gallery came from the open doorway.

'Quick, James!' Fen pulled him along with her and they left the gallery behind them, running down the colonnade.

'Look, there!' James had spotted two bodies lying on the ground at the end of the passage. In a few seconds, they were there with them, James strides ahead of Fen by now. She slowed as she saw him pull Simone off Magda, loosening the young model's grip from around the older woman's throat.

'I'd have been paid more if you'd died with your parents,' Simone was hissing at Magda.

'Simone!' James pulled her fully off Magda and held her against one of the columns.

'Magda, oh Magda, are you all right?' Fen fell to her knees beside her friend and, seconds later, Joseph was there too, comforting his wife. 'What happened?'

Through gasps of breath, Magda explained that she'd seen Simone fire the gun, her face lit briefly by the torch, and had run out of the gallery after her. By dashing after her into the late-afternoon drizzle and tripping Simone up, Magda had thwarted the killer.

Thoughts started falling into place and Fen spoke them out loud, as much to get it clear in her own head as to help the others piece it together. 'Simone, I was wrong, *you're* the murderer, aren't you? And The Chameleon!'

Simone struggled against James's arm, which was still holding her securely against the pillar. 'James, why won't you defend me? Why are you letting her accuse me like this?'

James just shook his head. 'Fen,' he said, his voice a little croaky. 'Carry on.'

Fen nodded, stood up and then looked back at Simone. 'I wasn't wrong about Henri though, was I? Except he wasn't actually the murderer. You are. You were his weapon.'

Simone rolled her eyes and then raised her eyebrows, inviting Fen to continue, if she dared. She did.

'You've told me enough times that you would do anything not to be poor again. How much was he paying you?' Fen's question was met with silence. 'I see,' she realised. 'It wasn't money. Ah… the apartment. You hardly seemed shocked at all when I said he'd agreed that we could stay on. You knew all the time that the apartment, and everything in it, would be your pay cheque.'

Simone struggled against James, but it was him, rather than Fen this time, who told her to stay still.

Fen continued to join the clues she'd noticed over the last few days together. 'Tipper doesn't bark at you. And Henri knew you had the stomach to kill, you were in the Resistance after all and had led many a Nazi officer to their death.'

'But Rose wasn't killed with a gun,' James took over, adding in his own thoughts to Fen's deductions.

'No…' Fen agreed. 'Mid-afternoon in a residential area… the weapon had to be quieter than that. Or more *improvised* perhaps. The countess's cat, Tsarina, got in a pickle over Tipper's barking at exactly the time we know that Joseph was calling to see Rose. You were already back in the apartment with her, though. And as soon as you heard him yapping, you knew you had to kill Rose quickly and quietly as whoever was approaching would more than likely let themselves in.'

'Did Rose not think it odd that Simone was home from work?' Magda had recovered her voice, though was still huddled on the ground in the arms of her husband.

Fen nodded and looked back at Simone. 'Possibly, though I don't think she suspected Simone at all. Your employer, on the other hand….' Fen paused, and rubbed her temples to help her think.

'What is it? James asked.

'Just something Christian said about you, Simone, that you were always "popping out to see James", though it wasn't so much James *as murder* you had on your mind those times, wasn't it? Anyway, you had the perfect opportunity to get as close as you needed to drive that paintbrush through Rose's throat without her even suspecting, right up until it was far too late.'

Simone just snorted in a derisory way and Fen felt that, far from denying the murder, she was almost itching to add in her own details.

Fen carried on while the stage was hers. 'You then hid in your bedroom, hoping that the visitor would go away, and luckily for you Joseph barely poked his nose in.'

'I thought I'd heard voices… I should have searched the apartment,' Joseph lamented but was quickly and kindly shushed by his wife. They were hugging each other tightly, Joseph's hand caressing the side of her neck where Simone had tried to strangle her.

'No one could blame you for leaving in a hurry,' Fen assured him, then turned once again to Simone. 'And to make it look like a burglary, you stole some of the paintings… And no doubt if we search your room now, we might find Rose's jewels too, do you think? I'm betting those pearl earrings you were wearing the other night weren't actually a gift.'

Simone closed her eyes and was breathing heavily through her nose, like a racehorse at the gate. James released his grip a bit and merely held her now by the wrists. He looked at her as he posed the question. 'Sold some of them, the paintings I mean, for a quick buck? Fen, what did the man at the kiosk say when you asked him about the Delance?'

'He was cagey about where it had come from all right… "it was a young man, I think, but it was hard to see".' Fen thought back. 'Simone, you said yourself you use fashion like a disguise. And I know how nifty you are with a needle and thread… James, your missing shirt!'

'Dear Lord, was that you, Simone?'

'Paired with some old trousers and a cap from Rose's portrait props, you could pass as a young man, just about.' Fen squinted at Simone.

'It was easy enough to find a cap and trousers. I missed that nice string of pearls you found down the side of that saggy old armchair though.' Simone raised one eyebrow in defiance.

James turned his back and Fen didn't want to assume, but she thought she might have seen him wipe his face with his sleeve. Simone currently had a lot to answer for and Fen carried on with the interrogation.

'Henri then told you to murder Gervais, didn't he?'

'He said it would be the last one,' she wore the expression of an employee forced to do a double shift. 'And then he would let me be.'

'What was his aim? Were we right in thinking he'd stolen the paintings?'

'Yes,' Simone confirmed. 'He was never as passionate about returning all the stolen artwork to the Jewish families as Rose was. He just hated to see such beautiful pieces be taken away and used as nothing more than decor by plump German hausfraus. He hated that they cared nothing about the art and only wanted to know the value. He sold some and planned on keeping others, a retirement gift to himself, I suppose.' She laughed. It was a hollow sound.

'And Gervais had worked out that something was amiss?' Fen asked her.

'Yes, he'd noticed the manifests were different. More paintings going to the auction house than there should be. He'd been blackmailing them both, but once Rose was dead, he had approached Henri with a deal. One hundred thousand francs or he'd—'

'Go to the authorities?' Fen interrupted.

'No, don't make me laugh,' Simone smirked. 'Henri *is* the authorities. Or as good as, with his connections. No, Gervais threatened something much worse. The Mob.'

'Blimey,' Fen took a step back and looked at Simone.

'I was sent to kill him as—'

'As you'd learnt to shoot in the Resistance?' Fen finished her sentence for her.

'Henri had recruited me back in the early years of the war. I was trained, among other women like Catherine, but in the end, I was used more as a lure to fool Nazi officers.'

'I know, you told me,' Fen bit her lip as she thought. 'And I bet Gervais would have been more than happy to see you that night in his garage.'

'I left you just before ten o'clock,' James said, looking at the beautiful young model, still held loosely by her wrists.

'And I wasn't back from the Louvre party until almost midnight, leaving Henri there, so he couldn't have done it.' Fen tutted to herself, then added, 'Plenty of time for you to commit a murder, though.'

'The hard part was getting lover boy here to leave me alone that night. I did quite a good job, though, I think, of putting you off. "James, you do love me, don't you?" "James, I think we should marry".' Simone pouted at James in the same way she must have done that night. He looked disgusted and, if he wasn't holding her captive, Fen was sure he would rather have been anywhere else but in her presence. *Poor James*, she thought, *the ultimate lion tamer*.

The sound of sirens filled the air and Fen knew her time for questioning Simone would soon be gone. Antoine Arnault and Michel Lazard had made it out of the gallery now, both looking pale and obviously in shock. Fen thought it might only be minutes before her own adrenalin gave out and she too would start taking on board what they'd all witnessed in that room.

'Just one more question, Simone?' Fen asked. 'Before they take you away.'

Simone looked at her and shrugged.

'Was it worth it, just for the apartment?'

'You think I only killed for that place? Once married, I would be in houses far more splendid.' She nodded towards James. 'But what Henri knew about me could have ruined any chance I had of becoming a rich man's wife. More than that, he could have had me executed.'

'For being a traitor... Surely if he knew you were The Chameleon, he would have turned you in long ago.'

'But he did know. He knew all too well. And he kept that knowledge, curated it like one of his paintings, ready to use when he needed it. He knew what lengths I'd gone to during the war to catch those SS officers. Sometimes they took more than just a wink to get down an alleyway. He said to me, "No English gentleman will marry a French slut" and said he would tell James, or Frederick, or John, or Jeremy...'

James shook his head. 'That wouldn't have mattered.' His voice was low and barely audible. 'But betraying your friends and murdering Rose, that is unforgivable.'

Simone didn't have the chance to reply as the gendarmes reached them and after a quick discussion with the stricken Magda and protective Joseph picked up the young model under the armpits and carried her back down the passageway to the waiting motor.

CHAPTER FORTY-FIVE

Fen poured the steaming tea from the pot and passed the teacups around. Magda was sitting elegantly on the chaise longue in Rose's apartment and Joseph was next to her, Magda's bandaged leg raised up on his lap. She'd taken quite a tumble when she'd tripped up Simone and it had done her ankle in something rotten. James, who had been exceedingly downcast since Simone had been revealed as the murderer, sat on the saggiest of the armchairs, with Tipper curled up on his lap, nibbling at his sleeve.

Fen sat down opposite him on the other chair and blew over her cup. 'Reverted to the mint concoction, I'm afraid. It seems you might be inheriting this place with the cupboards rather bare.'

'We are just grateful to Rose, and Monsieur Blanquer, for gifting it to us,' Joseph said, as he rubbed his wife's back.

The four of them were gathered in the studio, having paid their respects at Rose's grave in the Père Lachaise cemetery. She had been buried close to the Jewish graves, a nod to the families that she had died trying to help.

A few days before the funeral, Monsieur Blanquer, Rose's solicitor, had come to the apartment and interpreted her will, now that the main beneficiary, Henri Renaud, was dead.

'She had willed it to Henri, in its entirety, but she had acknowledged that both of them might have been exec…cuted by the Nazis if they had been c…caught.' Blanquer had explained to them all over a cup of proper tea, made with the last few leaves Fen had foraged in the tea caddy. 'But she made provision that in the event of Henri pre-deceasing her – and I feel that his recent death c… can be treated in that manner legally – that her estate should go towards helping those families who have lost everything. As her solicitor, I am happy to will the Bernheims the apartment and then we will decide later how the c…contents should be sold to provide monies for other families on hard times.'

The news had been greeted with tears of joy from Magda, and a very warm handshake from Joseph. Even James had smiled, his first for a few days. Fen couldn't have been happier with the solicitor's news and had thanked him profusely as she'd shown him out.

And so now the four of them were taking tea again, even if it was of the mint variety, and deciding how next to proceed.

'We can't thank you enough, Fenella,' Magda said, as she held her teacup up to her lips.

'I can't accept your gratitude, Magda, I feel like I've failed you all, and Rose in particular.'

'How so?' Magda asked and Joseph raised a questioning eyebrow too. 'You got her justice and even found two of Joseph's parents' paintings for us.'

Fen nodded. She had had the idea that Lazard, being the man Henri had been meeting that night she'd followed him, might have been the fence Henri had used to sell some of the paintings he had stolen. Lazard had accepted Fen's deal of her silence about his part in illegally selling paintings in exchange for the whereabouts of the stolen art. He handed five paintings over to her, having not had a chance to find buyers yet. They had been discovered, oddly enough, in the hotel room next door to James's and he had helped her carry them back to the apartment, just a few blocks away.

The problem was, apart from the Gainsborough and a Cezanne, which Fen knew belonged to the Bernheims, she couldn't work out who the other pictures belonged to. There was a sketch by Matisse, a study of boats in the water by Signac and even a small bronze figurine by Rodin. She felt very uneasy about sitting on these valuable artworks and just wished that she could work out to whom they belonged.

Fen looked over to where the two other brown paper–wrapped canvases were, and the small statuette. 'How can we decipher those codes on them if we don't know how Rose did it?'

'We can ask around the community,' Magda ventured, 'we may find that families have proof from old photographs that they owned those lovely pieces.'

'We can, and I can't think of better people than you two to do that,' Fen agreed. 'But what about Rose's *mission*? She wanted all of the art restored. Without her code, we can't even start to carry on her work, let along finish it for her. Those American chaps are finding more hidey-holes full of stolen art all the time, we have to be able to prove who they belong to.'

'Where would she have hidden it?' James asked, and Fen looked over to him, glad he was at least taking part in the conversation. She had been so worried about him after Simone was arrested, and had tried to talk to him, but he had refused to be drawn on the matter.

'Where indeed,' Fen thought out loud. 'The fact that she even used a code means she loved a puzzle at heart.'

'Didn't she mention something about puzzles, Fenella, when we first met?' Magda shifted her ankle slightly and sat up more on the chaise. Fen looked at her, as if studying her face would help her conjure up the memories of that first meeting.

'You're right… what was it she said… "The Impressionists were the finest puzzlers" or something.'

'Yes!' Magda looked more animated than Fen had ever seen her. Joseph and James suddenly looked a little more alert, too. 'Remember we all laughed about the pink splodges being a face.'

'And how if you look at something differently, you can work out how it was made…' Fen pushed herself out of the armchair and held her finger up. 'Hold that thought...' She went to the wall between the windows and unhooked the small Impressionist painting from where it had been rehung on the wall.

'Good thing I bought it for Simone...' James's voice almost cracked when he mentioned her name, and Fen squeezed his shoulder as she passed by him on the way back to her chair, painting in hand.

'I saw Rose once, correcting its position on the wall.' Fen felt around the edges of the painting where the brown backing paper was loosely taped to the frame. 'Aha...' She picked a corner of the framer's tape free and carefully unpeeled it from the frame and backing paper. 'That was easy,' she told the others, 'perhaps a little too easy. I think this tape has been removed and restuck more than once.'

Fen held the painting up and tipped it on its side so that anything hiding within would fall out from the untaped edge. And, sure enough, there appeared on her lap an envelope. Fen carefully put the painting down beside her chair and held the envelope up for the others to see.

'Go on then, open it.'

Fen quickly opened the envelope to find two discs of card within it.

'What is it?' Magda asked. Fen handed them to her and she passed them onto Joseph, who saw what they had seen: just two circles of brown card, one slightly smaller than the other, both with the alphabet listed around the edge of the circles.

'One of the circles has the alphabet in the right order...' Joseph noticed.

'... And one will be in random order.' James completed his sentence. He held his hand out and Joseph passed the discs to him. He looked at them and smiled to himself then told the others what he was thinking. 'This is a classic Alberti cipher.'

'Alberti?' Fen questioned.

'Leon Battista Alberti. A Renaissance architect. You should know that from your art lessons, Fen.' He looked up at her and she was pleased to finally see something of a twinkle in his eye.

'Of course,' Fen shook her head. 'How apt for an artist to use a cipher created by another artist.'

'He designed Santa Maria Novella in Florence,' Magda offered, but Joseph shushed her gently and asked James to carry on.

'He did indeed, Magda,' James agreed with her. 'He was also a linguist and cryptographer. We had a short cryptography lesson during our SOE training. The smaller disc sits on the larger one – easy enough to see how that works. Each letter on the disc then translates to one on the other one. The only problem is knowing where to place the smaller disc, which letter is the key.'

'Well, we know that.' Fen blurted out and got up again and fetched the Cezanne painting from where it had been sitting since the Bernheims had gratefully received it. 'Here, look. We know that EWJGZWON spells Bernheim. So you just have to spin it around to match B on the normal alphabet circle to E on the random one.'

James did just that and, sure enough, each letter of Bernheim matched up with the code chalked on the back of the painting.

'You've done it!' Joseph almost jumped up, but his wife's leg on his lap curtailed his celebrations. Instead, he clapped his hands together, but his excitement was infectious and soon all four of them were laughing and clapping, just so pleased to have finally found the cipher and have broken the code.

A few minutes later and they had decoded EWJWGYUG, which was chalked quite faintly on the base of the statuette, to Berenson, and then worked out that the Rensteins had owned the Matisse and Signac.

'She always said the Impressionists were the best puzzlers all right,' Fen remarked, holding the cipher in her hand. 'But I think Rose might have been right up there with the best puzzlers of the lot!'

EPILOGUE

Hotel de Lille, Paris
October 1945

Dear Kitty (and Mrs B & Dilys),

Your letter cheered me up no end, thank you! I must say, Paris hasn't been quite as expected, what with Rose's murder and James being devastated by the fact that he was growing rather attached to the murderess. I'll tell you all about it when I'm home, if an invitation stands to come and bed down with you three at the farm?

I just wish James could have such good friends as I have to help him through his grief at the moment. Thank you for looking into his family circs for me, I had no inkling that he'd been through so much. Well, that's not true – I had an inkling… he said he'd lost someone special when I first met him and told him about Arthur, and just recently he was so quick to throw his lot in with the first pretty girl who showed an interest. Finding out she was a cold-blooded killer – and double agent! – was a bit of blow for the poor chap. I think I'm starting to understand him now; he's noble all right, and not just in a born-with-a-silver-spoon type way. I'll keep an eye out for him, though; it's what Arthur would have wanted.

Good luck with the winter beet, ladies, and don't let Mr Travers name a cow after me like he did last time. One Fenella the Friesian is quite enough! Oh, and Kitty, here's one more clue to keep you busy til I see you again. This flower floated up, we hear (4). Hint: I think she's looking down on me now and hopefully laughing through her cigarette smoke.

Much love,
Fen xx

Fen sealed the envelope up and put it to one side, ready to take down to reception. James had, indeed, been very generous in stumping up the cost of a room for Fen, who felt it wasn't right to lodge with Joseph and Magda, even though they'd offered. She was just pleased that they could start their life anew, in a decent apartment and with at least a few of their old treasures and what remained of Rose's.

It was a small battle won against the evil that had trodden the world over the last few years and Fen felt Rose would have been pleased with the outcome. When she was packing up her bedroom, Magda had softly knocked on her door and limped in. She'd packaged up a few pieces and had made Fen promise not to open the parcel until she got back to the hotel, and even then, to promise not to return any of it to the Bernheims.

'Don't worry, Tipper isn't in there,' Magda had joked as the little dog had scampered in and jumped onto the bed, too. Fen smiled, thinking about him and how much Magda doted on her new pet.

Fen looked over to where she had laid out the contents of the parcel on the bed. Her first impulse had been to ignore Magda's stern instructions and package it all back up and return it to her, as she didn't feel she deserved such beautiful things. But Magda had said, as they'd kissed goodbye outside the apartment, 'Rose would want you to have those things. And those bits you chose for your parents, too. We want you to have them. It's the least we can do to say thank you.'

The Delance was the bulk of the package. Its backing paper still slit open where the Alberti cipher had been kept. Magda had slipped a note inside it though… *Since I have my own copy, this one can be yours.*

Fen smiled to herself, remembering Magda and Rose laughing about how many times the teacher had made her student copy it. A thought suddenly occurred to Fen – hadn't Rose called this "my little Impressionist"? She smiled. *I bet it's a forgery – or, as Rose would say, "an homage".* The thought didn't make her love the painting any less, in fact, if it was a copy by Rose, Fen would love it even more, as it would be *her* version of the painting, *her* soul put into it.

Wrapped up in a silken handkerchief was one of Rose's bejewelled hatpins, so often used to secure those bizarre turbans in place. It was made of a peacock feather studded with what must be fake emeralds and sapphires, and when Fen pressed it to her nose, she could just about smell the familiar scent of ylang-ylang and tobacco.

The last piece that Magda had saved for her was the long string of pearls that Fen had found down the side of the armchair. They had been carefully slipped into a black velvet pouch and Fen had poured the threaded beads into her hand in wonder as she'd opened it. The pearls were exquisite and, unlike most things in Rose's apartment, quite genuine. And, what's more, they would look fabulous paired with Rose's old bright yellow tea dress when James treated her to tea at The Ritz tomorrow afternoon.

A LETTER FROM FLISS

Dear reader,

I want to say a huge thank you for choosing to read *Night Train to Paris*. If you did enjoy it, and want to keep up to date with all my latest releases, just sign up at the following link. Your email address will never be shared and you can unsubscribe at any time.

www.bookouture.com/fliss-chester

I've always loved art, and although I never studied anywhere as grand as the École des Beaux-Arts, I have been lucky enough to go to Paris on several occasions. Art inspires such passions in people, and so I could easily imagine how it could lead to enviously coveting what isn't yours… and then murder!

I hope you loved reading *Night Train to Paris* and if you did, I would be very grateful if you could write a review. I'd love to hear what you think, and it makes such a difference helping new readers to discover one of my books for the first time.

I love hearing from my readers – you can get in touch on my Facebook page, through Twitter, Instagram or my website.

Thanks,
Fliss Chester

FlissChester

FlissChester

socialwhirlgirl

www.flisschester.co.uk

ACKNOWLEDGEMENTS

As always, it takes more than one person to bring a story to life, so huge thanks to my editor at Bookouture, Maisie Lawrence, and the whole editorial and marketing teams there, too. Also, my agent Emily Sweet is always on hand for advice and support – so thank you so much as always for all you do.

I've been down many research rabbit holes while writing this story, but once again the brilliant book *Parisiennes* by Anne Sebba was a great help, with so many fascinating stories, including that of Catherine Dior. Her name may have gone down in history as a perfume (Miss Dior is reputedly named after her), but she, and women like her, gave up their freedom, and in many cases their lives, to protect their friends and defend their country. As I read more and more accounts of the bravery shown by 'normal' people, I was awed by what those women and men went through and I salute them. Of course, I have fictionalised the characters of Christian and Catherine Dior, and their friend Pierre Balmain in this book and, beyond what is already historical record, any account I give of them is purely imagined.

A huge thank you to my art-dealing friends, Jessica and James from J&J Rawlin, who lent me books and told me about the darker side of the wartime art world. Paintings (and silverware, china and crystal as well as jewels and *objets d'art*) were stolen and thousands of pieces have never been returned, but the bravery of art lovers such as Rose Valland, who worked for the Resistance and did what she could to catalogue the art being removed by the Nazis, has not been forgotten. My Rose was inspired by Valland's story, but, of course, I had to put a few more puzzles and codes in!

My thanks as always to my family – you are my support network *extraordinaire* and I love you. My late grandparents were friends with the daughter of German 'degenerate' artists (Marg and Oskar Moll, pupils of Matisse) and I was lucky enough to grow up with pieces of Marg Moll's striking Fauvist artwork around the house. My husband, Rupert, has spent many a walk pondering plot points with me and although I don't take him up on all of his ideas, I'm sure a few of them have snuck in. If you spot any typos or random words, I blame the cat and his penchant for walking across my keyboard for no apparent reason except to get my attention!